SHERLOCK HOLMES

THE TESLA TELE-AUTOMATON

AND OTHER STORIES

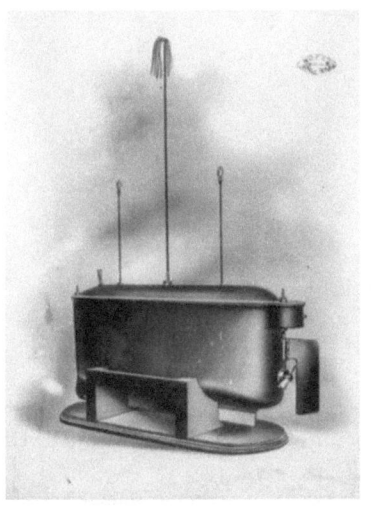

MIKE HOGAN

CONTENTS

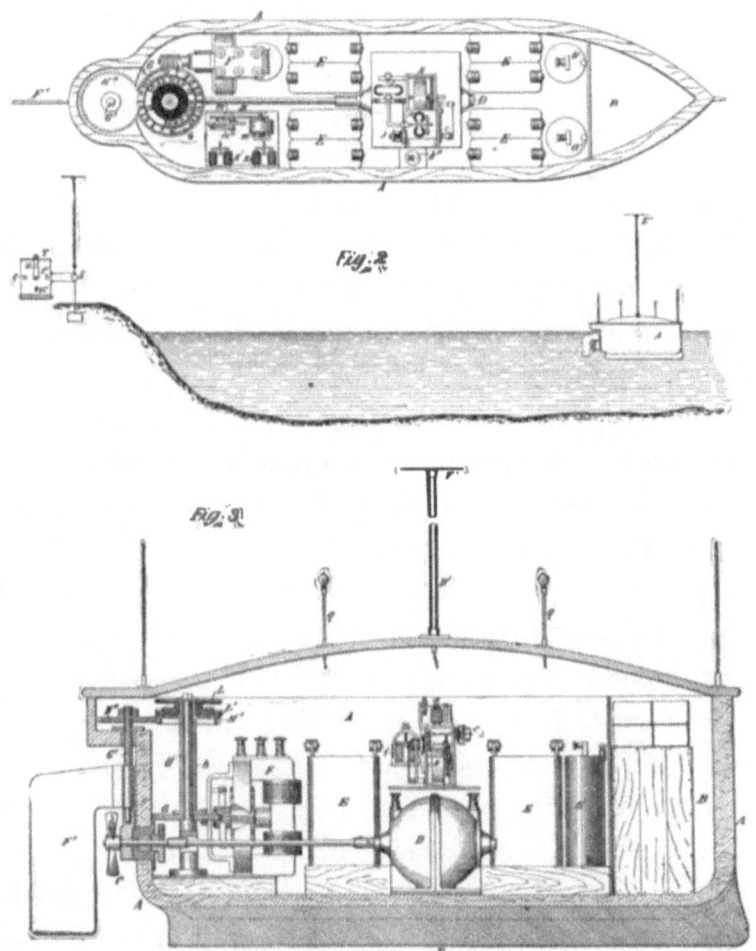

Fig. 1

Fig. 2

Fig. 3

TESLA'S DIRIGIBLE BOAT.

THE TESLA
TELE-AUTOMATON

"MAY I SEE THE soles of your boots?"

The gentleman blinked at Holmes across the bedroom he occupied in the Savoy Hotel, but he slowly lifted first one foot, then the other. Holmes inspected his boots through his magnifying glass, nodding sagely.

I could not contain an indecorous grin. Holmes had been summoned by messenger from the manager of the hotel just as Mrs Hudson was about to serve breakfast. With certain pangs (buttered kippers!), I had volunteered to accompany him.

A pageboy had ushered us into the grand suite of Mr Brown, an unusually tall, foreign-looking gentleman with a dapper moustache in perhaps his late forties or early fifties. The day manager and Sergeant Griffiths the hotel detective greeted Holmes' arrival with obvious relief.

The guest had explained in a high-pitched, faintly central-European accent that a satchel containing important documents was missing from his room. He had secreted the satchel atop the tall wardrobe that took up most of one wall of his bedroom while he went down to breakfast.

Holmes closely scrutinized the sitting room, then the bedroom.

"The maids at the Savoy are to be commended," he said to the manager, who hovered in the open doorway wringing his hands, the wide-eyed pageboy beside him. "There's no dust in which a mark might be visible, most unfortunately."

"We can take no credit, Mr Holmes," the manager answered. "Mr Brown prefers to clean the room himself."

I flicked a glance at Mr Brown, who stood, seemingly at his ease, one arm supporting the elbow of the other and a finger to lips curved in a half smile. He acknowledged Holmes' compliment with a slight bow.

Holmes surveyed the elegantly furnished bedroom. "The bedside table is sturdy, but on it are a vase, an ashtray and an alarum-clock. The side tables in the sitting room are similarly encumbered and the armchairs and sofa are massive, upholstered mahogany, hard to move. No, unless he is a second Chang the Chinese Giant, our thief used one of the four dining chairs from the window alcove to reach for the satchel."

"Not the pouf?" I indicated a corner of the bedroom. An embroidered footrest lay on the carpet before an armchair.

"Try it."

I dragged the heavy elephant's foot pouf to the wardrobe and attempted to clamber onto it so that I could see the top. The footstool sagged with my weight, and, unable to steady myself sufficiently, I slid onto the carpet. "Not the pouf," I confirmed.

Holmes picked up the nearest of the dining chairs and held it at an angle to the pale winter sunlight streaming through the windows. "What do you see?"

"An indistinct, grey-ish impression in the velveteen plush of the seat," I said. "Is it a number or a letter? Yes, I think I see an 'E', or perhaps a faint eight; and possibly another 'E' or another eight. The marks are blurred – wait! I have it! This is a room number marked in chalk on the thief's shoes by the boot boy." I knitted my brows. "And therefore, a reverse image."

"Just so. The most likely combinations are 88 or 83," Holmes said. "If the first number is a three, we have 33 or 38."

After checking Mr Brown's boot soles, he addressed the manager. "I assume the hotel has a photographer on call?"

The page was despatched to fetch the photographer, and Holmes examined the wardrobe. "Either you are not quite the hygienic paragon we have been led to believe, Mr Brown, or these stains are new." He peered through his glass at a splatter of pale, white-ish blots across the wardrobe door. "Still damp." He dabbed one mark with his finger and touched his tongue. "Salty."

He stood back. "I believe we have a pattern – a downward slash and a long horizontal, then another stroke, with three short horizontals."

"A cabbalistic sign," I said. "The thief is a member of a gang – the Sicilian *Carbonara*, perhaps. Or is it the ideograph of a Chinese tong brotherhood? Or the secret symbols of a tramp: they leave signs on houses they target."

The manager coughed.

"Not at the Savoy, of course." I peered more closely at the blots. "Could they be letters – a 'T' and an 'E'? What can they mean?"

Holmes addressed Mr Brown. "You hid the satchel on top of the wardrobe. Kindly show me how you did that."

Mr Brown stood on tiptoe and mimed sliding a heavy bag far back on the wardrobe top.

Holmes sat in the armchair and leaned back. "Would you care to tell me exactly what the missing satchel contained, Mr Tesla?"

The gentleman we had been led to believe was Mr Brown smiled. "I see you live up to your reputation, Mr Holmes," he answered, now with a tinge of Yankee discernible in his accent. "My alias does not hoodwink you. Yes, I am Tesla. I assumed a false name on the instructions of your Admiralty, who requested I come to England incognito to demonstrate my invention."

I had seen magazine illustrations of the brilliant inventor and electrical visionary Nikola Tesla calmly seated between huge electrical apparatus that shot gigantic sparks and vivid lightning bolts in every direction, and I was fascinated to see him in person. His face was oval, pale, and capped with sleek, oiled, black hair. Blue-grey, deep-set eyes were set above a prominent nose and high Slavic cheekbones. His ready smile and jaunty posture suggested both charm and self-assurance. But in an incongruous note, he wore white dress gloves with his otherwise conventional, if rather old-fashioned, frock coat and striped trousers. He gave the impression of a dapper, rather knowing gentleman's gentleman.

"May I ask how you saw through my charade," Mr Tesla asked, "if that is not a trade secret of your profession?"

"I attended your lecture at the Royal Institution in '92. You are a difficult person to forget." Holmes returned Mr Tesla's smile. "And your name is stamped on the suitcases and hatboxes piled by the sofa in the sitting room."

"So much for incognito," Mr Tesla said, his smile broadening. "I am sometimes obliged to travel under another name to avoid nuisances: business proposals from charlatans, invention ideas from crackpots, espionage by foreign agents and offers of marriage from lonely widows."

Mr Tesla glanced at his reflection in the mirror above the dressing table and adjusted his tie. "Such pretence is wearing to the soul." He turned back to face us. "On my last visit to England, my ideas were ardently received by engineers and men of science, but your admirals would not deign to grant me an audience; they laughed at my 'toy boat', derided my other inventions, and snubbed me." He smiled a thin smile. "Since then, the world has moved precisely in the direction I predicted, and now I am secretly requested to show my tele-automaton before a committee of your Naval grandees. They even paid my fare – first class on a crack steamer."

His smile died. "In the satchel are specifications of my tele-automaton and its control device, and blueprints of same. They are the fruits of many years of study and prototype construction. My notes are irreplaceable: they chronicle my thought processes, charting the many forks and turnings in the mental road I travelled before arriving at my theory. I intend to explore these byways in future research." He glanced again at his reflection and picked a fleck of lint from his lapel. "The data can be reconstructed, but that will set me back months: time I cannot spare. The loss is a grave blow to me, and the papers would be worth their weight in diamonds to certain foreign powers – and to the mountebank Edison."

"Tele-automaton," I mused. "There is an automaton in a glass case in the foyer of the Canterbury Music Hall on the Westminster Bridge Road." I chuckled. "A sheik in a turban who smokes a bubble pipe and tells faux fortunes, ha ha. You put the penny in a slot, and he, ah—"

Mr Tesla stilled me with a glare. Oddly, his stare was not directly into my eyes, but was focussed on my chin or neck. It was most unsettling.

"My device is not a frivolity, sir," he declared in a haughty tone. "It is a deadly torpedo, guided to its target by Hertzian waves and containing enough explosive to sink any ship in your Navy.

No warship, no matter how well-armoured or nimble, can survive within the range of the device. From the very moment the weapon is deployed by whichever enlightened naval establishment buys my patents, battleships will cease to be built. The most tremendous artillery afloat will be of no more use than so much scrap iron."

I felt my discomfiture keenly, and I bowed an apology.

Holmes favoured me with what I took to be a sympathetic glance. "Is anything else missing?" he asked Mr Tesla.

"Nothing, just the bag and its contents."

"At what time did you go down to breakfast?"

"I was working on various papers from about four o'clock to six," the inventor answered. "I seldom sleep more than a few hours a night."

"The first sitting for breakfast is at six," the manager said. "Mr – ah, Tesla is invariably our first guest."

A photographer appeared in the doorway, his cumbersome equipment carried by a young assistant. Under Holmes' direction, the boy placed the marked chair from the dining set in the window alcove and the photographer set up his camera, primed his flash stick and took oblique photographs of the seat.

"Open the curtains wide and photograph the wardrobe door," Holmes directed. "And kindly develop the prints in high contrast; the chair cushion in reverse, as a negative."

He turned to Sergeant Griffiths. "The obvious first: room numbers. Let me have details of the guests in rooms 33, 38, 83 and 88. And fetch the boot boys on duty on those floors last night."

Griffiths noted the room numbers and looked up. "Any notion of a suspect, Mr Holmes?"

"All I can say with probability is that we are looking for a tall man."

"But the thief used the chair to reach the satchel," I said. "He need be no more than ordinary height."

Holmes stood, took a cushion from the sofa, and tossed it onto the wardrobe. He raised his eyebrows.

"Ah, the fellow had to be tall to see the satchel."

Holmes turned back to the house detective. "I will interview the receptionists and the doormen on duty yesterday and this morning. Also, the maids, lift attendants, and anyone whose duties brought them to this floor during the time Mr Tesla was at breakfast."

"I'll gather the relevant staff in a vacant suite, Mr Holmes; Suite 1 on the first floor will do." Sergeant Griffiths poised his pencil over his notebook. "Regarding the saltwater stains, sir. I understand the gentleman's invention is of a nautical nature. Might we be looking for a sailor, or someone connected with naval matters?" He dropped his voice to a whisper. "Foreign persons perhaps?"

"At this stage, I will rule out nothing."

Sergeant Griffiths hurried away, and Holmes and I took our leave of Mr Tesla. We left him telephoning the Savoy telegraph office and arranging a telegraphic cable to New York.

The hotel manager closed the door of Mr Tesla's suite behind us, and heaved a long sigh. "Thank you so much for coming at such short notice, Mr Holmes. We are most reluctant to involve the police. With Mr Tesla being a prominent person, and American to boot, we thought it wise to ask you to handle the case." The manager hesitated. "For certain other reasons, we are averse to involving the authorities." He glanced towards the door of the Tesla suite and lowered his voice. "The gentleman's accommodation was engaged by telegram under another name. If Mr Tesla had used his own, we would have been reluctant to accept the booking. The gentleman has a reputation, if you take my meaning."

"I do not," Holmes knelt and closely examined the door lock and keyhole of the suite through his magnifying glass.

"Regarding the b-i-double-l, sir. Mr Tesla has been known to neglect his obligations in that regard."

I frowned. "You mean he leaves without paying? He does a midnight flit."

The manager winced. "He has, shall we say, overlooked payment on several occasions and at a number of reputable hotels here, on the Continent, and in the United States." He shook his head. "The suite was booked by a government agency for a gentleman named Brown, but the reception staff recognised Mr Tesla was our guest when the caller demanded a suite with number limitations, a telephone connection, no maid or valet service and eighteen fresh towels daily."

I frowned again.

"Mr Tesla displays various eccentricities, including an aversion to any number than is indivisible by three. Suite 66 meets his conditions. And we were obliged to prepare a special copy of the Savoy Grill menu with item numbers pasted over so as not to restrict Mr Tesla's dining choices. He insists on making his exact requirements, vegetarian demands gentlemen, known to Chef via the voice pipe in his room." The manager spread his hands. "Chef is a Gascon. He so far been persuaded from tendering his resignation, but the atmosphere in the kitchen is volatile."

The manager pressed his fingers against his temples for a moment, and then continued. "When Mr Tesla's identity became known to the management, we sent him a note requesting a deposit for ancillary expenses (food, wine, telegraph and telephone fees) to which we have not received a reply." The manager sighed. "Mr Tesla has very expensive tastes in wine and food, and, as you saw, he sends frequent international cables – lengthy international cables." He gestured towards the door. "It will be difficult to insist on immediate payment in these circumstances."

"You think Mr Tesla may have made up the burglary story to avoid paying?" I asked.

"Housebreaking story," Holmes corrected. "The theft occurred at breakfast time: burglary is robbery after nine o'clock at night."

I sighed. "You think the room-breaking story might be a ruse?"

The manager spread his hands. "With Mr Tesla, anything is possible."

Holmes stood and pocketed his magnifying glass. "How did the thief gain entry to Mr Tesla's room? I presume he locked his door when he left for breakfast. The key plate is heavily scratched from use, but I see no signs of tamper, or of forced entry."

"That's a puzzle, Mr Holmes," the manager answered. "The gentleman is adamant he locked the door. If he is mistaken, we may be looking at an opportunist thief."

"And if he is correct, an expert one."

The manager led us along the corridor towards the lifts. "Would you happen to know, Doctor, which part of America Mr Tesla is from?" he asked. "He has an accent that I cannot quite place."

"I believe he was born and brought up in Servia," I answered.

"Servia?"

"The one in Austro-Hungary."

"Ah," the manager said with a sniff.

I considered. "One reads of absent-minded professors and so on. I suppose one must make allowances."

"Mr Tesla has an assistant standing guard on his luggage in our storeroom," the manager said in a cold tone. "We are directed to make up a bed for the fellow each night next to his packing cases. It is most irregular."

A red-faced hotel clerk hurried along the corridor towards us and addressed the manager. "Come quick, sir, there's a kerfuffle in the lobby. Someone is stuck in the swing doors."

The manager bowed to Holmes and to me and hastened ahead to the lifts.

We strolled after him.

"Will you take the case?" I asked Holmes. "Are you not wasting your time on a nonsense of smoke and mirrors to avoid restaurant bills?"

"We shall see."

⸺◈⸺

We took the lift down to the first floor. Holmes opened the door of Suite 1 and ushered me before him into the sitting room where the hotel detective and a score or so of uniformed hotel staff waited. All chatter ceased as Holmes and I entered, and the staff clustered together against one wall, looking anxious.

Sergeant Griffiths introduced us, and Holmes interrogated the hotel employees one by one, beginning with the receptionists. The night shift staff firmly stated that nobody had asked for Mr Brown's (or Mr Tesla's) room number before the shift change at six that morning. And the day receptionists repeated that negative for the period six to seven, when the theft was discovered. Holmes frowned at one young man who was clearly ill at ease, fidgeting with his bow tie.

"It might be nothing, sir," the man said. He glanced nervously at a portly, red-faced man standing beside him. "But Mr Blake here, the night manager, was behind the reception desk at about ten-to-six this morning as we were changing over. He complained that the guest in Suite 66 had him up and down to his room several times during the night: street noise, room too warm, bed creaking and so on. He mentioned the name of the guest."

Mr Blake fingered his waxed moustache and glared at the young man.

"Brown or Tesla?" Holmes asked.

"Tesla, sir. We all know Mr Tesla is staying with us. His luggage—"

"Yes, yes – and?"

"I was obliged to shush him, sir, Mr Blake that is, because a guest was at the far end of the counter writing a note, an elderly clergyman, and he could overhear." He reddened. "It wasn't seemly."

Mr Blake gave the young man a dark look.

Holmes narrowed his eyes. "Describe the clergyman."

"In his sixties, sir, white-haired, wearing a black suit – ordinary quality – a clerical collar and a large black and silver cross on a chain around his neck."

"How did you know he was a guest and not a visitor?"

The young man considered. "I assumed, sir. It was early, when few visitors are about, but mostly because he was carrying a hot water bottle. I supposed he had asked the kitchens to fill it for him."

"India-rubber or earthenware?" Holmes snapped.

"India-rubber."

"Full or empty?"

"Full."

"Odd that he wanted it filled in the morning, not at night," I said. "Odder still that he didn't just call for an attendant, rather than getting dressed and going downstairs himself. And this morning was rather warm for the time of year." I turned to Holmes. "If he was connected with the theft, the clergyman may have been in disguise. Could an unscrupulous journalist have purloined the Tesla papers hoping for a scoop?" I lowered my voice. "Or was he an agent of a foreign power?"

A messenger entered the suite and gave Sergeant Griffiths a note. "Suites 33 and 83, unoccupied," the hotel detective read. "Lord Longeville, his lady wife and daughter in 38; Mr Schmetterling, the German actor, in 88." The sergeant chuckled. "Well, he says he's an actor, but his dummy does all the work."

"A ventriloquist," Holmes said. "Where is he performing?"

"At the Canterbury," I answered.

Holmes raised his eyebrows.

"I popped in one afternoon last week, when my Portsmouth train was delayed by points failure at Clapham Junction. I mentioned it to you at the time. He's rather good: you'd never know he was talking rather than the marionette." I chuckled. "The puppet is a Prussian drillmaster in a pickelhaube, barking at imaginary soldiers and sneering at the ventriloquist through his monocle: it's very droll. I doubt he'd get away with it in Berlin or Potsdam." I frowned. "Could it be an act? I mean, not a music hall act, but a sham—"

Holmes dismissed the reception staff and addressed the boot boys. "Which of you worked the eighth floor?"

A bright-eyed, fair-haired youth raised his hand, and Holmes sent the others away.

"Do you recall whether boots were left outside Suite 88?"

"Yes, sir. Black patents and a pair of tiddly riding boots. They had little spurs that I shined with *Brasso*."

"Show me how you mark the guests' shoes," Holmes said.

The boot boy produced a piece of chalk from his pocket and looked expectantly at Holmes. He turned to me, and I reluctantly removed one of my boots and handed it to the boy.

"Mark '88'," Holmes ordered the boy, "in your usual way."

Holmes pressed the marked boot onto the velvet seat of one of the dining chairs in the window alcove. "Perfectly readable." He frowned. "But not quite what I expected."

Holmes called the lift attendants forward and had them list their passengers between five and seven that morning.

It was difficult, they agreed, as the lifts had been packed with guests for the big society wedding taking place that morning. The groom was staying on the sixth floor, and gentlemen, including several clergymen, had passed up and down from an early hour. The groom's party came down to breakfast at about six thirty, while the bride's had their breakfast in their suites on the eighth floor, increasing traffic in the service lifts.

Sergeant Griffiths interrupted one of the service-lift attendants as he listed his passengers. "You say a waiter brought a tray up to the sixth floor at six ten?"

"Yes, sir. I'd just come on at six, and he was my first passenger."

Sergeant Griffiths addressed Holmes. "No Savoy waiter brought anything to the sixth floor between six and seven this morning, sir. That's why I didn't round them up for questioning."

Holmes turned back to the attendant and raised his eyebrows.

"He was a short fellow, sir, ginger hair, no moustache, all in black with a white apron, like the waiters wear. I didn't know him. We get temporaries on for special events, and some guests have their own valets and footmen and the like. He come from the direction of the kitchen, so I didn't think nothing of it, sir, and—" The attendant frowned as he lost his thread. "I hope I did right bringing him up." He looked at his toes. "He come down with me as well."

"How long after the waiter came up did you take him down?" Holmes asked.

"Maybe ten minutes, sir – no more than ten, prob'bly less."

"Was he carrying anything?"

"No, sir. Aside from the tray."

"What was on the tray when he went up?"

"Nothing, sir. Same when he come down."

"Very well." Holmes dismissed the lift attendants, sat in an armchair, took a cigar from his case and offered one to me. "So far, we have four possible suspects: the ventriloquist, the unknown waiter on his mysterious duty with an empty tray, the chilled clergyman and, if we are on a fool's errand and the robbery is a fabrication, Mr Tesla. We have the room number of the first. Aside from Mr Tesla, the others may or may not be lodging or employed here."

"The chalk had not yet rubbed off the thief's boots," I said. "He could not have travelled far from his hotel room on the thick Savoy carpets. If he came from outside, there's been no rain for a week and the pavements are dry. Ordinary walking would rub the chalk off in forty or fifty paces, so either the thief came a short distance to the Savoy from another hotel on foot—"

"—or he took a cab. And perhaps he took a cab back where he came from." Holmes addressed the remaining boot boy.

"Name?"

"Phipps, sir."

"You are temporarily deputised into the Savoy Hotel Irregulars, under my command."

The boy gaped at Holmes.

"At a bob a day, plus expenses."

Phipps grinned.

"Run to the cabstand at the hotel entrance. Find the cabby who dropped or picked up an elderly clergyman and/or a ginger-haired man, possibly in a waiter's uniform before six this morning. There's a half crown for the correct driver, and another bob for you."

The boy darted for the door, but I held up my hand. "Bring the wrong driver and you forfeit all. Be sparing with your description; let the cabby fill it out so you know he's not fibbing. That's the way detectives do it." The boy saluted and dashed out.

Holmes addressed the sergeant. "Kindly make a list of all clergymen staying at the hotel. And, on the chance the thief walked to the Savoy, procure a local map from the tourist information desk in the lobby—"

The sergeant produced a tourist map from his jacket pocket and spread it on the breakfast table.

"Your most experienced telephone operator must be assigned to me and provided with a local directory," Holmes ordered. "He will telephone the Cecil Hotel next door, state he acts in the name of the manager of the Savoy in a matter of robbery of a guest and request the names of the occupants of suites 33, 38, 83 and 88 last night. Then he must perform the same exercise with every hotel and boarding house listed within a radius of, let us say, a hundred and fifty yards." He ran a finger across the map. "Or from the Adelphi to the Gaiety theatres."

"There must be dozens if not scores of small hotels and guest houses in the alleyways on either side of the Strand," I said.

"We shall concern ourselves initially with establishments with more than thirty rooms. Our working assumption is that a hotel of that size will have a telephone connection, if only at reception. It will thus be on the directory list. The guest names by themselves mean little, but we can determine which rooms were occupied and make a schedule of suspects to interview." Holmes stood and glanced at his reflection in the mirror of an armoire by the window of the suite. "If there is any reluctance to cooperate, the operator may mention my name."

He addressed the sergeant. "Does Mr Schmetterling's suite have a telephone apparatus?"

"No, sir, but all our rooms are equipped with speaking tubes that connect to reception, our restaurants and the American Bar."

As if on cue, the speaking tube attached to the wall beside the door of the suite whistled. Sergeant Griffiths answered it and looked up, alarmed. "There has been an attempt against Mr Tesla's baggage." He listened again. "His servant has been wounded defending his master's possessions."

"Is the hotel doctor in attendance?" I asked.

"Not yet, sir. I believe he is with another guest."

"The theft has become tangible," I said to Holmes. "I must go."

"Very well." Holmes stood. "Sergeant, I want a watcher in the corridor outside suite 88; I am to be notified immediately if the ventriloquist leaves the room."

Holmes and I followed the sergeant down to the lobby, where he collected a box of medical supplies from behind the reception desk before we passed through a discrete green-baize-covered door and into the innards of the hotel. Open double doors immediately to the left revealed a storage room brightly lit by electric light and crammed with trunks, suitcases, and bags of every description.

Against one wall was a stack of wooden packing cases, and, incongruously, a neatly made-up camp bed. A man wearing a dressing gown sat on the bed, holding a bloodied towel to his head.

Holmes introduced us, and the man responded with a rueful smile. "George Scherff, at your service, gentlemen."

I examined Mr Scherff's head wound and sent a page for hot water.

"You serve Mr Tesla in what role?" Holmes asked him.

"General factotum." He winced as I dabbed his wound with alcohol from the first-aid kit. "The hotel staff are probably confused – it's not uncommon. Mr Tesla may have informed them I am his Turkish masseur, his wig maker, or his food taster. My employer has a well-developed sense of humour. It has caused us some inconvenience, particularly on our passage through Prussia. I handle Mr Tesla's finances, his travel arrangements, and other aspects of his life outside the laboratory – inside as well, in fact, as I am pressed into occasional service as his laboratory assistant. For the two nights since we arrived in London, I've been babysitting this." He tapped one of the wooden crates. "The end of warfare as we know it."

"As well as an odd sense of humour, your employer has several eccentricities," I said as I cleaned Mr Scherff's cuts and abrasions.

Mr Scherff chuckled. "Your pearl tiepin."

"Eh?"

Holmes invited Mr Scherff to explain exactly how he had been injured.

"Unlike Mr Tesla, I am not an early riser," he began. "I was disturbed twenty or thirty minutes ago by the concierge as he rummaged for a guest's bag. I got up, took a fresh shirt and my wash bag from my suitcase, and made my way towards the staff washroom, which I have been allowed the use of.

"I realised I had forgotten my razor, and I retraced my steps. The electric light was off in this room. In the faint light from the corridor, I saw the shadow of a man standing about where you are now, Doctor, slamming his fist against the packing case containing the tele-automaton.

"I shouted and darted forward. The man turned to me, and I was instantly doused with water: salt water." He displayed damp stains on his shirt and suit. "I wiped my eyes and attempted to grapple the fellow, but I was bludgeoned to the ground. My assailant fled, thankfully without having damaged the apparatus."

"Describe the assailant's weapon," Holmes requested.

"Oddly enough, I believe I was attacked with a tomahawk or something like it – a small hatchet. But perhaps that's my Yankee experience speaking. It was dark, so I cannot be sure."

"This wound was inflicted by a blunt instrument," I informed Holmes, "possibly with rounded corners."

"Was your attacker carrying anything else?" Holmes asked.

"Aside from the weapon? I don't think so."

Holmes nodded. He slid his hand over the rough wood of the nearest packing case. "This has been splattered with salt water in the same manner as Mr Tesla's wardrobe."

Mr Scherff started. "Was Mr Tesla attacked? Is he hurt?"

"No, no. He is quite safe," I reassured him. I fastened Mr Scherff's head bandage with a pin and stood back. "The wound is superficial, but you've had a crack on the head, so take things easy today. Contact the hotel physician or me if you feel nauseous or dizzy." I passed him my card.

"Thank you, Doctor. I'd best dress and report to Mr Tesla."

I fingered my tie pin. "You mentioned...."

Mr Scherff chuckled. "Mr Tesla has a strong dislike of jewellery, particularly pearls. If I wore a tie pin like yours, it would mean a day of sulks and bad temper."

I smiled a rueful smile. "I noticed Mr Tesla glaring at my collar."

"Jealousy," Holmes said with a smile. "Yours is a pin of singular beauty."

"Most amusing, Holmes." I followed him back through the service door and into the crowded lobby.

"May I see your boot sole?" Holmes asked.

I lifted my foot, feeling rather foolish. A gaggle of little girls in identical bright frocks and with flowers in their hair pointed and stared at me, tittering, their hands over their mouths. They were herded towards a bridal party by equally flowery young ladies.

"Still legible," Holmes said in a musing tone. He led the way through knots of wedding guests to the entrance.

"If the man or men who attacked Mr Scherff also purloined the satchel, what were they doing in the time between the theft and the assault?" I asked.

"A good question."

"And if our assailant was acting alone, he is a cool customer," I said. "He stole the papers from Mr Tesla's room then, rather than making his escape from the inevitable hue and cry, he tried to steal or harm the prototype of Mr Tesla's machine. He may have had confederates waiting with a carriage, the bogus waiter perhaps." I frowned. "At any rate, banging on the crate with his fist is a futile way to injure the Tesla device. I would have thought a foreign agent would have come armed with something more effective – dynamite, perhaps."

We passed through the swing doors and stopped on the pavement under the entrance canopy. An orderly queue of carriages and cabs dropped off guests and visitors at the swing doors. As each stopped, a corps of doormen and pages assisted passengers to alight and shepherded them into the lobby, loadin mountains of luggage onto trolleys in a well-drilled routine. Across the lane, another line of cabs served departing guests.

Sweepers scoured the gleaming pavement and roadway, and the all-pervading London stench of bitter dust, horse-dung, and creosote from the ubiquitous roadworks was replaced with a faint, perhaps imaginary, whiff of expensive perfumes. Compared with the frantic hustle and bustle of the Strand, just a few yards away, all was smooth, calm, and seemingly effortless efficiency.

I pointed to the cab rank from where Phipps waved, grinning.

"Miller's the cabby took the vicar, sir," the boot boy said. "And Dobbs is the doorman who saw him to his cab. No news of the cab that brought the vicar here, or of the waiter."

"Where's Miller now?" Holmes asked.

"On a job to Marylebone Station, sir. But he's a Savoy regular, and we've a big wedding on. I'm sure he'll be back soon."

"Unless he stops off for a late breakfast," I said.

"And Dobbs?" Holmes asked, surveying the doormen darting forward as each cab or carriage stopped under the hotel canopy.

Phipps slipped through the throng and returned with a tall, sombre-looking man in Savoy livery.

"A clergyman, sir, an elderly gentleman, was caught in the swing doors," Dobbs said in answer to Holmes' enquiry, "I helped him out and saw him to his cab. Miller was the driver."

"Distraught?"

"A bit befuddled, sir, not quite himself."

"Was he carrying anything?"

"No luggage." The doorman smiled. "Just a hot water bottle."

Holmes nodded. "And do you recall the cabman who brought the clergyman here?"

"I came on at six, sir. It was quiet till seven or so when things started to get busy. He didn't alight here during that time."

"I'm checking with the night men, sir," Phipps piped up.

I fumbled in my waistcoat pocket for a sixpence, but finding none, I was obliged to give the doorman a shilling. He saluted and returned to his duties. I noted the payment in pencil on my shirt cuff as Phipps made doe eyes at me that I ignored.

"It's clouding over," I said, sniffing the air. "I wouldn't be surprised if we had a cloudburst or two before lunchtime."

Holmes led Phipps and me through the swing doors. He surveyed the packed lobby with narrowed eyes. "Somewhere secluded, with a view of reception," he said. "The hotel library." We followed the boy across the lobby, weaving among knots of guests, first into an unoccupied room with desks laid with writing paraphernalia, then into an elegant library furnished in club-room style with comfortable leather chairs, sofas and potted plants. A pageboy leaning against the mantelpiece with his hands in his pockets sprang to attention.

"How long have you been on duty here?" Holmes asked him.

"Since six, sir."

"Did an elderly clergyman spend some time here earlier this morning?"

"Yes, sir."

"Did he have anything with him?"

"Yes, sir, a hot water bottle."

"Where did he sit?"

Holmes sat in the indicated armchair, close to the open doors. "I have an excellent view of the reception and concierge's desks and of the service door. I could easily slip into the baggage room when the staff are engaged." He smiled. "We are advancing."

Holmes instructed Phipps to look out for Miller and continue his search for the cabby who brought the clergyman to the hotel, and he motioned for me to take a seat opposite him.

"Let's reconstruct," he said. "Mr Tesla's bag was stolen between six and seven, when he returned from his meal. The door lock shows no evidence of being forced. That argues the room key had been purloined or borrowed from a confederate in the hotel, a skeleton key had been made (suggesting a long-matured plan) or an expert lock-picker was employed."

I nodded. "That is clear."

"A clergyman carrying a hot water bottle was at the reception desk before six this morning. He may have seen Mr Tesla pass through the lobby on his way to breakfast and overheard his room number from the irritated night manager. At six ten or thereabouts a man in waiter's uniform, or the clergyman after a change of clothing, took the lift to Mr Tesla's floor, and possibly did the deed.

After ten minutes or less, he came down again. Or, if the waiter is innocent, the clergyman could have easily mingled with the wedding crowd and come up and down without being noticed."

"Or he could have taken the stairs," I said."

"Unlikely," said Holmes. "The chalk mark would have worn off after six flights of stairs."

I checked the sole of my boot: it was clean. "Mr Scherff was attacked an hour after the robbery of Mr Tesla's papers was discovered," I said, "The clergyman watched from here, chose his moment and struck. Then he left in a cab, after a struggle with the swing doors." I considered. "Was his weapon concealed about him? I don't think he used his hot water bottle as a bludgeon."

"You will recall the evidence he wore a large cross on a chain around his neck."

"The blunt instrument." I said.

"Quite possibly."

"That seems almost sacrilegious." I frowned. "According to the doorman and the page, the clergyman did not carry a bag. Did the waiter leave by the service exit with the satchel, or he is still in the hotel? He could be Mr Schmetterling."

"Or anyone else. But you are quite right, my dear fellow: it's time we had a talk with the ventriloquist."

We stood and made our way to the lifts.

"Isn't it strange that Mr Tesla is so concerned about his baggage he requires Mr Scherff to keep a round-the-clock guard on it," I said, "but he stores his secret papers on top of the wardrobe? Why did he not put the papers in the hotel safe, or bring them down with him to breakfast?"

"Mr Tesla told us that he was working on them from very early this morning, but you're right. I have a feeling Mr Tesla is keen to keep up an impression of gentility, a certain elegance of dress and posture that would be spoiled if he were seen carrying a heavy bag. You noted his frequent glances at his reflection in the mirror in his suite."

⸺◆◇◆⸺

The lift attendant took us to the eighth floor. "A ventriloquist would be an excellent cover for a spy," I said as we alighted. "He could send secret messages to his confederates using his patter with the dummy. At any event, he is doing suspiciously well in his profession to afford the Savoy."

A young man in hotel livery loitering in the hallway gave us a dark look as we stopped at Suite 88. I whispered that we were working with Sergeant Griffiths, and he saluted and backed away.

Holmes' knock was answered by a balding, middle-aged man in his shirt sleeves, who opened the door a few inches.

"Good morning, am I addressing Herr Schmetterling?" Holmes asked. "I am Sherlock Holmes, and this is my friend and associate, Doctor Watson. Might we take a few moments of your time?"

"In what connection?" Herr Schmetterling asked in accentless English.

"This room number has been mentioned in relation to a circumstance that took place on a lower floor," Holmes said in an official tone. "It is a police matter of some moment."

Herr Schmetterling frowned, but he opened the door wide and ushered us in. "I hope this will not take long. I am about to go down to breakfast."

In contrast to Mr Tesla's immaculate suite, the ventriloquist's sitting room was strewn with a confusion of open bags, clothes and papers. Herr Schmetterling shrugged on a waistcoat and frock coat, and softly closed the door to the bedroom before turning back with raised eyebrows. He did not invite us to sit.

Holmes explained that a robbery had taken place on the sixth floor. Evidence suggested a connection between the theft and the eighth floor, and we were conducting enquiries in certain rooms.

"I was here all night, from midnight or so. I noticed nothing amiss," Herr Schmetterling informed us.

"Were your windows locked?" Holmes asked.

Herr Schmetterling frowned. "I assume so. I didn't check."

"It is possible a cat burglar may have scaled the building looking for an unlocked window. He may have climbed through while you were asleep. I wonder if I might have a look around. There may be traces of his passage."

Herr Schmetterling wrung his hands. "I'm a light sleeper, sir, and I am sure that I would have heard—"

A muffled sound came from the bedroom. Herr Schmetterling's eyes slid away from Holmes and towards the door. "I'm certain I would have been disturbed by an intruder."

Another sound, a shrill cry, came through the bedroom door. The ventriloquist paled and bit his lip. "Would you excuse me?"

He hurried into the bedroom. Before the door closed behind him, we heard a loud German-accented voice raised in anger.

Holmes quickly quartered the room, searching under and behind the massive Ottoman. He shook his head.

The bedroom door opened, and Herr Schmetterling came out carrying the Prussian officer doll I had seen at the music hall. Close to, it was tawdry. The silver pickelhaube helmet on its head was tarnished, its extravagant moustaches frayed, and the elaborate, bemedaled uniform it wore faded and patched, but the dummy's huge, bright-blue eyes glittered as they flicked from Holmes to me.

"He doesn't like to be l-left alone," Herr Schmetterling murmured with a nervous smile.

"Ha!" the dummy turned to its master and screamed in a harsh Teutonic accent. "It is not I who is the cry baby. It is not I who is fearful of the *Butzemann* under the bed *du willenloser mensh, du.* I do not my drawers wet before my performance. Not I."

"If I might just—" Holmes slipped into the bedroom.

The dummy leaned towards me and adopted a confidential tone. "He was the runt of the litter, you see. He boasts his mother was an Alsatian chatelaine. In fact, maman was a Lambeth washerwoman who on a church doorstep dumped him."

Despite my rational mind knowing that the dummy's voice was literally a stage trick, I gaped at it, half embarrassed for Mr Schmetterling. I attempted to diffuse the awkwardness of the situation by turning away from the dummy and addressing its operator. "I must congratulate you, sir. The effect is quite remarkable. I saw your performance at the Canterbury—"

"Washed her hands of him, his maman did," the dummy screeched over me. "And who could blame her for dumping the *dumkoft, nicht war?*"

The dummy slapped Mr Schmetterling hard across the cheek. "We know how to deal with such types in the Prussian service."

Holmes appeared from the bedroom, crossed the room, and loomed over the dummy. "You will be silent, if you know what's good for you. *Denkdaran, was mit Pinocchio passiert ist.*"

The dummy turned away, seeming abashed, and Mr Schmetterling looked down at his toes. "I know n-nothing of the matter you speak of gentlemen. I have no d-desire to be discourteous, but you can understand that I must get on. We have a matinee this afternoon. I m-must ask you to hasten this interview to an end."

Holmes closed the door of Mr Schmetterling's suite behind us and raised his eyebrows.

I shook my head. "If that man is an international spy, I'm the Sugar Plum Fairy."

"A hectoring, overbearing dummy, and the manipulator posing as the doll's assistant," Holmes said as we retraced our steps to the lifts and rang the bell. "A common, wearisome music hall trope, carried in a most wretched manner into real life. Would you characterise such nonsense psychopathic, Doctor?"

I considered as the lift arrived and we descended. "Possibly. Actors often stay in character offstage between acts, but this is behaviour of another order entirely. I suppose we must presume the ventriloquist has some acting skills, however rudimentary, so he could be our fake waiter, or even the clergyman, but I don't see him as a criminal mastermind."

"Perhaps the dummy pulls the strings."

"And *willen-* whatever the dummy called its master, and the *Butzemann* the ventriloquist is supposed to fear?"

Holmes smiled. "Ironically, a *willenlosser* man is a puppet, a weak-willed, spineless person, and *Butzemann* is the bogeyman under the bed."

"Ha." I frowned. "What did happen to Pinocchio?"

"He was hanged."

The lift doors opened. Holmes glanced across the foyer to the entrance door and chuckled. "Jupiter is descended among us."

I peered through the crowd towards the entrance door. "Is that Mycroft?"

"We are indeed pursuing a matter of considerable moment if it has extracted my brother from his lair," Holmes said as we threaded through the wedding guests. "Particularly on a Sunday."

Mycroft Holmes waited for us by the swing doors, his great bulk blocking traffic like a boulder in a swift-flowing river. He was physically the antithesis of his brother. Where Sherlock was slim and lithe, Mycroft was heavily built, verging on obese. But above his massive frame was set a head that reminded me of a bust I had seen of Cicero at the height of his rhetorical powers. Firm-browed, with steel-grey, deep-set eyes and full lips, the evidence of Mycroft's dominant mind was clear to see.

"I thought you might turn up," Holmes greeted his brother, "like a bad penny."

"My breakfast at my club was interrupted by a functionary at the Admiralty, which I am told, is buzzing like a demented beehive. Is it true Tesla's notes have been purloined?"

Holmes held up his hand. "A moment, Mycroft. Here is our boot boy."

Phipps waved through the glass of the swing doors. He beckoned Holmes, Mycroft and me outside and led us along a line of cabs to a hansom with a driver beside it in a grimy suit and battered top hat, holding a cab whip.

"Mr Dusty Miller, gentlemen," Phipps said with a bow.

Mr Miller sniffed. "The boy here says there's two bob in it for tellin' where I dropped a clerical cove this morning."

I glared at the boot boy, who assumed a cherubic air.

"A farthing tip on a one-and-thruppence fare," Mr Miller said. "And him a man of the cloth. I nearly flung it back at him. I dropped him in Great St Andrew's Street, Seven Dials, by the Crown."

"Did he go inside?"

"In the pub? Did he heck. He wouldn't even get down outside. I had to move the horse a dozen yards on before His Grace would care to set foot on the pavement. Going on he was about the Demon drink and the Sabbath and all that palaver." He chuckled. "Funny thing. He was carrying—"

"—a hot water bottle," I said.

Holmes held up a restraining hand. "Do not lead the witness, my dear fellow." He turned back to the cabby.

"That's right, a hot water bottle."

"Very well. Pay Mr Miller, would you Watson? And give the boy his fee, a shilling each for finding Miller and Dobbs."

I paid the cabby the full half crown and gave Phipps his florin after a stern lecture on the infamy of greed. He had the cheek to counter that he had merely subtracted sixpence from Miller's payment as his usual commission.

"I have more news, sir," the boy said with a grin. "I tracked the cabby who picked the vicar up from the cab rank in Jermyn Street and brought him here."

"Time?"

"Exactly five thirty this morning, so the cabby says, by St Martin's chime."

Holmes rubbed his hands together. "We move forward. We have the three loci pertinent to the case: Jermyn Street, the Savoy Hotel and Seven Dials. Another bob for Phipps, Watson, and half a crown to the second cabby."

I paid the boy again, vehemently impressing on him the sanctity of contractual obligations and the iniquity of avarice. Holmes gave him his new instructions, ordering him to scour the vicinity of Seven Dials, hunting an elderly cleric wearing a large cross and carrying an empty hot water bottle. He requested me to arrange cab hire by the hour with Miller and provide Phipps with small change for tips.

"Another half crown each if they mark our quarry," Holmes added.

I advised the boy to question local shopkeepers and policemen and enquire at guest houses, hotels, churches and chapels.

"Let him use his common sense," Holmes said. "He's young enough to still possess a vestige of native wit."

Mycroft and I followed Holmes back into the hotel foyer.

"The clergyman obviously used the hot water bottle as a receptacle for the salt water," I said. I made a note on my cuff, "but what the devil was the water for?"

Holmes smiled. "You may have answered your own question."

We found a quiet corner away from the crowd milling around the reception desk and the concierge's counter.

"Sherlock," Mycroft said in a sombre tone, "I cannot impress on you enough the grave consequences—"

"Just a moment, Mycroft." Holmes darted across the foyer, jostling aside members of the bridal party. He buttonholed the hotel photographer, who was setting up his equipment for wedding photographs. "What are you doing here? Where are my photographs?"

"All developed, sir. I'll print them out as soon as I'm done with—"

Holmes waved him away and jabbed his finger at his assistant. "Show me to the developing room." The young man glanced nervously at the photographer, and Holmes hooked him by the collar and stalked across the foyer, propelling the assistant before him.

"While you're busy, Holmes, your brother and I might think about a late breakfast or an early luncheon," I called after him. Holmes and the young man disappeared through the green-baize door by the concierge's desk.

Mycroft beamed.

The head waiter of the Savoy Grill greeted Mycroft effusively. He led us past centre tables of ladies in fashionably huge hats and groups of theatre people who lived up to the Grill's Bohemian reputation in a clamour of histrionic greetings and extravagant gestures. We settled at a quiet corner table away from the hubbub, surrounded by City and political gentlemen taking their solitary and sedate Sunday breakfasts.

Mycroft chuckled as he studied the menu. "Did you know that Mr Tesla cleans every dining implement he uses with napkins – he gets through a dozen or more at every sitting."

"Exactly eighteen, I would hazard a guess," I said. "He requires that many towels each day."

A waiter appeared, and Mycroft and he engaged in an earnest conversation in a mixture of English and French.

"We are too early for the *prix fixe* luncheon," Mycroft said at last, "I'm ordering devilled kidneys, black pudding, and Cumberland sausages for Sherlock and me – with scrambled, no poached eggs. They have an excellent house champagne I can heartily recommend."

"I'll have the same."

Mycroft and the waiter exchanged more culinary chat. "Maurice tells me French walnuts are just in; they will do well with a creamy goat's cheese the chef brought back from an epicurean pilgrimage to Saône-et-Loire."

The waiter left us, and Mycroft smoothed his napkin across his knees. "Our Admiralty demonstration is at a secret location at eleven," he said. "I suggested Sunday as more discreet than meeting in office hours on a working day. The First Sea Lord wasn't happy, and he is even less amiable after being dragged off a golf course to deal with the current crisis."

I raised my eyebrows. "Is it a crisis?"

Mycroft waited until Maurice was out of earshot before he answered. "It is; *entre nous*, the prime minister has been informed. The importance of Tesla's discoveries could hardly be exaggerated. I personally shepherded a sizeable sum through the Naval Estimates to acquire the patents for the tele-automaton. Tesla's device will revolutionise naval warfare; no vessel will be safe within its operational radius."

"Where have I heard that before?" I said.

Mycroft leaned back in his chair, looking uncomfortable.

"I remember now," I said. "The Bruce-Partington submarine of a few years ago was to make an end of naval warfare, was it not? No battleship could survive in the same ocean as one." I smiled. "Yet we are still building battleships apace. What became of the wonder submarine we made such a fuss of back in '95?"

Mycroft blinked at me. "There were certain difficulties." He brightened as the waiter returned with our wine. "Here is Sherlock."

"The prints are drying," Holmes said as he took his seat.

"We were discussing the Bruce-Partington submarine," I said, a little mischievously. "It seems, despite all the fuss at the time, it was never taken up by the Navy."

"I ordered eggs and sausages," Mycroft said, signalling a waiter to fill Holmes' glass. "I think you'll find this champagne rather fine."

"The Admiralty declares itself open to all innovations in naval warfare," Holmes said as he sipped his wine. "They form a committee to investigate the merits of each invention – submarines, heavier-than-air flying craft, automatic guns etc. The committee invariably reports that there is no merit in the device. The theory the government follows is, if our Navy is seen to deride and reject an invention, then other Powers are less likely to take it seriously."

"Even if the invention has merit?"

"Particularly if the invention has merit. The Admiralty is perfectly satisfied with the naval status quo. We have more battleships, cruisers, and torpedo-boat destroyers than anyone else, and the Navy considers itself superior to any two forces that might combine against us. If the Bruce-Partington submarine had made capital ships redundant, we would have suffered the most."

"You think that's why the Admiralty invited Mr Tesla here from America – to reject his invention?" I asked. "That is rather cruel."

"His case is an exception," Mycroft answered in a sharp tone. "The tele-automaton device is quite extraordinary. I saw a demonstration at the Electrical Exhibition at Madison Square

Gardens in New York a few years ago. It was uncanny. I had a sketch made."

He laid a drawing on the table. It depicted a rectangular pool surrounded by a crowd of onlookers in which a toy boat festooned with antennae circled.

"The boat performed whatever manoeuvres the gentlemen in the crowd called to it, turning, stopping and starting to order. If my mind were not entirely rational, I would have deemed it black magic." He chuckled. "In fact, several members of the audience looked uneasy, crossed themselves or hurried away. You see Mr Tesla in the background of the drawing, controlling the device via energy waves similar to those that travel along our telegraph wires; in this case the waves move unseen through the air."

"What is the operational range of the apparatus?" Holmes asked.

"A few dozen yards. But Tesla avers range is merely a question of output power. Theoretically, there are no limits. According to his submission to the Admiralty, the controller of the projected weapon may be miles from its target, outside gun range and thus operating in complete safety."

"How would the operator see the target at such a distance?" I asked.

Mycroft tone grew ominous. "That is the crux, and the reason the loss of the files is so disastrous. In his notes, Tesla outlines a completely new method of detecting ships across great distances using waves of energy. Once the enemy is detected, the tele-automaton can be aimed towards it. According to Tesla, the notes are speculative, but contain enough data to direct a wireless expert towards the solution."

"Germany has an abundance of wireless experts," I said. "And so does France."

Our food was served, and while we ate, Holmes and I brought Mycroft up to date with our progress.

"Very well," Mycroft said. "You will agree that the device must be in our safe hands rather than those of our bellicose Continental or trans-Atlantic neighbours."

I could not disagree.

"An agent could reap a pretty reward for the missing papers," Mycroft continued. "I draw your attention to this list of the top foreign agents in the country right now."

"Adolph Mayer, Louis La Rothiere and Hugo Oberstein," I read. "Could one of these be posing as our ventriloquist? It would be a cunning plan to play the Dr Jekyll while in reality acting as Mr Hyde."

"The ventriloquist is a pathetic specimen," Holmes told his brother. "The Prussian dummy, however, is capable of any nefarious act."

Mycroft called a waiter and requested another bottle of wine. "Our elderly cleric exhibited oddly amateur behaviour for a seasoned spy – getting stuck in the doors, ha. Or do both our reverend and the ventriloquist ape the dilettante to put us off the scent?"

"And then there is the waiter who travels up and down in the lift carrying an empty tray," I said. "What, if anything, is his role in the affair?"

I looked up and stood. "Mr Tesla, won't you to join us?"

Mr Tesla approached our table, looking quaint in his Prince-Albert-style coat and white gloves.

"You know Mr Mycroft Holmes, I believe." I called a waiter and requested a chair.

"Thank you," Mr Tesla replied, bowing to Holmes and his brother before sitting. "I have re-assumed my identity as Mr Brown."

The waiter proffered a menu, but Mr Tesla waved it away. "Kindly take the vase of flowers away and bring an unopened bottle of Evian water and a tumbler."

"We were discussing your machine and the end of warfare as we know it," I said with a smile.

"My device is much, much more than that, Doctor." Mr Tesla smoothed a ruck in the tablecloth, and moved the condiment cruets into line with the table edge. "My torpedo uses a 'borrowed mind', responding to orders from a distant and intelligent operator. But the day is not far off when I will endow a machine with its own intelligence, whereby it can act on environmental stimuli of its own accord."

The waiter returned with Mr Tesla's Evian water, a glass and a stack of napkins. I counted eighteen.

"So much for incognito," Holmes said.

Mr Tesla smiled and polished his glass with a napkin.

"I read in a *Strand Magazine* article that you believe humans have no wills," I said.

"Every human action is the result of external stimuli."

"Even your own?"

Mr Tesla discarded the first napkin and reached for another. "Indeed so, but I am particular about my stimuli."

"If we could return to our purpose, gentlemen," Mycroft said. "Mr Tesla's briefcase contains his plans for an automaton which, left to itself and without any control from the outside, will seek out and destroy enemy ships. The military possibilities of such an achievement are stupendous; it will mark the beginning of a new epoch in war. Imagine, Sherlock, a thinking weapon!"

Holmes smiled. "Let us hope the weapon reasons more logically than the vast majority of humans."

"This is no laughing matter," Mycroft said sternly. "It is a vital case. You must stretch all your resources to recover the missing papers."

I echoed Holmes' smile. "A reasoning machine sounds a little far-fetched. Will future man be expected to chat with his typewriter or let his horseless carriage determine which route he takes to Town—" I spied the photographer's assistant across the room and beckoned him.

Holmes pounced on the sheaf of photographs he offered, and held each under the electric wall sconce by our table. "Now we have it," he said. "I am dull indeed not to have seen this."

He tossed the photographs onto the table, and Mycroft and I examined them in the bright light. One showed the stained wardrobe. "I see a cross, and then an 'E'," I said. "It is perfectly plain."

"Edison filament globes," Mr Tesla said, peering at the electric lamp. "The bulbs in my room are Swan's, based on my own design." He sniffed. "These are Edison's."

"This is not a hotel room number," Mycroft said, tossing another photograph onto the table. "It's a locker number. For a sports club, a swimming bath, perhaps, or a Turkish bath."

"It's 'B 3'," I said, leaning forward to get a closer look.

Holmes checked his watch and stood. "Sports clubs and swimming pools will just be opening; but one can spend the night at some baths. There is one in Jermyn Street, where the cabby picked our fellow up." He stalked towards the doors.

Mr Tesla and I followed. I heard a cry from Mycroft behind me. "I shall stay and man our headquarters. Remember, Downing Street waits for news."

Holmes and I piled into a two-horse growler at the hotel entrance. Mr Tesla gestured to a hansom in the queue. "I will follow."

"Mr Holmes, sir!" A Savoy footman thrust a sheaf of papers through the cab window.

"A note of clergymen staying at the hotel," I said as the cab set off. "And a list of the occupants of rooms 33, 38, 83 and 88 at the Cecil and other hotels in the vicinity. The telephonist has done a fine job, Holmes. We must send a commendation to the hotel management."

Holmes nodded absently.

"I don't understand," I said as we turned into the busy clamour in the Strand. "Why will Mr Tesla not travel in our cab? With him, we would be three. Now he is alone in his cab. One is not divisible by three."

"You forget the horse and driver," said Holmes.

"Ha! By that reasoning, we two plus Mr Tesla and our two horses and driver would have been six – still divisible by three."

"We cannot expect reason to play a significant part in our electrical genius's dreads. If you sat down for dinner, let's say at the Savoy, and you were the thirteenth guest, would you not experience a twinge of anxiety?"

"I admit I might: it would depend on who was picking up the bill."

We made good time in light traffic and got down at the cab rank outside the London hammam in Jermyn Street. Compared to the hubbub of the Strand, the street was Sunday quiet, with just a couple of pedestrians and a few passing cabs and omnibuses.

"*Nota bene*, gentlemen," Holmes said as Mr Tesla joined us. "The cabstand is just a dozen steps across a swept pavement from the door of the hammam."

We passed under a faux Greek portico and into a spacious black-and-white-tiled lobby filled with a curious melange of marble statuary, silk hangings and Oriental *objets d'art*. Holmes tapped the floor with his stick. "Tiles, no carpet."

A young man was bent over a newspaper behind an ornate counter. He looked up, slipped the paper under the counter, and donned a red fez. "First Class is it, gentlemen, with shampoo? That'll be four shillings each, or monthly membership—"

"Four shillings," I exclaimed. "Daylight robbery!"

The man curled his lip. "We maintain a select clientele, gentlemen. But, if you prefer, Second Class is only half a crown. Kindly leave your hats, boots and sticks with the assistant."

"We wish to look around," Holmes said, "to inspect the premises to see if it meets our requirements.

"I'm sorry, sir, I can't let you past the – oy!"

Mr Tesla and I followed Holmes through a curtained doorway and into a room lined with lockers and furnished with long benches. An atmosphere composed of steam, chlorine, sweat, and perfumed soap instantly enveloped us.

A young attendant wearing baggy silk trousers and a fez sat with his elbows on a table piled with checked towels, smoking a cigarette.

He stubbed the cigarette, stood and bowed. "Good morning, gentlemen." He gestured to a rack of coloured bottles and other merchandise behind him. "Precious oils from the Orient, the latest Colognes to order, mineral water, alcoholic beverages and nibbles available from the Continental Café opposite, and hookahs for hire at a bob a go with aromatic Arabian tobacco that soothes the spirits and exercises the lungs. We offer shampoo service, vibro-electric massage, Harbutt's Vigour Tonic rub—"

Holmes held up a restraining hand. "Are you the only attendant on duty?"

"Yessir. It's just me right now, as the other shampooers are having their breakfast. If you'd care to take a glass of something or have a splash in the pool, I can sort you out one by one."

"Where is the boot boy?"

"You're looking at him, sir. I'm the all-the-bloomin'-work-and-then-some boy at eighteen bob a week. He grinned. "Plus tips."

Holmes glanced around the empty locker room. "That must keep you busy."

"Of a Saturday evening, you're not wrong, sir. The gentlemen come in at closing time to sleep it off, like. But then we have a half-dozen shampooers. We've had no more than three gents in today, sir. It's the cycling and golf crazes keeps them out on Sundays. I don't know why we bother staying open. Is it shampoo then?"

"Do patrons have their regular lockers?"

"No, sir, choose as you like."

"You write the locker number on the shoe soles in chalk, do you not?" Holmes passed a photograph to the attendant. "Did you write this last night or early this morning?"

"B 3, sir. Brown, lace-up brogues, size eleven, by Lobbs of St James's. Lovely leather, sir, worth taking a bit of care over." The young man smiled. "And the gentleman is grateful, sir."

"His name?"

"Reverend Pottinger. Tall old cove, but still stiff as a guardsman. He gives us improving literature, sir. Bible stories and the like."

"He's a member?" Holmes asked. "He comes here regularly?"

"Yes, sir. He buzzes through the hot room like a dose of salts, sir, then sits and reads his paper. Or oftener than not, he plants himself in the library, reading the magazines and dozing till we close up. A great one for books, is Reverend Pottinger – a very learned gent if you take my meaning. He showed me a letter he wrote what was printed in the newspaper with his very own name there with it."

"On what subject?"

"I couldn't rightly say, sir, but he gets right het up over the newspapers sometimes, tearing them up. We've had members complain."

"Did Reverend Pottinger stay here last night?"

"He did, sir. We've a dozen rooms in the Chambers upstairs, mostly for clients what have missed their train home. The reverend gets a bit fuddled like after a few gins and lemons, so he takes a room." The attendant fingered a chain around his neck with an ornament attached. "He gave me this. I'm to wear it at all times, even at night."

Mr Tesla leaned forward. "A Saint Benedict medallion: a sacramental expressing faith in Christ's protection from the Enemy. It wards against the Evil One."

I raised my eyebrows.

"My father was a clergyman, a Servian Orthodox priest, as was my grandfather."

"Where does the reverend live?" Holmes asked.

"Dunno, sir," the attendant replied. "Not nearby; he comes here by cab."

At a nod from Holmes, I gave the attendant a shilling and made a note on my shirt cuff. We trooped back into the lobby, and Holmes confronted the supercilious receptionist.

"I wish to enquire about one of your guests, a Reverend Pottinger."

"He won't be in today," the man replied. "He's upset with us for opening on the Sabbath. He's complained to the management."

"The reverend stayed here last night."

"Not the Sabbath, see." The receptionist smiled. "Yesterday was the day *before* the Sabbath."

"I need Reverend Pottinger's address," Holmes said.

The man slowly shook his head. "Against the terms of my employment, guv. I can't go around giving personal details of our clients to all and sundry. Unless you're the Law, and you don't look like the Law. By rights, I should call the peelers and have you done for trespassing."

"It is a matter not only of the utmost urgency, but of national importance," Holmes insisted. "I am Sherlock Holmes—"

"And I'm Marie Lloyd, the One and Only." The receptionist chuckled. "Pull the other leg, gents, it's got bells on." He leaned back in his chair. "Of course, I'd like to cooperate." He rubbed the fingers and thumb of one hand together in an unmistakable gesture.

"Damn your impertinence," I exclaimed. "Keep a civil tongue in your head or I'll know the reason why. We are willing to reward those who offer us information, but we will not bribe an employee of the hammam to procure information."

Holmes chuckled.

"There is a distinct ethical difference, Holmes," I said warmly.

"Of course, my dear fellow: I quite understand."

The all-the-work-and-then-some boy peeked through the curtains and held up his shilling; the receptionist frowned. "You'll make it worth my while if I tell you the old buffer's address, is that it?"

I bridled. "Cooperation with the agents of law and order is a civil obligation—"

"Yes," said Holmes.

The receptionist sniffed, pulled a ledger from under his counter, and slowly leafed through it. "Pottinger's address, you say? Agamemnon, 12 Neal's Yard, Seven Dials."

I reluctantly placed a shilling coin on the desk and made another note on my cuff.

"Do you have a *Crockford*?" Holmes asked.

"There's a set in the library, sir," the bath attendant answered. "The reverend always has his nose in them."

Holmes consulted the clerical directory. "As expected from his address, Reverend Benjamin Pottinger was a naval chaplain before he retired – served on HMS Agamemnon in the Crimea. Interesting."

"You cannot seriously think Reverend Pottinger is our thief, Holmes," I said. "What possible motive could he have? And if he were, who is the waiter?"

"I have a possibility in mind. A clergyman is in an excellent position to recruit experts in all criminal fields."

⸺◆○◆⸺

We got down from our cabs outside the Crown public house in Great St Andrew's Street, Seven Dials, ordered the cabbies to wait, and made our way through the narrow entrance to Neal's Yard, a triangular space lined with market wholesalers. Number twelve was squeezed between flower and basketry shops, all shuttered on a Sunday.

The housekeeper who answered the door rolled her eyes when Holmes requested Reverend Pottinger. "He's out in the backyard as like as not: at his devotions." She directed us along a narrow, dim corridor to the open back door.

A tall, white-haired gentleman in clergyman's attire stood in the backyard facing away from us. At his feet was a zinc bathtub. A slight, ginger-haired, middle-aged man in a server's smock stood beside him, holding open a book that was obviously, by its thickness, a Bible.

"Let us pray," the clergyman intoned. "God's creature, salt, I cast out the demon from you by the living God, by the true God, by the holy God, by God who ordered you to be thrown into the water spring by Eliseus to heal it of its barrenness. May all evil fancies of the foul fiend, his malice and cunning, be driven afar from this place."

"Amen," the server replied.

The clergyman took handfuls of salt from a bucket at his feet and sprinkled them into the bath. "O Lord, source of irresistible might and king of an invincible realm, in awe and humility we beg you, Lord, to regard with favour this thing of salt and water, to let the light of your kindness shine upon it, and to hallow it with the dew of your mercy so that every assault of the unclean spirit may be baffled, and all dread of the serpent's venom be cast out—"

The server saw us and tapped the clergyman on the shoulder.

The reverend turned, took off his pince-nez and frowned at us. He started back when he saw Mr Tesla. "Ye have your portion and lot with Cain the fratricide, with Simon the sorcerer and the traitor Judas," he cried, raising his hands as if to ward off a blow. "And with those who have said to God: depart from us, for we will not know Thy ways."

There was a long silence, broken by Holmes. "Reverend Pottinger, I presume?"

"What do ye with this ungodly man?" Reverend Pottinger stretched a crabbed hand towards Mr Tesla. "This man has sold his soul to the Old One in return for supernatural powers. What do ye with him?"

"I am Sherlock Holmes, and this—"

"Only God maketh man in His Own image. Only Man is endowed by the Almighty with will and an immortal soul. You bear the Mark of the Beast! 666!"

"Suite 66 on the sixth floor of the Savoy," I murmured. I glanced at Mr Tesla. "Three elements: 6, 6 and 6."

"You do the work of the Evil One: you are his minions. Do not attempt to deny it. Your cursed work is controlled by demons." Reverend Pottinger raised his hands in supplication. "Let them be ashamed and confounded together that seek after my soul to destroy it; let them be driven backward and put to shame that wish me evil. Let them be desolate for a reward of their shame that say unto me, Aha, aha."

The server added his amen, looking a little shamefaced.

"You slashed a cross and 'E' on the wardrobe door in blessed salt water," Holmes said. "'E' for *exite*, I would suggest, meaning 'Get ye gone', referring both to the demons and Mr Tesla."

"May ye perish in the day of judgment; may perpetual fire devour ye with the Devil and his angels, unless ye make restitution and come to amendment!" Reverend Pottinger fumbled beneath his robes, drew a heavy pistol, and aimed it at Mr Tesla. I darted forward, but Holmes was before me, slamming his stick on Reverend Pottinger's wrist.

I helped the clergyman to a wicker chair in a corner of the yard. His wrist was bruised, but not broken.

Mr Tesla gazed down into the tin bath in which a brown satchel lay submerged.

Holmes picked up the pistol. "An antique pepperpot with six barrels. Judging by the corrosion, it hasn't been used since the Crimea; it was obsolete even then. If all the barrels had fired, there would not be much left of Mr Tesla or, most likely, of the Reverend Pottinger." He turned to the server. "I know you."

"Dolly Murdoch, Mr Holmes." He saluted. "Reformed housebreaker, sir."

"One of my parishioners," Reverend Pottinger said softly, looking up, his face drained of colour. "He acted entirely under my direction."

Holmes ordered Murdoch to tell us what he knew of the affair.

"I opened the gentleman's door easy enough, Mr Holmes, but I couldn't find what the reverend wanted – secret papers and the like. So, I reported, and the reverend went for a looksee himself. He couldn't resist sprinkling the salt water to banish demons."

"I commend your professionalism, Murdoch," Holmes said. "You left no marks on the door lock."

Murdoch bowed. "The reverend filched the gent's bag and come down by the guest lift. We met in the lobby. I slipped out the service entrance with the bag and come here." He glanced across the yard to where Reverend Pottinger sat, quietly weeping. "The reverend stayed behind to curse the evil device."

"Why dunk the satchel in the salt bath?" I asked. "If you wanted to destroy the papers, why not simply burn them?"

Murdoch pursed his lips. "The landlady won't allow fires in the back yard, sir."

"How did Reverend Pottinger know that Mr Tesla was in England?" Holmes asked.

"An American reverend was on the same ship as him, sir, the Ada-something."

"The Adriatic," Mr Tesla said as he removed his coat and gloves, passed them to me, and rolled up his sleeves. "There was a pastor on board. He preached to the third-class passengers on the boat deck just below the windows of my suite in an irritating, shrill voice. He completely misinterpreted the meaning of the Parable of the Mustard Seed."

"You corrected him," I said.

"I thought it helpful to do so." Mr Tesla lifted the satchel from the bath and held it out as it streamed water. "And I suggested he move his flock farther along the deck out of earshot."

"How did he know of your device?" I asked.

"I needed to make certain adjustments to the tele-automaton. I borrowed the ship's swimming pool; it caused a stir." He laid the satchel on the ground and shrugged. "So much, as you say, for incognito."

Holmes, Mr Tesla, and I assembled in St Andrew's Street. The dripping bag lay on the running board of Mr Tesla's hansom.

"I owe you gentlemen my thanks."

I accepted Mr Tesla's plaudits as Holmes penned a telegram to his brother, using Murdoch's back as a writing desk.

"Are you sure you don't wish to press charges?" I asked.

"No, no. I bear no malice," Mr Tesla replied. "Reverend Pottinger acted according to his lights: strangely hued though they may be. My data is safe – I use an indelible ink of my own invention." He shook his head. "Humans do as they must do, Doctor. Our minds and bodies react to external stimuli and situations, nothing more."

He pulled on his white gloves. "In a few years, I will produce tele-automata capable of acting as if possessed of their own intelligence. Their advent will create a revolution. My torpedo is the first of a race of mechanical men who will do the laborious work of the human race.

"The present is theirs," Mr Tesla gestured towards the city around us. His lips curled. "And Edison's. But the future, for which I have really worked, is mine. I'll send you some of my writings."

He checked his watch. "I must go directly to the meeting with your admirals. My assistant will meet me at Great Smith Street Baths in Westminster with the apparatus." He chuckled. "I travel incognito."

"One question, if I may," I asked. "These rays you use to communicate with your device – do they pass through humans?"

"Waves, in fact, Doctor, but don't worry, we are all constantly penetrated by swirls of magnetism, Röntgen rays, alpha, beta and gamma rays, and many other phenomena we can only guess at. And the average human emits enough electrical power to illuminate a light bulb – even an Edison one, weak and untrustworthy though they are."

"Light bulbs or humans? Or Mr Edison?"

He laughed. "Take your choice."

———◆◇◆———

"I shall call this the Case of the Tesla Tele-automaton," I said, looking up from my desk at our lodgings in Baker Street that evening. "I have a subtitle: 'An affair of boot soles that became a one of immortal souls.' What do you think?"

Holmes snuggled down in his armchair, put his feet up on the fender, and blew a stream of fragrant pipe tobacco across the sitting room.

"Let's hope the Admiralty display a more enlightened attitude to Mr Tesla's invention this time." I blotted my notebook. "He returns to America tomorrow." I dropped into my seat by the fire and lifted my glass of tawny port in salute. Holmes returned my gesture with his glass.

"Mr Tesla spoke of mechanical men," I said. "When they become available, we might order one from Gamages and dispense with Billy."

Our page looked up bleary-eyed from the fireplace, where he stoked the fire. "Will that be all, Doctor?"

"Yes, get along to bed."

"How about some music to go with this excellent port?" I asked as the sitting-room door closed behind our page.

Holmes waived acquiescence, and I leafed through our growing collection of gramophone recordings with some pride of ownership.

"Do you mind something modern? I've a recording just in from Paris of Edvard Grieg, the Norwegian composer – you'll recall him from the Dreyfus affair. He's playing his '*Au printemps*' piano piece. It's rather charming."

I wound the gramophone, and as the music began, I reflected on how extraordinary it was that Holmes and I, sipping port wine in our homely sitting room in West London, could listen to music by a Norwegian composer performed months ago in Paris, and we could play it over and over if we wished. The gramophone machine replaced the human orchestra as Mr Tesla's mechanical man would soon replace our servant class.

The needle popped and crackled at the end of the disk.

"Mr Tesla's ship had a swimming pool," I said. "Extraordinary."

"Grieg has a light touch," Holmes said. "The melody is clear in its shape and dynamics, but, if you agree, we might try some Sarasate. We have his *Zigeunerweisen*."

Mr Sarasate's gypsy excursions on the violin were a trifle convoluted for my taste, and I thumbed through an American magazine given to me by the great inventor while Holmes leaned back in his chair, eyes closed, absorbed in the complexities of the music.

When the piece came to its extravagant conclusion, I flicked down my page. "Mr Tesla writes that life on Mars is a statistical certainty. In fact, he claims he has already received a communication from Space. It consisted of numbers, three of them, of course; they were one, two and three!"

Billy peeped through the door. "Telegram, Doctor, with one-and-thruppence to pay." He yawned. "And is there an answer?"

He handed me the flimsy, and I read, "Pottinger, Neal's Yard, Seven Dials. Expenses thirty-six shillings. Phipps."

Holmes smiled. "Succinct and economical, Young Phipps will go far."

I checked my watch. "Fourteen hours cab time at two-bob an hour, plus dinner and supper for the boot boy and the cabby, plus tips for his informants over and above the change I gave him; one pound sixteen is fair. I suppose we'll have to pay him from your Savoy fees. I'll tell Phipps to have the cabby call tomorrow morning."

I went to my desk and turned up the lamp. I wrote a short telegram and made a note of the additional expenses incurred in the case.

"We might tip the telephonist a bob or so," Holmes reminded me.

I handed Billy the telegram. "We should have called Miller and the boy off the scent when we found Pottinger; I have to admit I clean forgot them. I wonder how Phipps found our man."

"And our address."

"Yes, that too; a resourceful young fellow, if a little brazen."

"If I were asked to open communications with Martians," Holmes said, picking up the thread of our conversation, "I would begin with mathematics."

"But surely at a higher level than simple arithmetic, Holmes. The aliens must think us a very backward crew if they sent us such a rudimentary message." I chuckled. "One, two and three."

"In many respects, we are backward; I very much doubt an alien intelligence will bother with the Earth unless they are prospecting for minerals or a food source." Holmes tapped his pipe out on the fender. "As Mr Wells put it in his excellent story of Martian invasion, 'across the gulf of space… intellects vast and cool and unsympathetic, regarded this earth with envious eyes'." He stood. "I shall wish you goodnight."

With that uncomfortable thought resonating in my brain, I made my way upstairs to bed.

THE HYDE PARK MYSTERY

"I say, Holmes," I said as I eased the door of the sitting room open and edged through with my valise and rod case, "those cab rascals are on strike again and it's raining sheets. I'd like to – oh."

I paused in the doorway and blinked at Holmes and two gentlemen seated on the sofa and in my usual chair before our fireplace.

"Excuse me." I backed towards the hallway.

Holmes sprang from his armchair. "Come in, my dear fellow," he said. "Come, take a seat; I was hoping you might be back in time to join us."

I laid my luggage on the carpet and my gloves on the sideboard, slipped into a seat at the dining table and regarded Holmes' visitors with interest. One was a youngish man who exhibited the manner and dress of a gentleman, while the other, an older, sallow-faced, bearded man, wore a cheap, wrinkled suit and had the cloth cap of a working man on his knees.

Holmes settled back in his chair. "Doctor Watson, let me introduce Mr Renfrew of Addison, Chalmers and Renfrew, solicitors, and Mr Salmon, Secretary of the Amalgamated Cab Drivers' Society," he said with a mischievous smile. "Mr Salmon was just explaining the cabmen's grievances against the railway companies as a background to a case on which my opinion is requested."

I offered a frigid greeting. "I should be interested to know why no cabs were available at Waterloo Station this morning," I said stiffly, "much to the inconvenience of myself and many other passengers burdened with luggage. I was obliged to cross the bridge to the Embankment before I could induce a cab to stop and pick me up."

"I'm afraid that old chestnut 'railway privilege' is to blame," Holmes said. "That is the iniquity the strikers aim to redress, is it not, Mr Salmon?"

"The action is not a strike, if I may correct you, Mr Holmes, sir," Mr Salmon answered in a shrill tone. He turned to me. "I hope you will not blame the cabbies for your disruption, Doctor. Aggrieved street cabmen have temporarily and locally withdrawn their cabs from the vicinity of certain railway termini, as is their right under the relevant acts. Bluchers are voluntary, not contracted." He looked to Mr Renfrew as if for confirmation of his statement, but that gentleman merely smiled and gave a slight shrug of his shoulders.

"If I may summarise the position," Holmes said. "The street cabbies object to the system under which certain cab proprietors pay the railway companies for their cabs' privilege of picking up passengers at the mainline stations. Non-privileged cabs may drop passengers, but they are excluded from taking fares within the station."

"It is iniquitous," I conceded. "At busy times, cabs are scarce and long queues form at the stands. Station cabs, especially two-wheelers, are more knocked about than street cabs, and their horses are often inferior. Arriving passengers are anxious to get away, perhaps to catch a connecting train at another terminus, so they are less particular than one would be on the street." I frowned. "Bluchers?"

"Non-privileged cabs," Mr Salmon explained. "If the Boat Train, say, or a bunch of crowded excursion or race-day trains arrive together, the station staff have to call in street cabs to assist the station cabs – Bluchers as we call them."

Holmes stood and reached along the mantelpiece for his briar pipe. "Doubtless named for General von Blucher's Prussians at the Battle of Waterloo, who, according to partisan legend, reached the field of honour too late for combat and had to be content with merely mopping up stragglers from a French army already thoroughly beaten by the manly English."

"And Scots," Mr Renfrew said in his Highland accent.

"Quite." Holmes slumped back into his seat and packed his pipe. "And with those general desiderata understood, we may return to the purpose of your visit, gentlemen."

Mr Renfrew opened his briefcase, took out a brown file secured with silk tape and passed it to Holmes. "Crown v Thomas Long, cabdriver, for the wilful murder of cab company proprietor – or more accurately *erstwhile* cab company proprietor – James Ellerton Staines."

"The Hyde Park Murder," I said, leaning forward in my chair.

Mr Renfrew winced. "So the case has been termed in the gutter press, Doctor Watson, but I think we might allow my client his statutory right of reasonable doubt and call it the Hyde Park Shooting. My client maintains his innocence and contends that the deceased committed the abominable sin of self-murder."

I bridled. "I read of the case in *The Times*, hardly a gutter publication."

"A matter of perspective, my dear fellow," Holmes said with a smile. He stood. "Gentlemen, I shall examine the evidence and give you my opinion in due course." He confirmed an appointment at Mr Renfrew's chambers the following day and ushered our visitors to the sitting-room door.

I shifted to my usual chair and warmed my hands at our crackling fire. "At times, there are fifty or sixty empty cabs milling about the entrance to Victoria Station, impeding traffic. If they were allowed inside to the cab stands, a lot of congestion could be avoided."

Holmes resumed his seat and lit his pipe from the fire with a spill. "Anything to do with London cabs, be it fares, licensing, privilege or whatever, is bound to be contentious. Matters near to the hearts of the working class (beer), and middle class (cabs), are best left alone, as Viscount Cross, our Home Secretary of some years ago, wisely observed."

Holmes settled back in his chair and picked up the folder; he was instantly lost in its contents and soon wreathed in pipe smoke.

I busied myself unpacking my case, cleaning my fishing rods, and arranging with our housekeeper for my laundry to be seen to, before I considered the onerous task of catching up with my correspondence.

I returned to the sitting room as Holmes yawned and tossed the folder to the floor at his feet. "Pass me a couple of telegraph forms, will you? I am minded to do a little sleuthing before my appointment with Renfrew tomorrow. Are you game?"

"Certainly, it will make a welcome change from squatting by the Thames at Chertsey in a steady drizzle as I did all day yesterday, with just a half-dozen minnows to show for my efforts." I passed Holmes a sheaf of forms. "The cabby's barrister will try to prove his passenger committed self-murder. Suicides in cabs are, if not common, certainly not rare; I've often heard cabbies gripe about having to clean their cabs after an incident. But from the facts as laid out in that notorious gutter publication, *The Times,* the case looks to be a straightforward one of revenge murder."

Holmes stood. "There are singular elements to this matter that elevate it above the norm, if there is a norm for homicide."

"Not suicide?"

"No, no. I suspect Mr Renfrew's client may have been economical with the truth."

Holmes filled in two telegram forms at his desk and called for our pageboy. "Inspector Tobias Gregson of Scotland Yard, who we know to be competent despite his deductive limitations, is the agent assigned to the case. If the data presented in the file is correct, Gregson will see the cabby hanged."

I sent Billy to fetch a hansom from the stand, and we set off for the new Scotland Yard building on the Victoria Embankment.

———— ◆ ————

Inspector Gregson sat erect at his desk in the full glory of his befrogged uniform.

A mahogany ink stand, a silver-framed photograph of a white-haired gentleman, presumably a relative, a green-shaded Argon lamp, a telephone apparatus, and a single, slim folder lay in exactly symmetrical juxtaposition on the gold-stamped leather before him.

Empty shelves lined one wall of the room, which smelled strongly of new wood and furniture polish, with files and books in tea chests ranged below them. A narrow, as yet uncurtained, window offered a view of the Thames, slightly obstructed by a bare-branched tree. A framed map of London pinned to one wall was the only decoration.

A young constable, fair-haired like the inspector, sat in one corner at a desk covered with folders, evidence boxes, and untidy stacks of folded newspapers. He jumped up as Holmes and I entered and ushered us to a pair of upright chairs in front of the inspector's desk.

"How are you finding your new accommodation, Inspector?" Holmes asked.

"Well-enough," Inspector Gregson said. "Your telegram requested a briefing on the Long case, Mr Holmes." He opened the folder in front of him. "I have the cabby's statement."

"Perhaps you would be good enough to summarise?"

Inspector Gregson slid the file across his desk to his assistant.

"Long picked up a gentleman at eleven fifteen or thereabouts on Monday night from the night cabstand in Holborn Circus, his usual billet," the young constable began. "Long says the gentleman appeared to be slightly the worse for drink, slurring his words, but not drunk. He gave Paddington as his destination, specifically the Great Western Hotel. He requested Long pass through Piccadilly, without giving a reason.

"The ride was unremarkable until they reached Hyde Park Corner, where Long turned his nag north towards his destination. His passenger knocked on the roof and required him to take the Ring Road through Hyde Park instead."

"A straighter route," I said. "I've taken it myself; it's the only way through the Park open to cabs."

"You travelled in the daytime, I'll wager, Doctor," Inspector Gregson said. "The Ring Road is rarely used at night. It's pitch dark in the Park, save for the odd lamppost here and there, and the road is hardly more than a narrow bridle path. One or two cabs have missed a turn and ended up awash in the lake."

"Was Long suspicious?" I asked.

Inspector Gregson nodded to his assistant.

"He says he thought his fare was befuddled," the constable answered, "and like you, Doctor, the passenger wanted to take his usual route. The Queen's Gate was open, though the constable on the gate called to Long as they passed through to remind him that the Park closed at midnight."

Holmes nodded. "Go on."

"They followed the edge of the lake to a point between the Receiving House of the Royal Humane Society and the Magazine, where the passenger again banged on the roof and ordered Long to pull up. The Ring Road was pot-holed, and Long thought the fellow had been made unwell by the bumps.

"He stopped, and instantly both he and the horse were startled by a loud report. It took a moment to bring the horse under control. When he opened his hatch, a strong smell of gunpowder greeted Long, and he was shocked to see his passenger slumped across the seat.

"After vainly checking the man for a pulse, he drove on to the Victoria Gate where he alerted the constable on duty at eleven fifty-seven."

Holmes frowned.

Inspector Gregson leaned forward in his chair. "Yes, Mr Holmes, forty-two minutes for a journey that, in daylight and with moderate traffic, would take no more than twenty-two. At that hour of the evening, with no traffic to speak of, I would expect to do the journey in less time, not more. Long contends he has a slow nag, but I have examined his horse and found it to be above average for a cabber. In fact, Constable Boland here did the trip at the same time of night, in a police carriage mind, not a nimble cab, with the cabby's so-called slow nag hitched in front." He leaned back. "In how long, Boland?"

"Nineteen minutes flat, sir."

The inspector smiled. "So, what happened in the missing twenty-odd minutes?"

"An interesting question, Inspector."

On a nod from his master, the constable flipped a page of his report and continued. "The deceased carried no identification, just a wallet with a fiver in it and some coins. His overcoat and suit are not Saville Row but are good quality; his hat is Lock's of St James's, his gloves Dents." He smiled. "His bespoke boots have seen better days, but are very fine, crafted by Lobb—"

"An excellent company with records going back years," Inspector Gregson interrupted. "They recognised the boots, and we were able to identify the deceased as Thomas Ellerton Staines, owner of the Staines Cab Company with nine cabs on the streets of the metropolis. That many until a month ago, when one cabby had words with Mr Staines, pulled out the twenty-three quid saved with his hire-purchase scheme, and stormed off in high dudgeon, vowing revenge for various wrongs."

I frowned. "Long?"

Inspector Gregson gestured for the file, set it squarely before him, and put on a pair of gold-rimmed spectacles. "According to the cabby, Mr Staines fired one round into his own neck with his Galand and Sommerville .44 calibre pistol. And indeed, his pistol was found to have one chamber expended, and the remaining four loaded with unfired cartridges. Two more Webley centre-fire live cartridges were in his overcoat pocket."

Inspector Gregson looked up. "We live in a remarkable age for innovation, Gentlemen, and Scotland Yard is not behind in applying new methods in our investigations. Scientific evidence holds great sway with juries. The unfired cartridges in the victim's gun and coat were minutely examined by our experts at Woolwich Arsenal. One bullet in the gun and the two in the coat were clean and pristine. Three of the unused bullets in the gun were found to have traces of gunpowder—"

"That would be the case in any recently fired pistol," I said.

"—attached to the casing by smears of blood." The inspector continued. "Long's clothing and hands were also examined. Blood deposits and gunpowder residue were present on his right hand and sleeve, consistent, as you will agree, Doctor, with recently firing a pistol at close enough range to be blood splattered."

"May I see the weapon?" Holmes asked.

Inspector Gregson took a silvered revolver from his desk drawer. "The pistol is engraved with the victim's initials and has been confirmed by Mrs Staines to have been habitually carried by her husband."

Holmes closely examined the pistol, a rather old-fashioned-looking gun with a long extraction lever acting as a trigger guard. He returned the gun to the inspector, who replaced it in the drawer and stood.

"If you would care to follow me, gentlemen?"

The inspector led Holmes, me and the constable down a dusty staircase smelling strongly of fresh paint to an enclosed stable yard at the back of the police building where an unharnessed hansom cab stood.

"According to Long, Mr Staines shot himself in the confines of the cab interior," the inspector said. "Not a roomy place, as you will agree. Suicides almost invariably press the gun barrel to their temple or put it in their mouths, but Mr Staines chose to shoot himself in the neck from in front, so."

He mimed pointing a gun at his throat. "Awkward, no? The bullet passed through his neck. Where did it go? The cab has been closely examined and nothing found but this." The inspector pointed to a bright mark on the metal rim of one of the wheels. "Gunpowder residue was found on the victim's hand, but none on his neck, suggesting the fatal bullet was fired from a distance."

Inspector Gregson held out his hand. "Long's story is a tissue of invention, Mr Holmes. How he lured his ex-employer into his cab, I don't yet know, but I will stake my reputation on this being a murder."

Holmes and I shook his hand, made our farewells, and boarded our waiting cab at the gates of Scotland Yard. Holmes tapped on the cab roof with his cane, and the cabby opened the hatch. "Dufours Place, Soho, if you please."

The cab turned out of the gates and into heavy traffic on the Embankment. "Fifteen thousand cab drivers infest London," Holmes said. "I am surprised we experience so little cab crime."

I coughed and pointed to the hatch above our heads.

"The London cabby is the most anonymous of men," Holmes continued. "Unlike the bus driver, who plies a regular route, the cab driver may roam anywhere in the city. His relationship with his passenger is a fleeting one, encouraging brusqueness of manner or even downright fraud or worse."

"The same may be true for passengers," I suggested. "I have heard respectable men brag of bilking cabbies of their fare by darting into the Burlington Arcade or Swan and Edgar's, or of treating them with contempt – even men of consequence at my club who in all other matters are worthy of respect."

"It is an interesting collision of the working and middle classes."

We drove in silence as the cab followed the line of the River, turned north, and crossed Trafalgar Square.

"Inspector Gregson seemed a little – how shall I say – aloof, or even cold towards us compared with our previous encounters," I suggested.

"Really? I didn't notice."

"He didn't offer tea."

<hr/>

Holmes and I got down outside St James' poorhouse, and we were directed by a common loafer to a modern extension of the main building where a porter in his cubicle enquired our business. He conducted us along a tiled corridor to the coroner's office.

We were ushered into a pleasant room warmed by a merry fire and with its walls covered with maps and photographs. A trim, neatly dressed gentleman sat behind a heavy, cluttered desk. He stood, introduced himself as the coroner, Doctor Weaver, and waved us to seats set before his desk, without offering his hand. "I received your telegram, Mr Holmes. May I ask with what authority you are making your enquiries?"

"I act for Long, the defendant in the Hyde Park case."

"I see." Doctor Weaver adjusted a pair of pince-nez on his nose and peered down at a sheet of paper on his desk. "I am afraid I can find no provision in the parliamentary statutes regulating the conduct of my office that allows me to share information with private agents, however well-intentioned."

"I am retained by Chalmers, Addison and Renfrew on behalf of their client," Holmes answered in a stiff tone.

"All well and good, sir." Doctor Weaver pursed his lips. "But as coroner, my duty is to report my findings in this matter to the relevant agencies and to them alone. If you can provide me with an authorisation certificate from the police, the Home Office or another supervising body as listed in the decretum under which I operate," he tapped the paper on his desk, "then I would be pleased to cooperate with you gentlemen."

Holmes glared at the coroner and seemed about to make a possibly unhelpful remark, so I quickly interjected. "Coroner Doctor Ivor Purchase of the Middlesex Mortuary at St Laurence, Pountney Hill has condescended to work with Mr Holmes to their mutual benefit."

Doctor Weaver smiled a prim smile. "Again, that is all very well. Purchase is free to make whatever decisions he may in his district, but this is my little domain, Doctor, and I require my 'i's to be dotted and my 't's crossed."

"A man's life is at stake," Holmes said. "This is hardly a time for quibbles."

We sat in strained silence for a long moment.

I stood and went to the fireplace. "I couldn't help noticing this photograph above the mantel, Doctor. Netley Hospital, if I am not mistaken? I did my medical training at Netley in '79 and served with the Berkshires in Afghanistan."

Doctor Weaver's stern demeanour softened. "Maiwand?"

I nodded.

"You would have known Surgeon-Major Preston."

"Very well. Like me, he was wounded during the battle, but recovered. I saw him off at Tilbury a few years ago when he was taking up a position in Hong Kong."

"He graduated from Netley with me," Doctor Weaver said. "I was with the Buffs in Natal." He frowned for a moment, then stood and shook my hand. "This way, gentlemen."

Holmes and I followed Doctor Weaver along a green-tiled corridor to the mortuary, a long, narrow room, brightly lit, in which a dozen or so porcelain-topped tables stood in rows; naked or sheeted bodies lay on several, and the inevitable reek of corruption polluted the atmosphere. Doctor Weaver pulled the sheet from one table, disclosing an obese male, face up, with a bullet wound in his throat.

"The ball entered his neck, severing the carotid artery and causing catastrophic blood loss before exiting behind his ear," Doctor Weaver said. "The victim was instantly doomed."

"This man has been badly beaten quite recently," I said. "He has bruises on his body and arms and a cauliflower ear." I borrowed Holmes' magnifying glass, leaned over the corpse, and examined strange discolourations on the victim's chin and between his nose and upper lip. "What are these pockmarks on his face? A skin disease?"

Doctor Weaver frowned. "They are odd; I've taken samples for analysis. You can see where blood remains attached to the skin of the chin and could not be easily washed off. And the marks on his philtrum and around his nasolabial creases are equally puzzling."

I shook my head, and Holmes, smiling, said nothing.

"Those strange marks, Holmes," I said we climbed back into our cab.

"Hmm?"

"I saw your eyes light up."

Holmes tapped on the cab roof. "Fetter Lane."

"The coroner was as unwelcoming as Inspector Gregson," I said. "Everyone seems to have tipped out of bed on the wrong side this morning." I wiped the cab window with my sleeve. "Or perhaps this persistent rain is putting a damper on people's spirits." I grinned. "Lucky Doctor Weaver and I were alumni of the Army Medical School, eh?"

"Stop at the next telegraph office," Holmes called to the cabby.

<hr />

We got down by the White Swan public house, and I followed Holmes into a narrow alley lined with decrepit fencing, picking my way among mounds of loose cobbles and sand, stinking puddles, and heaps of horse droppings. The din of traffic in Fleet Street receded, overtaken by the ring of a blacksmith's hammer. The metallic tang of a farrier's hot iron tainted the air.

An empty cab trundled up behind us, and the driver hooted us out of the way as he turned sharp between open gates into a wide, cobbled yard, spraying my trouser bottoms with mud and worse from his wheels.

Holmes led me into the yard behind the cab. A smithy was to one side amid a heap of broken cab parts and twisted ironwork, and the other side was an extensive stable. A two-story house stood in the far corner of the property with a glazed box on the balcony from which the entire yard could be observed.

I peered through the stable doors and saw narrow stalls for perhaps a score of nags. The roof was low, no windows pierced the walls, but light streamed through countless cracks and crevices in the walls and ceiling. The stench repelled me.

Sheds lined the smithy side of the yard, their open doors revealing rows of harness, bags of feed and the like. A tuneless whistle came from one, and the scent of frying onions wafted from another, which despite the competing stenches, made my mouth water.

Five cabs stood in a row in the centre of the yard, including the one that had splashed past me. Holmes addressed the driver as he got down from the box. "Staines Cab Company?"

The driver, a muscular, middle-aged man with a walrus moustache and a knowing look about him, folded a leather jerkin across his arm. "Staines as was. Not sure whose yard it is now."

"You worked for Mr Staines?" Holmes asked.

"Who's asking?"

"I am Sherlock Holmes, consulting detective. The solicitor for Mr Long has requested my help in his current misfortune. My companion is Doctor Watson. You are?"

"Joe Maudsley. I drove a Staines' cab till two weeks ago, four years in all; I was the senior man."

"You knew Long?"

"I did."

"I am here to enquire into the circumstances of the shooting in Hyde Park, particularly the relationship between Long and his employer."

The cabby laughed. "That's easy; they hated each other's guts."

"Why?"

Maudsley looked about him. I noticed the hammering has stopped, and several men in cabby's capes or leather aprons clustered outside the sheds, staring.

"Best come up." Maudsley led Holmes and me to a rickety staircase attached to the main house, up to the balcony and into the glazed shed at one end.

"Mr Staines' eyrie, where he kept his eye on us and did his books," Maudsley said. He leaned against a rough-hewn table and indicated a pair of stools. "Mrs Staines is gone to live with her mother, down Chippenham way. I'm looking after the place till things are sorted."

"What caused the rift between Long and his employer?" Holmes asked as we perched on the stools.

Maudsley sighed. "Look, gents, runnin' a cab business or driving a cab. It ain't easy with fodder at ten shillin' a week per nag, wear and tear on the cabs, and all the regulations on the boss's side. And on the driver's side, the daily cab hire is twelve shilling in January, going up a bob a week after the Boat Race to as much as eighteen in Derby Week."

Maudsley shook his head. "At the regulated fare rates, a cabby's to drive thirty-odd miles or more just to pay back the cab hire; that's before he makes a penny for himself. And add to that yard money for stablemen and carriage washers, and tips to buck riders, hotel doormen and the like. No, it ain't easy for boss nor cabby."

"Were all Staines' cabbies on daily hire?" Holmes asked.

Maudsley nodded. "Till a month ago. That's the story behind all the trouble." He wiped a windowpane with his sleeve and peered out. "Cabman's weather. A fine morning, so people go out without their umbrellas, and now a drizzly afternoon so they regret it."

"We won't keep you long," Holmes said coldly. "The trouble?"

"I don't like to speak ill of the dead," Maudsley took a clay pipe from his coat pocket and gently tapped it out on the table edge, "but it's well known Mr Staines liked his liquor. I won't say he was a drunk, but I can't say I've ever seen him completely sober. He'd a bad temper on him, and he was an unlucky wight." Maudsley opened a drawer under the table and took out a cloth bag. "Last year he bought seven horses from the Gypos fair down Brighton way, but only two was what we call a right 'cabber', a proper well-made-up cab horse. Then one of them was lost when the stable boy watered him at a public trough, though told not to, and he caught glanders and died."

He took a pinch of tobacco from the bag and filled his pipe. "A proper cab master must be sharp. The trade is overcrowded, sirs, what with trams and omnibuses and the underground railway. And the telephone. Time was, we'd get easy shilling fares in the City – gents passing to-and-fro from Throckmorton Street to Leadenhall, say, well within a mile. Now the toffs do the work by telephone or messenger."

"The trouble?" Holmes persisted.

"Like a lot of drivers, Long put some of his money aside each week with the guv'nor toward buying his own cab. He'd no money to get one new, but bit by bit he was saving and dreaming of buying his cab second-hand and being an owner driver. That's the only way to survive in this game."

Maudsley tapped his pockets and peered into the drawer. I passed him my matches, and he lit his pipe and nodded thanks. "One day, Mr Staines turns up in the yard gloating on how he's made a deal with the London, Brighton and South Coast Railway. We were to move the depot to Clapham and be privileged at Clapham Junction station."

"Lane was to become a privileged driver," I said. "What had he to complain about?"

Maudsley blew a stream of pipe smoke across the room. "Aside from having to pick up sticks and move his wife and little 'un across London, Long was dead against privilege: all street cabbies are. Privilege means a higher daily cab rent to the owner to compensate for the money he pays to the railway.

"Long gave Mr Staines notice and demanded his savings from the guv'nor's kitty. Mr Staines tried to talk him round, but Tom's stubborn nor hammered iron, and he damned Mr Staines' eyes and dragged his money out. He borrowed from his wife's brother, and they went in together on a second-hand rig as owner-drivers. He joined the Amalgamated Cab Drivers' Society and encouraged others to do the same. That put him right up against his ex-master. Words were spoken on both sides."

"That was all?" Holmes asked.

"It was enough, if you know Mr Staines and Tom. The drivers met together down the pub. Long stirred them up, and there was talk of a strike against the move to Clapham. I calmed the men, and it fizzled out."

Maudsley took a long draw of his pipe. "But Tom had set us thinking. I run a street cab. I don't want my cab weighed down with trunks and cases at the railway station with the roof needing fixing every six months. Nor chips and scratches on the cabinet work from the horses shying when the locos let off steam or hoot their whistles. And there's the penny fee you pay to enter the station. No, I leave all that to the four-wheelers. The railway companies fleece us cabbies both ways and backwards."

He folded his arms. "And I didn't fancy moving to Clapham. So I joined the Amalgamated Cab Drivers' Society too, and I took out a loan to set up a solo rig. As did three other Staines men. The guv'nor was furious – he has a temper on him – and he blamed

Tom Long. They were at hammer and tongs. Yes, they had a row right there in the yard, and it came to fisticuffs. Between you and me, Tom gave Mr Staines a right drubbing, and they parted on bad terms, both vowing to make the other pay for their wrongs."

Maudsley brushed tobacco strands from his coat. "Things went downhill for the guv'nor from then on. More men left, the bank pulled in loans, and he drank more. His missus told him she'd had enough and she went to her mother."

Holmes stood. "Thank you, Mr Maudsley. You have been very helpful. I assume the police are aware of the facts you have detailed?"

"The inspector asked a lot of questions."

"Mr Holmes?" a shrill voice cried from the yard below.

I went to the window. "A telegraph boy calling for you."

We descended the stairs to the yard and the grim-faced boy handed Holmes a telegram slip and bent to wipe the mud and horse dung from his once-shiny boots with a piece of rag. I tipped him thruppence, but that did not improve the boy's mood. He stalked across the muddy yard, muttering to himself as he picked a path between the pools of filth.

Holmes checked his watch. "We have an appointment at the scene of the crime in forty-four minutes." He turned to Maudsley. "But I should like to get to the Park a little early."

We watched as a groom and boy changed Maudsley's horse for a fresh one, wiped down the cab, and filled and trimmed his lamps, then we climbed aboard.

The trap was open and Maudsley leaned forward and looked down on us. "After the fight, Mr Staines boasted as how he'd chair-marked Long's cab licence before he gave it back to him. Tom learned of that in the pub that evening, and it was all his mates could do to hold him back from coming here and pummelling Mr Staines again."

Maudsley pulled on his driving gloves. "Tom has a fiery temper on him, and he can be main stubborn on top. I should not like to be his employer, and that's a fact." His expression became grave. "But Tom's no killer; at least, I should be surprised if he was proved to be one." He closed the trapdoor, flicked his whip, and the horse took the strain and started off.

"Chair-mark?" I asked.

"A secret mark added to the cabby's licence by his previous employer warning other proprietors that the man is unreliable or a troublemaker." Holmes pulled his briar pipe from his coat pocket, his tobacco from another, and stuffed the bowl.

"That may have exacerbated the bad blood between the men to breaking point."

"Quite possibly."

<hr />

"I received your message with surprise," Inspector Gregson said as he stepped down from his cab onto the Ring Road in the Park. A closed police carriage pulled up behind. "Yes, yes, your continued interest in the case surprises me, Mr Holmes. I won't say the matter is open-and-shut – if I may wax metaphorical, the case required a certain amount of teasing out." The inspector twisted imaginary fibres in his hands. "But I can safely assert that the vital threads of the matter are in my hands."

"There are one or two small questions that might be of relevance, Inspector," Holmes said with a smile. "How did Long lure Staines into his cab for a journey across the city to Hyde Park?

If he planned a murder, why did he not provide his own murder weapon, rather than relying on his victim bringing his pistol? And why did he handle the three unused cartridges in the cylinder?"

"And what are the strange marks on the victim's face?" I added.

Inspector Gregson pulled his watch from his waistcoat pocket and checked the time. "Yes, yes, a quibble or two may remain, I'll grant you." He put his watch away. "I have accepted your request to meet you here with the prisoner, against the advice of my superiors, and you'll forgive me if I answer your questions with another. If I can prove the cabby lied about the vital circumstances of the incident, if I can categorically exclude suicide, would you not agree that would leave Long in a very invidious position? The prosecuting counsel, Sir Vandissart Bullimore QC, could make much of that; he is pitiless in cross-examination."

Holmes pursed his lips and said nothing.

"I contend that Long lured Mr Staines to this out-of-the-way place intending to do him harm in revenge for alleged wrongs," the inspector continued. "He stopped his cab and pounced on his unsuspecting victim. At some point in the struggle, he gained possession of the victim's pistol and shot Mr Staines at close range, close but not close enough to corroborate his suicide story. There is no powder residue around the death wound." He smiled. "Scientific analysis, Doctor – as I said, that always impresses a jury."

Holmes pointed to a set of wheel marks in the muddy road. "The cab stopped here. The marks are still evident, although the rains have washed away blood and tracks in the mud. Did you make a thorough search of the undergrowth, examining the trees in particular?"

"What for, Mr Holmes? What of relevance is missing?"

Holmes shrugged, and we watched as Constable Boland and two detective sergeants helped their handcuffed and leg-ironed prisoner from the police van and escorted him towards us.

"Do I detect a gleam in your assistant's eye, Inspector," Holmes asked.

Inspector Gregson smiled a thin smile. "We have a witness, Mr Holmes."

"Inspector, now you have surprised me," Holmes said, returning his smile. He waved an expansive hand across the verdant grass, bushes, and clumps of woodland that stretched for hundreds of yards around us. "This is one of very few places in this busy city where I had expected mayhem could be committed with reasonable confidence of privacy."

"My witness lives no more than fifty yards from here, gentlemen." Inspector Gregson leaned back on his heels and grasped his lapels. "He heard four shots fired."

Holmes nodded. "That makes more sense than the single shot in Long's story."

Inspector Gregson blinked at Holmes.

"A witness in Hyde Park at near midnight?" I asked, looking about me. I could see no habitation within several hundred yards, and no building except the Royal Humane Society's Receiving House about a hundred yards farther along the road.

"Barnabas awaits us at the Receiving House," the inspector said curtly.

A hansom drew up and Long's solicitor, Mr Renfrew, got down.

Holmes drew his watch and checked the time. "We are assembled. Before we meet the mysterious Mr Barnabas, might we attempt to re-enact the crime?"

He faced the prisoner, a sullen-looking, sallow faced man in his thirties in broad-arrow prison dress with his cab driver's caped overcoat across his shoulders. "Good afternoon, Long. I am Sherlock Holmes, the consulting detective. I am your only hope of avoiding the Rope. Unless you cooperate with me and tell us the whole truth without equivocation, I regret to inform you that you will be hanged for the wilful murder of your ex-employer."

Long glared at Holmes. "I did not murder Staines."

Holmes returned the cabby's glare. "I believe you did not, but you do no good with this nonsense of suicide. The inspector has a witness. Will you not do yourself the favour of telling us how Mr Staines' life ended here?"

"I've said my piece." Long spat on the grass and looked away.

"Watch it, you." One of the detectives guarding the prisoner jerked the chain binding his wrists and arms. "Answer the gentleman nice."

Holmes balled his fists. "The man is as stubborn—"

"—nor hammered iron," I said.

Long remained silent. His solicitor murmured in his ear and then addressed Holmes and Inspector Gregson. "My client reserves his defence."

"I have followed your tracks to Long Water," Holmes said in an exasperated tone, "where you disposed of the evidence."

Long looked up, startled, and the inspector regarded Holmes through narrowed eyes, "Evidence, Mr Holmes?"

"In good time, Inspector. If Long will not cooperate, let us meet your Mr Barnabas."

We walked along the Ring Road in a huddle, stepping around puddles and in silence but for the jingle of the prisoner's chains.

The drizzle had abated, but the clouds were low, grey, and threatening.

"Is Barnabas a first or family name?" I asked as we followed Inspector Gregson into the Royal Humane Society Headquarters.

The director, a Mr Wick, met us at the door and ushered us through the handsome main building with its elegant rooms furnished in the Regency style. We came out to the lake shore and to a rather incongruous faux Elizabethan structure that I must have seen a dozen times on visits to the Park, but took no notice of. Inside the high-roofed chamber were several hospital beds, a hot water furnace and bath for warming frozen limbs, a hook in the ceiling for hanging the semi-drowned by their feet, and a large bellows for blowing reviving cigar-smoke into their lungs.

Everything was modern and sparkled with cleanliness, everything except for a wizened old man in a tightly buttoned, patched grey suit with a threadbare blanket across his shoulders who sat in a chair by the door. He looked up as we entered the room and gave us a rheumy-eyed, gap-toothed smile.

He was introduced as Barnabas.

"Your witness is a tramp," I said. I frowned at the old man's downcast expression. "I mean, ah, a gentleman of the road."

"Mr Barnabas worked for the Post Office for many years until he became sick and was obliged to give it up," Mr Wick said. "He gave the *view halloa* when a small boy fell off the bridge, and the child was saved. Since then, he has been allowed to make a nest under a tarpaulin against the wall of the equipment shed where we keep lifebelts and the like. During the day, he earns a few pennies by picking up litter. The park attendants and police turn a blind eye."

"Hyde Park is the only royal park patrolled by the Metropolitan Police rather than the Parks Constabulary," Inspector Gregson explained. "We perhaps take a broader view of public order than the specialised force. We are plagued with slum-dwellers washing their grubby offspring and filthy laundry in the lake, but Barnabas does no harm, and we're used to him."

The inspector addressed Barnabas in a loud voice. "You heard shots on the night in question – two nights ago, on Monday. Is that right?"

"Indeed, sir. Shots. Bangs, they were," the old man answered.

"How many bangs?"

"Four – four bangs." He lifted his arm and waved a trembling hand in the air, his finger pointed at the inspector. "'D T', sir."

"Inspector," I said, "your star witness's mind is befuddled by drink and circumstance. You see his shaking, crabbed hand. He admits he suffers from 'D T'. *Delirium tremens*." I lowered my voice. "I don't think even the majestic Sir Vandissart Bullimore would care to offer a trembling alcoholic as a witness in a capital case."

Holmes pulled up a chair and sat knee to knee with Barnabas; they conversed in murmurs.

The inspector rounded on Long. "What have you to say? This witness contends there were four shots."

Holmes looked up. "But we know better, do we not, Long?"

Long looked down at his feet, Mr Renfrew put a consoling hand on his client's shoulder, and Inspector Gregson glared at Holmes.

"How do you account for the single fired cartridge case in the pistol if four shots were fired?" I asked the inspector.

"You may think we at Scotland Yard are not scientifically minded, Doctor, but you would be wrong, sir." Inspector Gregson addressed Mr Renfrew. "Under normal circumstances, the prosecution would spring this on your client during the trial, but I am being as open as I can be. I think we can save ourselves a deal of trouble and save the Queen some money by showing you how tight my web is about your client.

"Mr Staines' pistol is a five-shot. If he decided to carry a reload, it would be logical, would it not, for him to carry five more bullets? I believe he did so. Long fired four shots at his victim; one chipped a wheel rim, and only one hit home and answered his purpose. Thinking to outwit the police and mimic a suicide, he took three unfired bullets from Mr Staines' pocket and replaced the fired cartridges with new ones, accidentally smearing them with blood in the process. His hands were bloody when he was examined at the station." The inspector turned to Holmes. "How is that, sir?"

"Yes, I believe that is exactly what happened."

Inspector Gregson frowned at Holmes. "You do? Then that's an end of the matter."

"Not quite." Holmes stood and shook Barnabas' hand.

"Mr Holmes, you spoke of further evidence," Inspector Gregson said as we stepped back onto the Ring Road.

Holmes looked up. "The heavens threaten. It's only four hundred yards or so, but we might save time and ride. Follow me."

"I spoke with Constable Boland, the inspector's assistant," I said as I sat with Holmes in our hansom, leading the convoy towards the northern gate of the Park. "It seems Inspector Gregson has been criticised by his superiors for attempting to introduce some of your deductive methods into his department. His detective sergeants went over his head with complaints of the inspector's apparently oppressive zeal in avoiding contamination of crime scenes, his arduous systematic techniques, and his insistence on detailed record-keeping. Gregson has been warned off too close a collaboration with you. That may explain his cool attitude."

Holmes smiled a reptilian smile. He tapped on the roof and called to Maudsley to pull up, and he and I jumped down. "Come along," he called to the vehicles behind us.

Holmes marched past a 'Kindly Do Not Walk on the Grass' sign towards the lake, whistling, his cane over his shoulder and his silk hat at a jaunty angle. I grinned as I followed him. With Holmes in this mood, I thought, anything was possible.

"Please do not step on the wheel tracks," he called to the police, prisoner, and Mr Renfrew straggling behind us.

"Marks of a loaded hansom, Mr Holmes," Inspector Gregson returned. "I noted the tracks when I surveyed the scene yesterday."

"I expected that you had done so, Inspector. I know how systematic and thorough your investigative methods are."

We followed the wheel tracks to where they stopped by the edge of the lake and turned back towards the road.

"As you know, Inspector," Holmes said. "Long paused here. Let us consider why."

One of the detective sergeants with the prisoner answered. "He pulled off the road to be better concealed while he reloaded the victim's gun and prepared his story."

"Four shots, Mr Holmes," the other detective said. "That amounts to cold-blooded murder in my book." He grinned at his companion, winked at Long, and mimed a jerking a noose above his head.

"We know that Mr Staines habitually carried a revolver, and his foreman says he had a fiery temper," Holmes continued, unabashed.

"These cab fellows stick together, Mr Holmes," the same detective said. "Look at that recent strike at Waterloo—"

"It was a temporary and localised withdrawal of service, Sergeant," I corrected him, "not a strike."

The detectives exchanged amused looks, and sauntered to the lake edge, lighting cigarettes.

Holmes beckoned to Inspector Gregson. "If you thought you might be stalked by such a fellow as Staines," he murmured, "what would you do?"

"I'd carry a weapon to defend myself." The inspector narrowed his eyes.

"And if you were Staines attempting to wreak your revenge on Long, you would not wish to—"

"—be recognised." The inspector's frown faded, and a slow smile spread across his face. He turned away, calling his men together.

"The marks on the victim's chin," I said.

Holmes echoed the inspector's smile.

Inspector Gregson picked up a fallen tree branch about a foot long and heaved it into the water. "Search in an arc from at that radius," he ordered.

"In the water, sir?" One of the detectives murmured something, and the other laughed. "Looking for what, sir?

Inspector Gregson frowned. "For what? Haven't you been paying attention? For a pistol and disguise, of course. How else do you suppose four—"

Holmes coughed twice.

"How else do you suppose *six* shots were fired?" the inspector asked.

The detectives took off their boots and stockings with a great show of reluctance. Constable Boland tittered behind his hand.

"You too, Constable," Inspector Gregson ordered.

We joined the inspector and watched with amusement as the policemen rolled up their trousers and waded into Long Water, shivering and cursing. I turned to Holmes. "More than four shots?"

"My dear Watson, not only have you looked but not seen, you have listened but not heard," he answered. "Mr Barnabas will make an excellent witness – for the defence. The hand that you described with some exactness as shaking and crabbed is the key to his testimony."

"I noticed the cramped fingers of the telegraph operator," I said with a sniff.

"Exactly. You were precisely correct."

I gave Holmes a suspicious glare and said nothing.

Holmes mimed tapping a Morse key. "Barnabas was hunched over a telegraph apparatus for twenty years, until, as you saw, his fingers became stiffened and fixed by arthritis into the crablike claw with which is now burdened. He was obliged to give up his employment. Incapable of using a Morse key, and having no other skill, he is as we now see him, a gentleman of the road, but not as you so rashly diagnosed, a drunkard.

"Barnabas informed me that he is fiercely temperance; he eschews all alcoholic beverages. His befuddlement is not due to drunkenness, but rather to shyness: he has had little commerce with people for many years, other than begging for his bread. We must make some allowance."

"But he clearly said he heard four shots, and he suffers from – wait, Morse!"

Holmes nodded. "As Inspector Gregson and I instantly apprehended, Barnabas was not admitting to bouts of *delirium tremens*, he was describing what he heard on that fateful night in the precise language of his erstwhile employment. Dah di dit dah: the letters 'D T' in Morse code. BANG, bang, bang; BANG."

Constable Boland cried out, stooped, and held up a mass of hair wrapped around a shining bright revolver. He waded back to shore, handed the gun to the inspector, and held up a sodden false beard.

"A Webley .44 with two shots fired," the inspector said as he snapped the cylinder closed. "Those, plus four from Mr Staines' gun; six shots in all."

He turned to the prisoner. "You have a reputation as a stubborn fellow, Mr Long, and that will be the end of you if you persist. I have built a fine web of circumstantial evidence around you, but you have a glimmer of hope. Six shots were fired that night – two from your revolver—"

"Four shots or six," one of the detectives said as he struggled to put on his stockings. "Long still killed Staines and covered it up."

"That's wilful murder in my book," said the other detective.

"No, gentleman," the inspector corrected him, "Six shots. Four from Mr Staines' revolver, and two from Mr Long's, but Barnabas heard four bangs. You must try to develop a more deductive approach to your work." He beamed at Holmes.

Holmes addressed Long. "Let me stimulate your memory. You carried a pistol for self-protection against your erstwhile employer. It was in your pocket when you picked up a fare in Throckmorton Street at eleven-fifteen, a bearded gentleman well wrapped up in an overcoat and scarf and wearing a bowler. The journey went as you have described it. When the customer ordered you to stop in an out-of-the-way place, you opened the hatch to see what was up.

"The inspector and I cannot reconstruct the details without your help, but we know this. You and Mr Staines exchanged shots:

he fired four times, and you twice. Your first and last exchanges were simultaneous, and that final shot was the fatal one."

Long looked from Holmes to grim-faced Inspector Gregson, and he slowly nodded. "You have it down pat, sir," he answered in a throaty rasp. "I got a gun because I knew Mr Staines of old: he knew not the meaning of Christian forgiveness, nor of bygones. He thirsted for revenge.

"I didn't recognise him in his false beard and heavy coat sir, in the black of night, and I drove him here all innocent, thinking nothing of it 'cept my passenger was in drink. We stopped right where you said, sir.

"I opened the hatch, and he was staring up at me, his face twisted and a pistol in his hand. I knew instantly who he was, beard or no beard. I slammed down the hatch, jumped from the cab and ran for my life towards a clump of trees by the roadside, pulling my pistol from my pocket as I ran. I turned to a shout; Staines was out of the cab pointing his gun. I did the same, and we fired. We both missed.

The horse reared at the noise and slid into the ditch, taking the cab with it. I turned, ran again, and heard two more shots; one hit a tree just as I dived behind it.

"Staines was coming towards me, waving his gun and shouting as to how I'd ruined him and his family and I was going to pay the price. I tried to reason with him, but my fear mounted as he advanced. He aimed, and I did the same. We both fired; his bullet again hit the tree I was sheltering behind, and mine struck him down.

"I left my hiding place and ventured to him. The bullet had passed through his neck and blood was spurting out. I could do nothing. I took his gun and pocketed it and my own before I calmed my nag and drew her and the carriage out of the ditch.

"I thought to leave him and ride on to the Victoria Gate and fetch help, but although I had little hope he could be saved, and he was my sworn enemy, I felt it was my Christian duty to make the attempt. I dragged the body to the cab, heaved him aboard and set off.

"I had to pull up the horse after a short distance as the body had shifted and was in danger of falling out. I checked on Staines. There was no doubt he was dead. His red-soaked false beard was half off, his eyes were open and staring, and his chest was drenched in his life's blood. I sat by the side of the cab and tried to make sense of what had happened. I could see the lamps of the Gardens across the Bayswater Road. The police box was there, but I was afeard to give myself up – I knew my hot temper and our row when I left Staines' employ would be black against me.

"I looked through his pockets and found Staines' wallet, with a fiver in, a few coins and a letter from his wife. In his other pocket were five cartridges. That gave me pause."

Long hung his head. "It was a mad thought, borne of fear I would be charged with his death, gentlemen, but I thought if he were not identified and no connection was made to me, the police might accept he was a suicide. I reloaded the gun, all save one chamber, leaving two bullets in his coat."

"Tut-tut," said Holmes. "A foolish move."

"I turned the cab and crossed the grass back to Long Water. I ripped up the letter, God forgive me, and threw the pieces, my pistol and the false beard into the lake."

Holmes addressed the two sergeants. "Of the six shots, the first two were fired simultaneously, as attested by Barnabas and

Long. Then two shots came from Mr Staines' gun, and finally two more simultaneous shots, one of which killed the victim. Murder, manslaughter, or justifiable homicide, gentlemen?"

"We shall enter a plea of self-defence, Mr Holmes," Mr Renfrew said, rubbing his hands together, "with every prospect of acquittal. The disguise will prove premeditation on the part of the victim and help corroborate my client's account." He smiled. "Perhaps the police might review the facts and decline to prosecute."

Inspector Gregson returned his smile. "Not my decision." He offered his hand to Holmes, Renfrew, and me, turned away and marched back towards the carriages. His assistant grinned and trotted after him, carrying his boots, leaving the bewildered detective sergeants with the handcuffed prisoner.

Holmes held out his hand. "Key?"

<hr />

Holmes and I stepped down from our hansom outside our lodgings and I paid our cab fare, adding a half-crown tip.

"Very decent of you, Doctor," Maudsley said. "Without tips I'd starve, and that's the honest truth of the matter. Women never tip; I look for a swell nob with his lady, or a City man who puts his fare down without a murmur and adds a tanner on top. They're the fellows for me." He raised his whip to his hat in salute and trotted away.

"I wonder why people hire a cab to commit self-murder?" I said as Holmes and I divested ourselves of our coats in the hall.

"I imagine they don't want to cause their relatives any inconvenience. Or perhaps their housekeepers. I believe Mrs

Hudson would be quite vexed if you decided to shrug off your mortal coil in her second-best bedroom."

I considered that hopefully unlikely prospect as we made our way upstairs to the sitting room.

"I'm not sure I approve of trade unions," I said as we settled by the fire and Holmes poured us restorative brandies after our busy day.

"You needn't be concerned," Holmes answered as he passed my glass. "The great bulk of cab drivers are too underpaid, overworked, and isolated to combine; as long as they are underpaid, overworked, and isolated, so they will remain. Becoming an owner-cabby is one of the few ways in which a working-class man may be master of his own destiny with no boss to kowtow to, so the best of the class aspire to the avocation. His middle and upper-class passengers fear that independence, and that is why cabs are so intensively regulated."

Holmes smiled. "If ever the poor rise up against their masters, the cabbies will be their leaders."

THE STRONGEST AND MOST EXTENSIVE VAULTS IN THE WORLD
FOR SAFE KEEPING SECURITIES & OTHER VALUABLES.
Erected at a cost of more than £200,000.
FIRE, WATER, BURGLAR & BOMB PROOF

VIEW OF ONE OF THE 8 VAULTS ON 3RD TIER, EACH OF WHICH IS FITTED WITH ABOUT 700 PRIVATE SAFES.

VIEW OF THE NATIONAL SAFE DEPOSIT COMP'Y BUILDINGS, THE MANSION HOUSE AND ROYAL EXCHANGE.

VIEW OF THE COMPANY'S INTERIOR ARMOUR CLAD VAULTS, 40 FT. UNDERGROUND – FIRE, BURGLAR, WATER & BOMB PROOF, GUARDED NIGHT AND DAY BY ARMED WATCHMEN. FOUNDATION 80 FEET BELOW LEVEL OF STREET.

VIEW OF ONE OF THE 8 VAULTS ON 1ST TIER, IN WHICH PLATE CHESTS, AND DEED AND OTHER BOXES ARE STORED.

1 Queen Victoria Street, Mansion House, London, E.C.

FOUNDED 1872.

SUBSCRIBED CAPITAL, £296,000.   **PAID UP CAPITAL, £216,000.**

Directors:
THE MARQUIS OF TWEEDDALE (Chairman).
GEORGE ARBUTHNOT, Esq.   H. S. COULSON, Esq.   SAMUEL PETO, Esq. (Stock Exchange).

Manager: Bankers: Assistant Manager:
J. S. WILKES, Esq.   UNION BANK OF LONDON.   B. M. YOUNG, Esq.

Safe Deposit Company, Ltd.,

TO LET PRIVATE SAFES, fitted in Great Fire, Water, Burglar and Bomb Proof Vaults, to the public by the year at moderate cost.

TO RECEIVE DEPOSITS OF PLATE CHESTS, Boxes of Deeds, and other valuables for safe keeping, by the year, or, for shorter periods.

TO GUARANTEE OR INSURE THE SAFETY OF BONDS and other securities deposited with the Company for safe keeping and management.

TO ACT AS TRUSTEE, RECEIVER AND ADMINISTRATOR for Private Persons.

TO ACT AS TRUSTEE FOR PUBLIC COMPANIES.

THE PROPER JOB

"WATSON."

"Eh?" I poised, shaving brush in hand. "Holmes? What is it?"

"This really is too much," Holmes called through the bedroom door.

I sighed. I had been hoping for a quiet breakfast with the morning papers and a peaceful Saturday away from my surgery, strolling in the Park perhaps or taking a run on my bicycle, and I was not in the mood for fuss and bother. Early-Spring hypochondriacs who had undermined their constitutions by dosing themselves with quack-salves and patent remedies had plagued me all week. And while I was overtired and a touch brittle, Holmes had been mildly tetchy for a fortnight or more, exasperated by what he considered the dearth of worthwhile, proper crimes and the plethora of triviality presented to him by a succession of time wasters.

I splashed water over my face and reached for a towel.

I opened the sitting-room door. A short, bald gentleman with a full white beard was warming the tails of his old-fashioned, Prince-Albert-style frock coat before the fireplace in our sitting room.

"Mr Grigoryan has some disquieting news," Holmes said in a bleak tone as he passed me our visitor's calling card. "He attempted to access his deposit box at the New York and Continental Bank on Cornhill this morning and was unable to do so."

I glanced at the clock on the mantel, which read twenty past eight. "Is the bank open at this hour?"

"The bank opens at ten on working days," Mr Grigoryan answered in a cultured Eastern European accent, "but the deposit vault opens at seven. I was the first customer. The bank manager informed me there was a minor hiccup in the arrangements; in fact, the vault door would not open. I watched the concierge turn the combination locks to the correct setting and insert the key, but the unlocking wheel would not turn." He spread his hands in a Continental gesture. "Perhaps I am a Cassandra, and there is no cause for alarm, but I would be grateful if you gentlemen would condescend to accompany me to the bank and represent my interests in the matter."

Holmes leaned one elbow against the mantel, his fingers tapping on the shelf as he glared at our visitor. Holmes' demeanour made it clear he cast Mr Grigoryan's problem in the same time-wasting category into which I placed my valetudinarian patients.

I hesitated. It seemed likely the matter would peter out as a misunderstanding or mere mechanical dysfunction, but Mr Grigoryan was clearly disturbed. All Holmes and I need do was accompany him to the vault and watch as it was repaired and opened. I had never visited a safety-depository, and I was curious to see how they operated. I thought that after inspecting the vault, Holmes and I might have a pleasant breakfast or early luncheon in one of the plentiful chop houses or cafes in the financial district.

"I would be delighted to help you, Mr Grigoryan," I said, avoiding Holmes' eyes. "I'll get my coat and hat and have our page fetch a cab."

The day was clear and bright, chilly, but not at all unpleasant for early March, and Baker Street was busy with clerks and shop assistants on their way to work. A hurdy-gurdy man had set up by our lamppost, playing a lively tune, and a couple of street sweepers leaned on their brushes, watching a newsboy perform an impromptu gig. His boards were plastered with the latest sombre news of the seemingly never-ending war in South Africa and the almost equally protracted American election hoopla.

Billy held open the door of a four-wheeler, grinning and tapping his feet. Holmes preceded Mr Grigoryan and me into the cab and sat beside the window, his hat low over his eyes, his face half covered by his muffler and his arms tight folded. I tapped my stick on the roof and ordered the cab to the City.

"You start your day early," I remarked to Mr Grigoryan.

"My business is often conducted outside normal hours," he answered over the rumble of the cab wheels. "I buy precious metals and rough diamonds on the European and American bourses, and I must keep up to date with prices at the mines in South Africa. I am in regular telegraphic contact with DeBeers here, in New York and in Johannesburg. The long conflict with the Boers has made the diamond and metals trades more volatile than usual.

"A customer looking for a yellow diamond of a particular size and quality contacted me recently. I put out feelers, and early this morning I received a telegram from DeBeers' London office offering just such a stone. In such matters, one must act before another dealer makes an offer, so I instantly replied that I would take the stone and make payment to DeBeers' representatives in the City. The banks are closed until ten, of course, but I keep a contingent supply of gold in a deposit box with the New York and Continental Bank on Cornhill for just such occurrences – many diamantaire transactions are in cash, on a handshake."

Mr Grigoryan fingered a slim wedding band on his finger. "I hurried to the bank and waited on the pavement until St Mary's bell struck the hour of seven. And I waited. The doors did not open. Then at seven ten or so, a cab pulled up and the bank manager, Mr Peters, got down. I followed him inside and to the strongroom. The concierge who usually opened the vault in the morning was manipulating the combination dials and trying to turn the unlocking wheel."

"There were no signs of tampering?" I asked.

Mr Grigoryan considered. "No, and Mr Peters did not seem unduly perturbed. He suggested there might be a technical fault with the door, and he informed me he had sent a district messenger to contact a locksmith."

"A sensible move," I said.

"Well and good," Mr Grigoryan said, "but after several failed attempts to open the vault, I believe I detected something in the bank manager's eye that gave me pause. I am an Armenian who lived for many years in the shadow of the Ottomans; I have seen a great deal of foreboding. As I feared the problem may not be so easily solved, and may, God forbid, attain a darker hue, I thought it best to seek expert advice. My anxiety propelled me to Mr Holmes' door."

Holmes said nothing, but I thought I observed a faint smile about his lips.

"I knew of Mr Holmes from a copy of an illustrated magazine I picked up in the waiting room at my dentist's surgery the other day," Mr Grigoryan continued. "It contained the first part of your interesting report on Mr Holmes' investigation of an unexplained death in the garden of a house by a desolate moor, in Devonshire, I believe, or Derbyshire." He smiled. "I looked in vain among the stack of periodicals for the next episode of the narrative and the solution to the mystery of the old gentleman's death."

I opened my mouth to answer Mr Grigoryan, but Holmes roused himself and pre-empted me. "The titular hound did it," he said with a sniff. He turned to me. "Really, my dear fellow, your romanticised accounts of my cases do me no service. I owe it to myself as the world's only consulting detective to insist that you confine your literary efforts to the cold, hard facts of each case and the logical steps by which I unravel the mystery." He waved a dismissive hand. "*Sans* literary flourishes and unnecessary melodrama."

I made no reply, and Holmes subsided. Mr Grigoryan again fidgeted with his ring, and we continued in strained silence along Fleet Street and into the City proper.

※

We skirted St Paul's in a tangle of omnibuses, carts and cabs and stopped at the corner of Cornhill and Lombard Street outside the triangular, Palladian-style premises of the New York and Continental Bank.

A City of London police sergeant stood before the imposing brass-bound double doors, arms akimbo, facing a half-dozen or so gentlemen gathered on the pavement who, judging by their dress, their gesticulations, and the babble of tongues in which they demanded attention, were mostly foreigners.

Mr Grigoryan and I followed Holmes as he edged through the crowd. A gentleman in a long grey coat and bowler bumped into me and apologised in what sounded like Spanish before requesting the policeman allow him entrance. The policeman waved him away and saluted Holmes.

"Good morning, Mr Holmes. Halloran, sir. You won't remember me, but I was with the Reigate force when you investigated the burglaries there—"

"Of course, Halloran. Congratulations on your promotion."

The sergeant beamed.

"These gentlemen are with me."

Halloran tapped on the double doors. One opened, and a porter ushered Holmes, Mr Grigoryan and me inside, slamming the door behind us and instantly muting the hubbub.

We found ourselves in a cool, spacious lobby in the three-sided form of the building. The floor was pink and ochre marble, and tall, delicately fluted iron columns supported a panelled ceiling from which crystal chandeliers hung, providing a bright electric light. A porter's desk stood to one side and iron grills secured a long counter against the far wall.

"I don't recall Halloran during the Reigate inquiry," I said.

"Neither do I," Holmes glanced around the lobby and snapped his fingers at a page leaning against the wall. "His sergeant's stripes are new, so the supposition of promotion was obvious."

The page pinched out his cigarette and led us down a narrow staircase to the basement, along a tiled corridor and through an open grill door. The room before us was square and as brightly lit by electric fixtures as a butcher's shop. Straight-back chairs surrounded a long table, bare but for glass ink pots, stationery, and ashtrays. Against one wall was a waist-high shelf divided by privacy screens, and on the right, dominating the room, was a circular door of gleaming steel at least eight feet in diameter framed by a massive steel buttress and with a metal-spoked wheel and three combination dials at its centre.

"The vault is still closed," Mr Grigoryan murmured.

A strong smell of cigar smoke together with a taint of disinfectant in the air tickled my nose, and I sneezed and scrabbled in my pocket for my handkerchief.

A gentleman stood by the vault door smoking a long cigar, a uniformed porter beside him. Mr Grigoryan introduced Mr Peters, the manager of the New York and Continental Bank, and Roberts, the vault porter.

"I have read of your exploits, Mr Holmes," Mr Peters said in a strong American accent. "I regret we will have no opportunity to test your powers today."

"Is the door still locked?" Mr Grigoryan asked.

"I'm afraid so," Mr Peters said, "but there is no cause for alarm."

"It's temperamental, that door is," Roberts said in a London accent. "Sometimes she opens as smooth as butter, but now and then, she needs a good kick."

I frowned at the ponderous mass of metal before me. I would have been astonished if anything but a traction engine could have made the slightest impression on the door.

"Did you try kicking?" Holmes asked.

Roberts shrugged and tapped a cigarette from a packet. "We've called in the Herr."

"The locksmith who performs occasional maintenance and resets the combination every three months," Mr Peters said. "He's a Hollander. I've sent for him."

"Who is responsible for opening and closing the vaults?" Holmes asked Mr Peters.

The manager frowned. "Doctor Watson's memoirs have an avid readership in the United States, Mr Holmes, but I cannot submit to an interrogation on bank procedures from a person, however prominent, who is not an authorised agent with a legitimate interest." He blinked at Holmes. "I don't believe you have an account with us."

Holmes took his watch from his waistcoat pocket, glanced at it, and turned to me. "Short's is around the corner. They do a good shilling breakfast."

"I have an account with the New York and Continental," Mr Grigoryan said, addressing Mr Peters. "And I hereby authorise and request Mr Holmes to act on my behalf."

Holmes faced Mr Peters and raised his eyebrows.

"Very well," he said. He grasped his lapels and rocked on his heels. "I say that there is no cause for concern, and that is no idle boast. You must understand, gentlemen, that deposits with the NY and C Bank are utterly secure. We stand in a twenty-foot-deep basement protected by four feet of best concrete and then by armour plate so superior in hardness that in US Navy tests an iron ingot of thirty-two hundredweight dropped from eighteen feet failed to penetrate. The same armour served the Navy well against the Spanish fleet during the recent war. Our vault doors weigh no less than four long tons." He gestured to the porter beside him. "Faithful watchmen control access to the boxes and the system of business we have inaugurated is precise and accurate in all its details."

Mr Peters dropped his voice to a whisper. "I may tell you gentlemen that the bank has certain other defences on which I cannot elaborate. We are safer than the Bank of England just across the street."

"Who locks the vault and on what schedule?" Holmes asked.

Mr Peters nodded to the porter.

"Hobbs and me close the vault at seven every evening except Sunday," Roberts said. "I lock the door with this key, arming the alarm." He held up a long key with a complicated tang. "Hobbs then twirls the combination dials twice round to start the timer for eleven hours and forty-five minutes. The lock cannot be opened until the timer runs out. A bell sounds at a quarter to seven each morning, and only then does the mechanism release the dials."

"Like an alarum clock," I said.

"I twirl the dials to the right numbers," Roberts said, "and the plate covering the keyhole drops, so I can insert the key, like this. I twist it twice and hear a click. Now I should be able to turn the wheel that withdraws the bolts surrounding the door." He grasped the wheel in the centre of the door. "It won't move."

"You wind the clocks for the timer?" Holmes asked.

"I do, daily – there's a sixty-hour movement with two backups, just in case."

Holmes gestured for the key and closely scrutinised it.

"A double-bitted stamp aligns with grooves and wards cut into a stack of sixteen steel plates," Mr Peters said, puffing on his cigar. "The lock is unpickable. Only the bank chairman, myself, and Roberts here have copies of the key, and we keep them about our persons or in a secure location at all times." He indicated a red box high on the wall beside the vault door. "I said there is no cause for alarm, gentlemen; in fact, there has been no alarm."

I peered up at the box. Stamped into the cover plate was the company name, 'The Holmes Electric Protective Company, Boston.'

I turned to Holmes and raised my eyebrows.

"No relation."

"The electric alarm is set into the door frame," Mr Peters said. "It is enabled and disabled by the vault key. Attempting to open the doors without the key sets off a bell outside the bank. If the supply of electric ether is interrupted by tampering, the alarm rings. It is a foolproof system – from America." He took his watch from his waistcoat pocket, glanced at it, and slipped it back. "If you will excuse me, gentlemen, I must make certain arrangements upstairs before we open."

He bowed and hurried away.

Holmes gestured to the combination wheels and addressed the porter. "May I?"

Roberts waved permission, and Holmes passed me his silk hat. "Did you bring your stethoscope?"

"I did not. I failed to anticipate the need for an auscultatory examination."

Holmes laid his ear against the door and gently twisted the first combination wheel back and forth.

"One can hear a faint click as the cogs rub against the bar that prevents the insertion of the key," I explained to Mr Grigoryan.

"Ssshh." Holmes manipulated the wheel for several minutes, then moved to the second wheel, and to the last. "The lock is not the problem; it's working normally," he said, retrieving his hat. "The cover has dropped, revealing the keyhole, as it should."

Holmes inserted the vault-door key and gently turned it anticlockwise. "The key engages normally." He tried the wheel handle in the centre of the door, but it would not move. "I can only surmise that the opening mechanism is jammed from the inside."

He stood back. "There's nothing I can do. Even if a locksmith drilled through the door and managed to reset the combination, the door will not open. It is obstructed."

"But we must be able to open the door," Mr Grigoryan said, looking pale.

"I suggest you contact the manufacturer," Holmes said, addressing the porter. "But they may not have a solution other than drilling a big enough hole to pass through: a tremendous job."

"The Herr's been called," Roberts said, casting a disapproving glance at Holmes.

Holmes smiled, looked down and seemed to examine the floor for a moment before he nodded to himself and turned to me. "I must insist that any record of this affair be limited to the facts, without stylistic or dramatic embellishment of any kind."

"And those cold, hard facts are?"

"All in good time." Holmes tapped the floor with his cane. "The bank is in an interesting location. Below us are the ancient sewers of London." He strode to the vault wall and tapped. "A hundred feet in that direction is the Bank of England. At the same distance in the other is the crypt of St Mary's Woolchurch."

"You needn't bother yourselves with tunnelling," Roberts said coldly. "The basement walls are concrete reinforced with iron bars and faced with flame-hardened brick and tile. It'd take a corps of Irish navvies a month to hack through."

Holmes tapped his finger against the corner of his mouth in a thoughtful gesture. "Do you clean this room and the vaults?" he asked.

"I do."

"Where do you keep your cleaning materials?"

Roberts gave Holmes an odd look before he crossed to the right side of the room and opened a door set flush with the wall, revealing a good-sized utility room with walls of bare brick. I followed Holmes inside. Along one wall were shelves lined with tins of metal polish and packets of soap flakes and other cleaning materials, and a rack of brooms, mops and feather dusters. Various buckets and pails hung on hooks below them. In a corner was a sink and a small stove with a kettle. A simple table with four chairs set with a teapot, cups and saucers was in the opposite corner.

Taking up the centre of the room was a waist-high steel and brass apparatus with several hand wheels and dials. A mass of pipes and tubes of various diameters emerged from the mechanism and disappeared through an iron grill in the concrete floor. A deep, rumbling roar emanated from below, and a strong draught ruffled my hair on the back of my head. I peered through the grill and saw the gleam of water twenty or thirty feet below.

"A six-foot-deep cistern under the building holds thirty thousand gallons of water," Roberts explained. "That's why we don't worry about tunnels. Woe betide any foolhardy person digging into the vault."

"Fed by the River Walbrook, I presume," Holmes said.

"One of the lost rivers of London," I said.

Roberts nodded. "The Walbrook flows through a wide pipe controlled by the valves you see before you. Even if someone navigated the torrent, he'd have to break through two steel grills to get to this room." He smiled. "Leaving him with the vault to tackle; and as you saw, the door isn't damaged."

Holmes pointed to the ceiling. "A hatch."

"Access to the electrical wires and gas pipes."

"Could someone pass through that hatch and cut the wires, disabling the alarm?"

Roberts shrugged. "The vault timers are mechanical, so they'll not be affected, and the alarm will operate for sixty hours on an electric accumulator. If the wires are cut, the lights go out till we light our gas system, but the alarm has back-up accumulators – it'd ring and the coppers would come arunning." He gestured to the lights suspended above us. "Our electric lamps are burning bright."

"What time do you arrive at work?" Holmes asked.

"The hall porter, me, and the boy are here by six thirty or twenty-five to seven. I sort out the vault, Hobbs organises the lobby, and the page does any errands and the like. We might have one or two early birds at seven, but we don't get busy till eight or half past."

Holmes ran his finger over one of the pump dials. "When did you last clean the anteroom and vaults?" he asked.

Roberts bridled. "I clean every day."

"This morning?"

"Not today. I usually unlock and open the door, then I mop the vault floor and the anteroom before we open the doors upstairs for customers. But when the safe door wouldn't open, I sent to fetch Mr Peters."

"You didn't mop the anteroom this morning."

"No."

I stifled a smile. Holmes had often emphasised the importance of minutiae in investigations, but I could see no material relevance in the mopping of the floor. Perhaps, I thought, he suspected Roberts had a hand in some nefarious activity connected with the malfunctioning door, and he was putting him off balance.

The fellow was pasty faced, and I detected a redness in his eyes suggestive of nervousness, if not guilty knowledge. I leaned forward in anticipation of a rapier thrust of interrogation.

Holmes gestured to the pot and cups on the table. "Who makes the tea?"

Roberts frowned. "The boy."

I blinked at Holmes. His questions suggested random arrow shots from a thin quiver rather than rapier thrusts. The porters' catering arrangements hardly seemed relevant to the problem of the locked door.

"And you did not mop the anteroom this morning," Holmes persisted.

Roberts folded his arms and glared at Holmes. "I thought it best to inform Mr Peters."

"You did right, Roberts. Nobody is blaming you," Mr Peters said.

Holmes and I turned and found the bank manager at the door with a short, heavyset man in a tweed overcoat whose grey hair spilled from under the rim of his bowler hat, joining ample side-whiskers framing a flushed and heavily dew-lapped face. His deep-set eyes blinked at us with no trace of warmth.

"Inspector Jones," Holmes said. "How charming to see you again."

"A bit of bother, is it?" Inspector Jones asked in a faint Welsh lilt. "There's a crowd outside, foreigners for the most part, screeching and carrying on." He addressed Mr Peters. "I might ask you to have a word with them. We don't want any unnecessary how-dyer-do. You may tell 'em I've personally examined the vault door most thoroughly, and in my professional opinion, it's not been tampered with."

The inspector peered at Holmes. "I am surprised to see you here, Mr Holmes. I don't see any sign of hidden treasure, peg-legged men or giant dogs."

Holmes favoured me with a dark look as the inspector chuckled. "No, sir, I see no scope for your detective powers here today, if you don't mind me saying. We have a mechanical problem before us, gentlemen, or my name's not Athelney Jones."

Holmes bowed, but made no reply, and he, Mr Grigoryan, and I followed Mr Peters and the inspector out of the vault room. Roberts hung back, but Mr Peters gestured for him to join us as we passed through the grill door to the staircase. We climbed towards the lobby, and I quizzed Roberts on the procedure for customers accessing their boxes and noted his answers.

"What staff are on duty on days when your offices are closed?" Holmes asked Mr Peters. "You mentioned faithful watchmen."

"On weekdays, when the vault door is open, the two concierges and messenger boy are on duty," he said. "Hobbs has the key to the outside door. He lets in any clients who wish to access their boxes. Roberts mans the grill at the bottom of the stairs and holds the master box key – both the renter's key and the master key are needed to open a box. The concierges have rattle alarms and police whistles to hand if there is any trouble, and the boy can summon help at need."

He shrugged. "Even if a miscreant managed to enter the vault, he would be faced with the box doors, which are not easy to pry open. We would have plenty of time to deal with him."

Holmes nodded. "And when the safety repository is closed?"

"A police constable makes his rounds every fifteen minutes," Inspector Jones said, "or each half hour at the very most."

"He patrols the outside of the building?" Holmes asked.

"Checking the locks, yes." The inspector smiled. "I know what you are thinking, Mr Holmes – why does the bank not have a watchman in the building at night and on the Lord's Day? Well, sir, we do not encourage banks and other premises to employ one for the simple reason that they afford ne'er-do-wells an opportunity to bribe or intimidate their way inside without breaking into premises and leaving a trace. We're in the shadow of the Bank of England, gentlemen, in the most secure square mile on earth, patrolled by City police constables who check all doors, shutters and windows on their beat; they know every property and every soul in them, and the tiniest anomaly stands out like a sore thumb."

"So, nobody is inside the bank at night." Holmes turned back to Mr Peters. "Do you have the blueprints of this building?"

"They are in the bank vault in the second basement." Mr Peters checked his watch. "The door is locked on a timer until a quarter to ten o'clock, nine minutes from now."

Holmes smiled. "Let's hope that door performs its duties."

———— ◆◇◆ ————

Mr Peters gave Holmes a frigid look as he led us into the lobby. A score of soberly dressed men who I presumed were bank employees clustered before the banking counter, looking perturbed. The iron grill protecting the counter was still down. Sergeant Halloran stood by the entrance doors with the other lobby porter and the boy. The hubbub outside was now clearly audible through the doors, and Mr Peters stiffened.

Inspector Jones pursed his lips. "I've sent for a half-dozen constables; we'll wait for them before we venture out."

"I should like to see the offices on this and the upper floors," Holmes said to Mr Peters.

"There's nothing to see, Mr Holmes. The offices are still locked and empty. I have kept our staff here in the lobby to help with the crowd when we open."

"Nevertheless, if it's not too much trouble."

Mr Peters nodded to Hobbs, who unlocked a tall cabinet beside the porter's desk and took a keyring from a hook.

Mr Grigoryan excused himself, having urgent business to attend to, and I promised to contact him as soon as the problem was resolved. He was escorted by Roberts to the back door.

Inspector Jones sat at the porter's desk and shook a cigarette from a packet of *Wild Woodbine*. "I shall establish my headquarters here while we wait for reinforcements. Halloran, you trot along with the gentlemen."

Hobbs crossed the lobby, opened one of a pair of glazed double doors, and operated a switch to ignite the electric globes hanging from the ceiling, revealing a long, unadorned corridor lined on both sides with closed doors.

I instantly sneezed. "I think I must be coming down with something. Or last night's fog has affected my sinuses."

Holmes took a deep breath. "Do you smell anything?"

I sniffed. "Is that smoke?"

Holmes and Hobbs led the way along the corridor, Holmes murmuring questions and the porter answering distractedly as the acrid smell grew stronger until it was swamped by the bitter stench of chemicals and stink of burnt wood. The linoleum floor became increasingly gritty with dust and the walls soot stained. I turned to Mr Peters to make a remark, but he was in a daze, stumbling after Holmes, white-faced and with trembling lips.

Holmes paused and pointed to a canvas hose that emerged from a door on the right, snaked along the corridor and disappeared through a part-open office door on the left.

"There's been a fire," I said to Mr Peters. "Did the fire brigade attend?" He stared blankly back at me and made no answer.

Holmes followed the hose farther along the corridor, pointing out grimy footprints in patches of damp sand and fragments of wood and bits of plaster littering the linoleum, to a battered door hanging on one hinge. "We are above the vault."

He pushed the door wide, revealing a shadowed modern office with panelled walls and shuttered windows. The reek of chemicals and smoke was intense.

I followed Holmes inside and operated the electric switch by the door, but the lamps did not ignite. I lit a match and gasped. Smashed desks and chairs were piled against the walls, and they and the floor were blanketed with swathes of wet sand, shredded paper, and lumps of broken masonry and plaster. Wooden panelling was torn from the walls, and splintered joists were visible in the blackened ceiling. In the centre of the room was a ragged hole from which poked the top rungs of a wooden ladder.

Mr Peters entered behind me and staggered back against the wall. "Dear God."

Holmes and I picked our way forward and looked through the hole. I lit another match, but I could see nothing but darkness below.

"Where did all this sand come from?" I asked.

Holmes scanned the room. He darted to a corner, pounced, and held up a ripped canvas sack and shreds of rubber. "They tamped the explosives with india-rubber bladders filled with water and heaped with sandbags."

He went to the window and tapped the buckled steel shutters. "Give me a hand, old man."

Holmes and I dragged the screeching shutter up halfway, as far as it would go, letting in shafts of pale sunlight.

We returned to the hole and peered in. The concrete floor had been pierced, eighth-inch thick iron bars were bent downwards and the armoured steel composing the roof of the vault had been penetrated by a tremendous force.

Holmes addressed Mr Peters, who stood wide-eyed, pressed against the wall of the room. "We'll need more light: candles, or preferably, electric torches."

He swung himself onto the ladder, carefully wriggled through the hole, and disappeared. I followed him, trying not to catch my shoulders on the rough concrete and squeezing inch-by-inch past metal shards, until I stood beside Holmes in a pool of water on the debris-strewn floor of the vault.

He struck a match on his boot heel and held it up. Racks of safety-box doors ranging in size from four-inch letter boxes to three-foot-tall safes lined the walls. The massive door, straight ahead of us, was in shadow, but the flaring match caught the gleam of shiny rods, wheels and cogs.

A dozen or more boxes hung open, their doors bent outwards at strange angles, and the puddled floor was littered with lumps of concrete and empty metal drawers and strewn with a mess of bags, cases and sodden papers.

I struck a match, and Holmes bent and picked up a heavy hammer, a chisel and then a length of steel bar attached to a heavy metal coil and with three hinged legs.

"A giant corkscrew," I suggested, my voice echoing in the small chamber.

"A specialised tool that works on the same principle," Holmes said. "They used it to pry open the boxes."

Something in the debris glittered in the flare of the match, and I retrieved a gold coin the size of a waistcoat button from a half dozen scattered across the floor. "My God, Holmes, if they discarded gold, what did they take?"

Holmes lit another match, examined the coin, smiled, and dropped it. "Twenty Spanish pesetas, worth about ten shillings. It seems the robbers didn't bother with them."

He stooped and picked up a part-smoked cigar lying on a heap of sand, a wisp of smoke rising from the ash at its tip. He read the band. "A three-quarter-smoked *Henry Clay*, an excellent Havana."

"Not a brand I know," I said.

Holmes replaced the cigar and stepped carefully to the far wall. He examined the back of the vault door and pointed to a crowbar jamming the cogs and sprockets that inserted and withdrew the rods securing the door. "Pass me that hammer."

Holmes knocked the crowbar from the cogwheel, and it clanged to the floor. He lit another match, held it high, carefully examined the back of the door, then blew out the match. "Give me a hand, old chap."

Holmes and I pushed against the door. It swung smoothly open, flooding the vault with electric light from the anteroom and revealing a middle-aged, blond-haired man in a dark suit and the wide-eyed bank pageboy. The man nodded a greeting and held out his hand. "Mr Holmes and Doctor Watson, a pleasure to see you again," he said in faintly accented English.

Holmes smiled. "Watson, you will remember Mr Van den Boorn?"

I gaped as I recognised one of Holmes' many acquaintances in the criminal fraternity, known among his nefarious confrères as the Dutchman. From his metalworks in a shady part of South London, he specialised in the construction of unbreakable locks for the wary, while to his shady clients he offered sophisticated implements designed to defeat them.

Holmes had employed the Dutchman on several occasions, most notably in the fabrication of a crutch forged from costly aluminium that had been used in circumstances remaining, after the passage of many years, murky and uncertain.

I watched with considerable disquiet as the Dutchman entered the vault.

Holmes held up the crowbar. "This was jammed in the mechanism."

The Dutchman nodded. "That would do it." He picked his way among the debris and examined one of the buckled safety-box doors. He indicated an untouched, locked box. "You see the door edges are flush with the frames and the hinges are internal – that's to inhibit chisels. Steel brackets fix six-inch brass deadbolts to the back of each door, and three inches of the bolt passes through the strike plate to secure it. Difficult to pry open."

Holmes picked up the giant corkscrew device and passed it to the Dutchman.

"Interesting, Mr Holmes. A metal tip at the end of the rod has evidently broken off. It is inserted into the keyhole and twisted, exerting tremendous pulling force and wrenching out the door. A clever design."

The Dutchman stifled a yawn as he glanced around the vault. "Looks like they started at the far wall, unfortunately for them, as most of those boxes are not yet rented. Safety deposits have never really caught on in this country. The English keep their silver in the butler's strongroom; their notion of security is having the boot boy sleep across the doorway."

I made my attitude to such impertinent remarks by a guest in this country clear by my silence.

The Dutchman pointed out a box with its door buckled but not broken open. "Here and on these other doors, they tried and failed."

I watched as Holmes ranged along the line of smashed-open boxes, closely examining each one. He stopped about a third of the way along a row and turned to Mr Peters, who stood ashen faced at the open door of the vault. "Do you have a list of box renters?"

"A list? "Yes, I am sure we do. Yes, we must have."

"I should like to see it," Holmes said softly.

Inspector Jones called through the hole in the ceiling. "Oh, deary me, here's a pretty business: what a mess. I said the door was not the problem, and I was perfectly correct. I'll make my way back to the vault room and be there in a trice. Kindly refrain from touching anything."

Holmes chuckled. "Let's make way for the inspector and see how the robbers made their entry."

He and I climbed back up the ladder and wriggled slowly and carefully through the hole. We left the wrecked office with Sergeant Halloran in tow, following the hose across the corridor to a lavatory where it was attached to a tap. A circular hole three feet in diameter had been bored through the wall.

Holmes tapped the wall. "Shoddy construction. They poked through from the adjoining building in minutes."

We clambered through the hole into a large room with palliasses laid in rows on the floor. Across the far wall 'Soap, Soup and

Salvation' was painted in two-foot-high letters, and on the other walls were exhortations to repent and pray. A hole in that wall let us into another lavatory stall. We passed a line of urinals and through the door into a dim corridor, its mould-stained walls lined with doors. To our right was darkness, while to our left, dim light filtered through the filthy skylight above a street door. The bitter smell of strong tobacco pervaded the atmosphere.

Holmes turned to the muffled sound of voices and thumping coming from the street direction. "Perhaps our navvies are still burrowing." He strode along the corridor, swung open a door, and I followed him into a workshop in which two rows of long tables stood on a sawdust-strewn floor. Women sat at each table rolling tobacco leaves into cigars, and in one corner of the room a man operated a mechanical press, punching what looked like coloured labels.

A short man in his waistcoat and bowler hat hurried across the room, waved us back into the corridor and shut the door behind him. "The office is across the corridor, gents. This is private." He frowned at Sergeant Halloran. "Police?"

"Who are you?" Holmes demanded.

"Are you here about the burglary?" the man asked Sergeant Halloran.

"Who are you?" Holmes repeated.

The man folded his arms. "I'm the works manager of the Marlborough Cigar Company. When I opened up this morning, I found the office in a right old mess."

"Kindly show me."

The manager led us across the corridor and ushered us into a small office and shop combined, its walls lined with shelves stacked with colourful cigar boxes. A young clerk sat with his elbows on a long counter. He slipped his racing paper out of sight.

"They jumped the backyard wall, fiddled the back door I suppose and helped themselves to our stock," the manager said.

"How many did they take?" Sergeant Halloran asked.

"Three."

"Just three cartons?" The sergeant frowned, his pencil poised over his notebook.

"Three cigars." The manager bridled at my smile. "They made a right old mess, with their rubbish all over the shop. Took us best part of half an hour to clear up."

"Show me the rubbish," Holmes said.

We followed the manager back along the corridor, past the closed lavatory door and out into a cemented backyard. A row of metal dustbins stood against a six-foot-high wall amid a clutter of wooden packing cases and barrels. The manager opened the lid of one bin, disclosing the remains of beef pies and mash wrapped in greased paper and parcelled in newsprint, and six empty ale bottles.

"They had their supper in the office. We found this." He held up a dusty, false beard. "Must have been drunks on a jolly. We didn't bother reporting."

Holmes picked up one of the bottles. "Daniell's Dinner Ale." He turned to Sergeant Halloran and raised his eyebrows. "Pie and mash?"

"There's a stall on the corner of Cornhill and Pope's Head Alley, sir. They open about noon. I'll have a word." Halloran said to the manager. "Come and have a look at your lavatory. You've had mice."

"A moment," Holmes said. He faced the manager. "Withholding evidence is a serious crime."

The man paled. "I don't know what you mean."

"You found a coat or cloak and a hat."

"That old thing? I thought someone might have a use for it is all." The manager led us back to the hall, opened a cupboard, and removed a threadbare black overcoat and a well-worn flat cap. "I thought to give it to the Sally Army girls next door. I didn't know anything about evidence, Sergeant."

Holmes snatched the coat and hat and examined them thoroughly before handing them to Sergeant Halloran. "English cut, woollen coat, no tailor's label, bought second or perhaps tenth-hand. The front is faded, and the shoulders are pinched, so it hung for a long time on a thin hanger in a window or outside a shop door. It stinks of mothballs, as does this nondescript workman's cap – misshapen as you see by being stored flat in a pile. Nothing much of interest, other than the fact they exist, and they were purchased recently. Those are salient facts."

<hr />

Holmes and I passed out of the front door of the cigar premises and into Cornhill. The pavements were almost empty. The City clerks were at their desks in the tall office buildings on this side and in the hulking, windowless edifice of the Bank of England across the street.

"Someone must have heard an almighty bang during the night," Holmes said.

"The City is practically deserted from office closing time on Friday till Saturday morning," I said.

"Even early in the morning in the empty City, someone heard the bang and saw the escape carriage. It would stand out all the more in the absence of other traffic. Carters and market workers start at an early hour and there are the plethora of beat constables the inspector is so proud of." Holmes rubbed his hands together. "A proper job after all, my dear Watson, and I'd wager you thought this would be an inconsequential affair."

I was saved from having to make an answer by Inspector Jones, who bustled along the pavement to us from the cigar shop, also rubbing his hands together.

"I have reached certain conclusions, gentlemen."

Holmes smiled. "I have no doubt of it."

The inspector waved an expansive arm at the shop behind us. "The gang drilled their way from the cigar factory through the party walls of the Salvation Army building and into the bank's lavatory on the floor above the vault, correctly assuming there would be no alarm mechanisms or patrols."

"This seems a very sensible way of gaining access to the building," I said. "A tunnel would have taken much longer – far simpler to smash through brick walls rather than worm their way through thirty yards of London clay."

"Obviously so, Doctor. That part was very clear to me from the beginning." The inspector narrowed his eyes. "They chose a Friday night, do you see, when the Jewish sabbath begins and bankers are in a hurry to get off home."

"Why not Saturday night?" I asked. "That would have given them all day Sunday and Sunday night to complete the work."

"That is a question I shall ask the robbers as and when I bring them to book." Inspector Jones hooked his thumbs in his waistcoat pockets and leaned back on his heels. "Speaking of books, your own endeavours in that regard are well spoken of, Doctor, even by some of my colleagues, but I confine my reading to the Lord's Word, and I shall focus my attention on the facts of the case, not wild surmises about whys and wheretofores."

Holmes murmured an annoying "Hear, hear."

"The gang blasted a hole in the vault ceiling in the early morning," Inspector Jones continued. "They ransacked thirteen boxes before they made their escape."

"Why did they jam the door?" I asked.

"Devilment, Doctor. These type of fellows don't care what mayhem they create."

"The locksmith suggests some boxes may have been empty," I said, "not yet rented."

The inspector tapped the sheet of paper in his hand. "I have all the details, Doctor. No speculation is necessary."

Holmes held out his hand. "May I?"

Inspector Jones drew back, then smiled and passed the paper to Holmes. "I've nothing up my sleeve, do you see, gentlemen? As the Good Book says, 'Let each one of you speak the truth with his neighbour, for we are members one of another.' Methodical police work will beat the band in this case, as it has in all my previous investigations. My record speaks for itself."

"Doctor Watson and I were contemplating the clues the miscreants left us," Holmes said as he made notes on his shirt cuff. "A fine cigar, and three stolen cheroots, the debris of three pie and mash dinners and the disguise discarded in the cigar shop dustbin."

"Working class food, gentlemen," Inspector Jones replied. "I'll have my men infiltrate the public houses in Spitalfields and Whitechapel, sniffing for whispers. One of the gang will let the cat out of the bag sooner rather than later: the criminal classes love to prattle. 'When words are many, transgression is not lacking.'"

Holmes handed the paper back to the inspector. "Mr Grigoryan's name is not on the inspector's list."

"I'm relieved to hear it," I said. "What did the gang get, I wonder?"

"We may take it for granted that they stole cash and anything that can be easily sold or melted," Inspector Jones said. "The vault is in the financial centre of London, gentlemen, where one would expect box-holders to store financial instruments, gems and cash. Some items will be useless to the thieves – deeds, private papers, wills and unique items that might link them to the crime. They dumped those."

He shook his head. "Mr Peters has directed his staff to interview each box holder, but how the insurance companies will assess their liability, I do not know. It's just the renter's word that he has something valuable in the box. And between you and me, I expect most of the contents will be uninsured."

"They must have visited the vault to check the lay of the land," I said. "Perhaps the bank staff will recall suspicious characters."

"All in hand, Doctor," Inspector Jones said. He checked his watch. "Thank you for your interest in the case, Mr Holmes and Doctor Watson. I think you can now leave it to the professionals. You might keep an eye on your morning newspapers. I wish you good day." He turned away.

"There are one or two aspects of this case make it interesting, are there not, inspector?" Holmes said.

Inspector Jones paused and narrowed his eyes. "And what would they be?"

"The hole in the vault ceiling is narrow and obstructed by twisted iron rods and protruding shards of metal. Doctor Watson had difficulty worming his broad, rugby-playing shoulders through, and I see he has nicked his jacket sleeve. The robbers had tools; why did they not enlarge the hole to make ingress and egress easier?"

"Time, Mr Holmes. As I have said, they had only a few hours—"

"Again, Inspector, Doctor Watson quite rightly asks why they did not attack on a Saturday night, leaving the whole of Sunday to work on the boxes."

"Logic is your strong point, Mr Holmes, but not all criminals are blessed with your gifts."

Holmes smiled. "You are too kind, Inspector, but sometimes simple observation will suffice without the necessity for deep analysis. There was a strong carbolic soap smell in the vault anteroom when we entered this morning, yet the porter stated that he had not mopped the floor since yesterday morning."

The inspector chuckled. "Carbolic lingers, Mr Holmes. I can sometimes smell the taint two or three days after Mrs Jones's washday. The smell you speak of obviously came from the mops and cloths we saw in the pump room and is of no consequence."

Holmes nodded. "I bow to your professional expertise, inspector, and I look forward to reading of your solution over my breakfast egg tomorrow morning." He turned to me. "Talking of which – a late breakfast?"

I blinked at Holmes. My fellow lodger seldom took notice of mealtimes when he was on a case, and I was pleasantly taken aback. "An excellent suggestion."

We left the inspector and sauntered along Cornhill, past the still-closed entrance doors of the New York and Continental. The pavement was now thronged with gentlemen and even a few ladies, many waving their fists at the stoic police constable on guard.

"I believe the inspector may have missed a couple of possibly salient points," I said.

"You astonish me."

"The manager at the Marlborough Cigar Company was anxious to usher us out of the rolling room – why?"

Holmes smiled. "You are about to enlighten me."

"He did not want us to see that his workers were crumbling used cigar stubs, doubtless picked up from the streets of London, and re-rolling the old tobacco in fresh wrappers. It is no wonder the thieves stole just three cigars; we can assume they were vile."

"Bravo, Watson. What more? You will call into evidence the *Henry Clay* to adduce – what?"

"Three of the gang gorged themselves on pie and mash and were content with penny re-rolled stinkers, but one had more refined tastes: he was no East End thug. He smoked a much finer cigar, and he wore fashionable chisel-toed boots."

"The prints in the mud on the vault floor and the dust in the office corridor," Holmes said. "Workmen's boots and one set of prints, as you say, in the latest style."

"Exactly."

Holmes bowed. "Excellent observation, old man, and cogent deductions with which I am in complete agreement." He stopped and looked at his watch. "It occurs to me that I have one or two little things to do. Let's meet at the Black Friar public house in an hour for an early luncheon – if you can hold back hunger pangs until then?"

"Certainly, I have some errands myself. We are almost out of pipe tobacco." I took Mr Grigoryan's business card from my pocket. "And I'll give your client the welcome news if he hasn't heard it already."

Holmes darted across the street and waved for a hansom from the stand under the duke's statue.

It was a pleasant day, and I considered walking to my tobacconist in the Strand, but I did not wish to leave Mr Grigoryan in suspense, so I too hailed a cab and directed the driver to Hatton Garden.

I was in a jaunty mood. It was clear that my years of association with Sherlock Holmes and his deductive methods, combined with my experience in medical diagnosis, had honed whatever native wit I possessed to the point that I could make a not inconsiderable contribution to the evidence in the case. I had noted the implications of the footprints and the cigar stub, as well as the unpleasant and unsanitary processes at the cigar factory which might or might not be relevant to the case. My sensitive nose had detected the taint of carbolic in the vault room, although the exact significance of the smell I had yet to determine. I thought one more observation I had made might throw an interesting light on the robbery, but I needed confirmation before I offered my theory to Holmes.

Altogether, I was not displeased with myself, and I resolved to visit my tobacconist as soon as I had conveyed the welcome news to Mr Grigoryan.

———◆———

"Yes, I am one of the lucky ones, Doctor," Mr Grigoryan said. "One of my acquaintances was not so fortunate. He lost a considerable sum."

I perched on a rickety chair in a tiny, cluttered office on the top floor of a grimy building in an alley off Hatton Garden. The ceiling was low, the walls bare whitewashed bricks, and the single window was tight-curtained. A bright Argand lamp illuminated a desk covered with files and heaps of small paper packets. The only other item of furniture was a battered workbench strewn with tools, clamps and grinding apparatus and with a large magnifying lens on a swivel. Above the bench, an icon of the Madonna gleamed gold and lapis lazuli in the lamplight.

"How long have you had the box?" I asked.

"Less than a year." Mr Grigoryan leaned back in his chair and regarded me from under his green eyeshade. "I was one of the first customers of the bank, and I thus claimed a discount on safety-box fees. There are only four deposits in London: the New York and Continental, Harrods' emporium, Chancery Lane, and here in Hatton Garden. The New York Bank is the cheapest, its location is convenient, and some of my American connections are clients of the Manhattan branch, which makes transfers easy. The New York and Continental is a merchant bank, but they offer the usual banking services to safety-deposit key holders."

"I understand many of the boxes are not yet rented."

"Safety boxes are a relatively new concept, Doctor, and many British people prefer to keep their valuables at home or entrust them to solicitors' safes or vaults at their usual bank. I and my fellow diamantaires require access to cash at odd hours, and we are used to maintaining boxes in New York or Amsterdam."

Mr Grigoryan slid the little paper packets across his desk, making small stacks, and then redistributing them again. "I was shocked at the inadequate security provisions at the bank. Not even a watchman on duty at night or all day Sunday! Despite the extra cost, I will move my account to Chancery Lane, where the vaults are patrolled night and day by armed custodians. That will deter the most die-hard villains."

"Inspector Jones suspects an East End gang in the business," I said.

Mr Grigoryan leaned forward and lowered his voice. "Rumour has it the robbers focussed their attention on the medium and letterbox-sized boxes rather than the larger ones. Is that not strange? Would one not expect them to smash open the bigger boxes as likely having more to steal?"

I nodded. "Go on."

"I believe this vault may have been targeted for a reason, Doctor." Mr Grigoryan's voice sank lower. "Everyone in the industry knows that DeBeers in South Africa have a monopoly on diamond supply; Cecil Rhodes bought up all the small claims or ran them into bankruptcy. Diamantaires like me have no choice but to deal with DeBeers. They release diamonds to the market in amounts carefully calibrated to market conditions, and sight holders, as we are known, buy the rough gems and have them cut and polished, mostly in Antwerp, Amsterdam and here in London."

He indicated the stacks of paper packets on his desk. "Sales take place every five weeks when parcels of diamonds are sent to each sight holder. Ironically, we buy sight unseen; we know only the specifications of the stones. Sometimes we are pleasantly surprised (if you are supportive of DeBeers, you might find a few 'specials' – larger stones) and sometimes we are disappointed."

"How does this relate to the robbery?" I asked.

"DeBeers maintain a diamond warehouse in London in which the stones are graded and divided into 'sight' packets. I happen to know the location of that secret warehouse.

Mr Grigoryan's voice descended to a whisper. "It is in this building. At one time the mass of stones were kept in a vault in the basement, but rumour has it the stock was moved earlier this year to a New York and Continental safety box as more secure – not under DeBeers' name of course."

He leaned back in his chair. "The depository contained a king's ransom in uncut diamonds, Doctor. The thieves knew exactly what they were looking for. They got away with a colossal haul."

Mr Grigoryan reached into a desk drawer. "I made this out to Mr Holmes in the amount of a guinea." He held out a cheque but did not meet my eyes. "I expect that will be an adequate payment for his services, under the circumstances."

I took the cheque and stood. "I will pass this to Mr Holmes and apprise him of your suspicions." I looked down at the little packets on the desk. "I wonder, might I ...?"

Mr Grigoryan obligingly opened one of the packets and held the contents up to the lamplight for my inspection. Three pea-sized, milky-white stones lay on the paper, disappointingly dull and lustreless.

"How much might they be worth?"

Mr Grigoryan folded the stones in the envelope. "Cut and polished, maybe forty guineas."

"Each?"

He nodded absently and returned to his stacks of paper packets.

I left Mr Grigoryan's chambers and stood on the pavement outside. The sky had clouded over, and I could smell rain in the air. I looked for a cab, noticed a tobacconist across the road, and decided to save myself a trip to my usual shop in the Strand.

"Do you know *Marlborough* cigars?" I asked the elderly clerk after I had made my purchases.

The clerk wrinkled his nose. "Not a proper brand, sir: they are a stain on the escutcheon of the trade. They re-wrap the sweepings of the street, sir, and trick their cheroots up in fancy boxes."

"And *Henry Clay*?"

"Ah, now – four guineas a dozen, when we can get them, sir. All these recent upheavals in Cuba have played merry hell with the trade, if you will excuse my vehemence. We've not had any stock since '97, sir, or perhaps the year previous. I did hear that Baron Rothschild had two hundred dozens smuggled out of Havana, on condition the seller had them wrapped in gold leaf."

I nodded. "I have a question of etiquette. In what circumstances would a gentleman smoke his cigar with the band still on?"

The clerk recoiled. "Never, sir. It would be considered bad form – showing off, as it is commonly termed. It would be the equivalent of wearing one's tailor's label on the sleeve of one's jacket."

"That is a general rule, observed even outside this country?"

"Most certainly, sir, in the better circles both here and on the Continent. We have a number of foreign gentlemen of distinction on our books, some of whom condescend to make use of the cigar divan on the floor above us. They observe the niceties to a tee, sir, almost as if they were English born."

I secured a paper bag for my purchases and, a little disappointed with my visit, I wished the clerk good day.

He offered me the same salutation, then frowned. "There was just one gentleman I recall, sir, oh it would have been at the end of the eighties or thereabouts. He took a light for his cigar from the lamp we keep by the door for the convenience of passers-by, a *Partagàs*, it was, as I remember, sir, a fine Cuban. And he did not remove the band! He wished me a very good day, sir, as you just did, and walked on as bold as brass." The clerk shook his head. "Not one of our regulars, of course, sir. A Yankee, sir, as I surmised from his tone and accent – from America."

I found a cab and got down outside the Black Friar public house, a modern building that I understood was favoured by City men and clergy from nearby St Paul's. I checked my watch against the clock above the statue guarding the entrance. Either the Black Friar was off by three minutes, or I was.

Holmes was in a seat by the window with a pint glass on the table before him. "The investigation has taken an interesting turn," he said with a smile.

I slid onto the bench opposite him. "I agree."

I called a waiter, ordered a beer, and passed Holmes Mr Grigoryan's cheque, which he glanced at and folded into his pocketbook.

On Holmes' request, I summarised my interview with Mr Grigoryan and his suspicions regarding the DeBeers Company diamond cache. "That explains why the gang gave themselves so little time in the vault and their unhurried attitude," I concluded, "the pie and mash and beer and so forth. They knew exactly what they were after."

Holmes considered. "Interesting, although Inspector Jones might think the notion speculative." He glanced over my shoulder. "Welcome Sergeant."

I turned and found Sergeant Halloran and a young constable behind me. The sergeant introduced his colleague as PC Laidlaw, the policeman who had patrolled Cornhill and Lombard Street the previous night. Holmes invited them to join us.

"Take off your helmet, boy," Halloran growled as they sat. "I'm sorry, Mr Holmes, Laidlaw's only been on the job six months. He's not yet learned his manners."

"What was your previous employment?" I asked to put the young man more at his ease.

Laidlaw reddened. "A taproom boy at the Duke of Sussex, sir. A public house down Lambeth way: no connection with His Grace."

On cue, the Black Friar boy appeared at our table, and I ordered a pint of ale for the sergeant, and on Halloran's insistence, just a half for the constable.

"How long have you been on the Cornhill beat?" Holmes asked Laidlaw.

"Four months, sir, in three-week cycles of Early Turn, Late Turn and Night Duty. I was on Night Duty yesterday, sir, from six in the evening to six this morning, with a forty-five-minute dinner break. I passed by the bank every twenty-two minutes, sir, and I checked the doors front and back."

"The backdoor is the tradesman's entrance?"

"Yes sir. Also used for deliveries, cash and that, so we keep a special eye on it during the day."

"What was the traffic like in the early morning?"

"Quiet, sir, once the evening rush died down. The only movement between three o'clock and when things got going at about six thirty was maybe a dozen cabs, some hay and vegetable carts to Spitalfields market and the usual procession of coal carts to and from the big depot behind Whitechapel Station. Around five, I saw a couple of early omnibuses and a pantechnicon – I stopped that for a routine look-see, sir. It contained theatrical sets and so on for a play the company was moving to Brighton. They were to load the sets on the eight-fifteen train from Waterloo."

"What theatre were the theatricals from?"

"The Varieties Theatre, Hoxton, sir. I told Inspector Jones, and he's sending word to Brighton."

"Very well," Holmes said. "We will leave the theatre folk to the industrious inspector. What line were the omnibuses?"

"London Road Car, sir, a green 'bus limping home with a sprung axel, and its replacement a little later."

"Time?"

"Coming up from Queen Victoria Street, about five, sir, then he turned around on Cornhill and went home. The replacement passed me at five to six or a bit before while I was waiting for my relief."

"You spoke to the driver of the omnibus?" Holmes asked.

"As he turned the duff carriage, sir. When he came back with the new rig, I just waved."

"Did you see any carriages stopped near the bank?"

"No, sir." Laidlaw considered. "Just a coal cart, sir. They stopped by the Marlborough cigar premises while the driver jacked a stone from his horse's hoof."

Holmes' eyes gleamed. "Time?"

"Just after four. The cart was on its way back to the yard with a few dozen sacks and three higglers, coal-heavers, sir, on the back. I asked what was up, and one of 'em called back about the stone. When I passed by on my next round, they was gone."

"What side was the lame horse?"

"Offside, sir." Laidlaw blinked at Holmes. "It wasn't them, was it, sir?"

Holmes sat back for a moment, steepling his hands under his chin. "Had anything delayed you in that circuit of your beat?"

"Yes, sir. A woman outside the Pope's Head pub – a woman of a certain type sir – was in drink, and she'd laid into a man who claimed to be her husband come to fetch her. I tried to calm things down, sir, but she was in a lather. Luckily she slipped and knocked herself out. We loaded her on a borrowed wheelbarrow, and her man took her away."

"How long did that take?"

"No more than ten or fifteen minutes, sir."

"Very well. What other disturbances were there in the night?" Holmes asked.

"You mean the bang, sir? It was at two minutes past six this morning. I was at the corner of Clement's Lane and Lombard Street, sir. The noise sounded far away, muffled like, but I turned back for a look-see, just in case. I found PC 87 Rourke at the corner of Birchin Lane with an official of the Empire Gas Company. He told us a gas main had blown in Smithfield Market and blowback had caused a reburberation—"

"Reverberation?" I suggested.

"Yessir, as I said, what was being dealt with by the gas company with no harm done."

"Describe the official," Holmes asked.

"An ordinary fellow, sir, in company uniform and carrying a manhole-cover hook like gas men do."

"Did you investigate further?"

"No, sir. I left that to the Metropolitan Police. Smithfield is outside the City of London proper, sir – it's a Met manor. They don't like the City force interfering, sir." Laidlaw sniffed. "Nor do we."

"You went back on your beat."

"I did, sir." He glanced at the sergeant.

"I interviewed the stall holder of the pie and mash stall," Halloran said. "He caters for caretakers and street sweepers and so on, including us coppers. At ten to five this morning, he received an order for three portions, two with liquor, one without. The man who ordered was in workman's dress with a London accent. He said he and his mates were repairing the roof of the cigar premises down the road which was damaged in last month's storms. The cook made up the pie order and was paid."

Holmes frowned.

"Liquor is parsley sauce, a cockney speciality," I explained. "It traditionally accompanies minced beef pie and mashed potato."

"I am perfectly aware of that. I was considering the importance of that information in relation to what we know of the gang." Holmes smiled. "And wondering what deductions Inspector Jones will derive from their sauce preferences."

I returned Holmes' smile. "I agree with the inspector that their cigar choices support his notion that three of them were lower class."

"What do you know of the Marlborough cigar factory?" Holmes asked Laidlaw.

"Dustmen take cigars from the refuse, street arabs pick up stubs from the street, and waiters and pages collect used stubs from the gentlemen's clubs; they deliver them to the back door." The constable looked to the sergeant. "It's not an offence, is it?"

I sipped my beer as I considered the constable's evidence. Although I had seen loafers pick up fag ends and cigar butts from the street, it had not occurred to me that anyone could make and market a cigar composed of street sweepings. I wondered whether the Marlborough company's unsavoury practices might be a cover for even more nefarious activities, and I made a mental note to suggest we should dig deeper into their affairs.

"When did you come off duty?" Holmes asked Laidlaw.

"At seven, sir." Laidlaw nodded to the sergeant. "It was supposed to be six, but Sergeant Halloran sent a message that the relief was delayed an hour."

"Did you see any of the bank staff coming to work?"

"Hobbs and the boy, sir; they passed me at about six thirty and said hello. I see them and Roberts often when I'm on Early Turn. They usually arrive about then or a bit after."

Holmes nodded and turned to Sergeant Halloran. "What caused the delay in relieving Laidlaw?"

"We had a scare, Mr Holmes. One of the relief bobbies turned up covered in spots, and we suspected he might have the smallpox that's going around. We called in the police doctor, but it turned out he'd had whelks for breakfast, and they disagreed with him and caused a rash."

Holmes addressed PC Laidlaw. "When did you take your dinner?"

"Three fifteen, sir. I often have a plate of jellied eels and a bun at the stand beside the duke's statue just before they pack up at three thirty."

"Very well," Holmes said. "One last question. The robbers drilled through the premises next to the bank. I presume that's a Salvation Army mission house."

"Yessir," Laidlaw answered. "They have Bible study early on Sunday morning and give out bread and cheese, then another meeting in the evening with soup, free baths and a place to sleep for a night for them willing to pray for it."

"Thank you," Holmes said, glancing out of the window. "You had better be off. I have a feeling your inspector might find his way here. They do an excellent one-and-six luncheon."

Sergeant Halloran led the constable out. I beckoned the tap-room boy, and Holmes and I made our order.

"After the explosion, the gang calmed the local policemen with the gas leak story," I said, "then spent forty-five minutes or fewer levering and drilling open the deposit boxes and ransacking them." I paused as a thought struck me. "Or did they continue to smash open the boxes even after seven – is that why they jammed the door?" I shook my head. "What a cheek, and dangerous with the neighbourhood becoming busy.

"Whatever the reason, they put themselves under a time constraint by attacking early Saturday morning and went to a great deal of effort for a short time actually robbing the boxes, which supports Mr Grigoryan's suggestion they knew exactly what they were after."

"Yes, our gang seems poorly focussed on the job in hand," Holmes said. "They wasted their already limited time having supper and set off the explosion as the City was waking up. The affair seems inexpertly planned."

"You mentioned an interesting turn, Holmes," I said as we settled to our luncheon.

"And I believe you have more than Mr Grigoryan's speculations," Holmes said. "Your news first."

I took a sip of beer. "I checked the cigar brand, *Henry Clay*. According to the tobacconist's clerk I spoke to, they have been unavailable in this country since the start of the Spanish-American War in Cuba in '97, although the Rothschilds got hold of some through their connections."

"And?"

"You identified the cigar from its band. An English gentleman, or even a well-mannered European, would remove the band on his cigar before lighting it. I contend the chisel-toed smoker may be a foreigner, and from farther afield than Europe. The bank is a branch of an American company, which may be a factor." I leaned back in my chair. "There is more. Mr Peters smoked a cigar in the vault room, and he had left the band on!"

"Bravo, Watson."

I smiled. "You agree?"

"It's an engaging observation." Holmes sipped his beer. "We might skip dessert, if you agree; we have a couple more ports of call this afternoon."

"The coal yard?" I asked.

"As a last resort. I don't expect much from the coal heavers; like dustmen, they are a tight-lipped group in my experience." He glanced at his watch. "I suggest we hire a cab by the hour."

Holmes glanced out of the cab window and tapped on the roof with his cane. "Just past the corner of Shoe Lane, cabby."

We got down, passed through a set of gates marked 'The London Road Car Company' in faded white letters, and entered a wide, cobbled yard. A substantial brick building formed one side of the yard, an office and a long line of horse stalls were on the ground floor, and a wide ramp led to more stalls above. Two dozen or more unhitched omnibuses liveried in brown, green and red were parked in the yard with gangs of cleaners wielding brooms, mops and buckets.

Holmes addressed a man in a bowler who was watching the work and smoking a reeking pipe.

"Do you rent omnibuses?" Holmes asked.

The man gestured with his pipe towards the building on the other side of the yard. "That's office business." He turned away.

"What a rude fellow," I murmured as I followed Holmes across the yard and into a cluttered office with a counter by the door and a dozen or so clerks seated at high desks behind it.

"Yes, we rent 'buses at very reasonable rates for private hire, company transport of employees or as charabancs for pleasure trips," a young assistant with oiled hair and a scant moustache answered Holmes' question. "There's a forty-shilling deposit on wear and tear. You'll need to make a change of horses every four hours, three in inclement weather, either here or at our Grosvenor Road stables. Our standard London rates are—"

Holmes held up a restraining hand. "This is an official enquiry regarding omnibuses in your livery seen on Cornhill in the City between five and seven this morning."

The clerk frowned. "The City at five in the morning? Not our scheduled runs; we start at seven, so the first buses through Cornhill would be seven thirty or thereabouts." He took a ledger from a shelf behind him and leafed through it. "We had two hires yesterday and one on Thursday for return on Monday. Let me see."

He ran his finger down lines of entries. "Thursday was the Mile End Baptist Choir, Friday was the Arden Players and then Rollins and Co. The choir's in a do at the Exeter Hall and Arden is a theatre company. I don't recall the pickup, but the drop was Waterloo Station."

He consulted another ledger. "Pickup was the Hoxton Varieties Music Hall. And Rollins were a works evening-out to the Victoria Temperance Hall, picked up from Aldgate."

"You provide drivers?"

"Of course. Can't let just anyone drive our rigs."

"And have the Rollins and Arden 'buses been returned?"

"Yes, both are in. We'll expect the choir rig later for a spruce up and change of nags." The clerk peered at the ledger. "There's a note here that the first rig we sent to Hoxton had a problem, and we sent a replacement." He looked up. "Are you making a complaint?"

"I need to speak to the drivers and conductors of all three omnibuses on a matter of official business."

"Just drivers of hire vehicles, no conductors." The clerk flipped the page. "Phipps, Leman and Mooney. Phipps is still out with the choir, and the other two are off rota till six. Mooney will have gone home down Lambeth way, but Leman's probably in the canteen or maybe the yard." He frowned. "What's this about, then? Are you the police?"

"I am investigating a serious criminal case," Holmes answered. "Kindly conduct me to the canteen."

Holmes and I followed an office boy into the yard. The boy stopped and pointed to the unfriendly fellow Holmes had addressed earlier. "There's Leman."

Holmes introduced himself and me to the driver and continued in a stern tone. "I require your cooperation in a criminal investigation. I must inform you that the participants in the crime, when caught, as they shall be, may not see the light of day for years, if not decades. Any persons wittingly or unwittingly involved must immediately cooperate in the investigation or face the consequences. The police inspector in this case is indefatigable and relentless in pursuit."

"You're after the dynamite gang," Leman said. He tapped a rolled afternoon paper sticking out of his pocket.

"You passed through Cornhill early this morning," Holmes said.

Leman puffed on his pipe. "I'd to pick up from the music hall at seven. I made sure I was well in time – I don't like to rush, me; I take things slow and steady. I thought to rest the nags for a bit and 'ave a bite of breakfast before the pickup; lucky I did, for the front axle pin bent as I passed the Exchange."

"At what time?"

"About five." Leman gave Holmes an arch look. "That's when I saw what I saw."

"Describe."

Leman smirked. "What's the reward?"

"That depends whether anything you have to say is of material assistance in the case."

Leman nodded. "A coal cart was parked a little ways up from the bank with a few bags of coal in the back and no one on the box, but a fella in a higgler's hood was having a fag in a shop doorway. I gave him a wave and he likewise. I got back to the yard, changed my rig, and passed through Cornhill at about five to six. The same coal cart was parked in the same place but facing the other way, towards the Mansion House, with a different fellah on the box. I 'ad a shufti as I went by, slow like; I said hallo and that."

"The driver?"

"Middling young with a thick, black beard." Leman chuckled. "He was in a coal-heaver's hood and jerkin, but he was the cleanest bleedin' higgler you'd see in a month of Sundays. His shirt under the jerkin 'adn't seen coal dust that day or any other, his face was white as a milkmaid's, and he was smoking a big, fat cigar." He held up his left hand and wiggled his ring finger. "He had a flashy fat ring on his hand – width of a shilling and yellow gold. And close up, I saw the horse under some old coal sacks was a fine grey fit for an alderman. Where outside of Holy Heaven would you see a good horse on a higgler's cart?"

"Language, my man," I admonished.

"You are an observant fellow, Leman," Holmes said. "What more?"

"I wished him good morning, but no reply come my way, so I wished him goodbye, with brass knobs on." Leman made a rude gesture. "I knew they was up to no good."

"You did not inform a constable," I said.

He shrugged. "Not my business. And no word in the paper about a reward."

"Did you see anyone else or anything else of interest?" Holmes asked.

Leman chuckled. "I heard the bang."

"Very well. You will be contacted if your evidence proves of value." Holmes nodded a curt dismissal.

"Mr Peters wears a gold ring, admittedly not a very large one, and he would have avoided speaking for obvious reasons," I said as we re-boarded our cab and Holmes directed the driver to Chelsea Village. "A beard is a simple disguise."

"Mr Grigoryan also wears a ring and has a strong accent," Holmes said, "and he already has a beard."

"Mr Grigoryan smokes a pipe; I saw a pipe rack on his desk. Mr Peters smokes cigars, and he leaves the band on."

"True," Holmes answered, "but Mr Peter's cigar was a Brazilian panatela, not a Havana."

I chose not to pursue the point. While I did not believe for an instant that Holmes suspected his erstwhile client, Mr Grigoryan, of dynamiting the bank vault, I also had to admit that Mr Peters was an unlikely perpetrator of such a sensational scheme. As the manager, he had access to the boxes without resort to explosives, and he and Roberts, perhaps in collusion with the Dutchman, could surely have concocted a simpler plan.

"What now, Holmes?" I asked. "To brace the coal heavers in their den?"

He shook his head. "The how of the robbery is evident, but that is not the crux of the matter; the why is much more interesting. I'm afraid we are no closer to the centre of what is undoubtedly a convoluted affair and possibly a dark conspiracy."

"The reason for robbing the safety deposit boxes seems plain to me," I said. "Whether the target was the DeBeers' diamond hoard or just the contents of the boxes, I can see no evidence of a motive other than greed." I frowned. "Unless the interesting turn you mentioned has uncovered one."

"It concerns your suspect, Mr Peters," Holmes answered. "The first name of the manager of the New York and Continental Bank is Marick – a name I have come across only once before. The Marick Peters I recall from the deaths column of *The Times*, was a Boer general who died in British captivity on the island of Saint Helena three or four months ago."

"You think he may be a relative? Perhaps the general's son?" I considered the implications of Holmes' discovery as we travelled west across London. The scorched earth policy of our army pursuing the Boer commandos and the conditions in the British 'concentration camps' we had set up in South Africa were shameful to any person of sensibility. Boer families had been herded into camps with little consideration for sanitation or sustenance, and I could well imagine how the death of a close relative under such inhumane circumstances might prompt an act of revenge – more particularly an act that materially strengthened the rebels' cause.

The Boers were in disarray after the capture of their capital, but they had not immediately surrendered as we had hoped. Many had retreated into the veldt to engage in hit-and-run tactics against our outposts and supply lines. Their bitterness and resentment were still strong. What could they not do with a fortune in diamonds!

We would be mad, I thought, to let them re-arm and thus risk another of our regular military disasters when out of hubris and conviction of our innate superiority, Horse Guards sent too small a force under an ass of a general. The Boer leader, Kruger, had mobilised twenty commandos within a week at the start of the war, all armed with the latest magazine-loading rifles and excellent artillery: twenty-five thousand men, a formidable force that, if reconstituted, would stretch Britain's resources to the limit.

"The name Marick be of no relevance," Holmes said, reading my thoughts. "It is thin straw on which to erect a framework of inference."

Our cab turned beside the River into Cheyne Walk, and Holmes requested the driver slow as he scanned the numbers on the elegant houses lining the street. He tapped the cab roof. "Stop behind that horseless carriage."

We parked in front of a charming house, brick built in the Regency style.

"The gentleman we are to visit has moved not only farther west, but further up in the world," Holmes said as we stepped down.

I spent a moment admiring the gleaming auto-mobile, as these fascinating new vehicles were beginning to be called, before I followed Holmes through the gate and front garden.

I was astonished to find that instead of a regular front door, a rectangular steel vault door complete with wheel handle and combination locks had been installed. Holmes pressed the electric bell, and the door was heaved open by an elderly servant wearing a stained leather apron who ushered us into a conventionally furnished hall. I noticed with distaste the man's yellow, cracked and grimy fingernails as he took our hats and canes and gestured for us to follow him along a central corridor towards the back of the house. He smelled strongly of engine oil and tobacco smoke.

We passed open doors to well-appointed reception and dining rooms to our left and right, then through a kitchen and scullery into a yard lined with three long wooden sheds.

The servant turned to Holmes and smiled, revealing a motley collection of blackened teeth. "You won't remember me, Mr Holmes."

"On the contrary, Janssen. My evidence had you sent down for four years for larceny in the Hatfield case."

The door of a shed opened, and the Dutchman stepped out, wiping his hands on a rag. "How good of you to call, Mr Holmes and Doctor Watson. I've been expecting you." He held up the rag. "I won't shake hands. Come."

We followed him into the shed. The interior walls were packed with tools neatly arranged on hooks, and on a workbench stood a pair of bright argon lamps, a microscope and other precision instruments I could not name. Against the far wall was a huge safe, its door ajar, and on a table under the window I recognised several safety-box doors, bent and buckled.

"What do you think of my front door, gentlemen?" the Dutchman asked. "It graced the vault of the City of Glasgow Bank, which foundered in '78. My neighbours contend it diminishes the tone of the street."

"It's certainly unusual. And you've come a long way since we last saw you in a garret in the Borough," I said with a gesture encompassing the house and yard.

"Yes, Doctor. At that time, I operated in two independent but intertwined spheres, as you might say. With my respectable bowler on, I was the fellow one goes to when the key is mislaid, or the lock mechanism needs maintenance —"

"And at your forge, you were tool-maker for some of the finest yeggmen in the business," Holmes said.

The Dutchman raised his hands in a deprecatory gesture. "All behind me now, Mr Holmes, you have my word on that. The safe-cracker trade has moved on, or rather dwindled almost to extinction. Time was, a master yeggman tickled open a lock with just a stethoscope, a set of my patent lock picks and some key blanks. Now it's all dynamite, or even more fickle nitroglycerine. These new young fellows know nothing of finesse.

"It was time for me to bow out of the game. I had always wanted a neat locksmith's shop offering the more discerning clients both security and discretion. I owe it to myself to admit that I have prospered; I maintain two premises, one in the City and the other in the West End. Business is booming, gentlemen. I employ eleven men and three boys, not including my man Janssen."

"I'm delighted to hear it," Holmes said.

The servant appeared on cue at the shed door with a tray of tulip glasses, a brown bottle of Hollands gin and a plate of fish slices on black bread.

Janssen filled the glasses to the brim, including one for himself, and the Dutchman offered a, hopefully playful, toast.

"To crime!"

I followed the example of the others in the company and swallowed the fiery liquid in one gulp. The juniper flavour was strong, but I managed to get it down without embarrassing myself, and I accepted a slice of bread.

"I was retained by the bank officials after they realised that using a vault manufacturer based in Ohio has its inconveniences when things need adjustment or maintenance," the Dutchman said as Janssen refilled our glasses.

"I maintain the bank and the safety-box vaults every three months. I test the alarms, and oil and change the combinations by opening a panel at the back of each door, loosening the screws that hold the plate covering the combination wheels and averting my eyes while Mr Peters struggles with the mechanism. The three combination wheels are marked in ninety-nine gradations plus zero, giving one hundred million possibilities, which ought to be pretty safe."

"What of the alarm?" Holmes asked.

The Dutchman shrugged. "It's simple, but effective. Metal plates bolted to the door and jamb have an electric flow sent between them. If it is broken, a second circuit activates an alarm. The key turns the electric connection on and off. The circuit could be shorted, but it would be risky."

"Roberts winds the clocks every day before he and Hobbs lock up," Holmes said. "Is that a difficult or time-consuming job?"

The Dutchman considered. "It usually takes seven or eight minutes, longer when the clocks need adjusting on Saturday and Monday evenings. That's fiddly, and hinged steel plates protect the knobs for moving the hands and setting the alarm from customers interfering with them. Each plate is separately padlocked."

"How long would that adjustment take?"

"A further seven or eight minutes; more if Roberts has had a restless night." He mimed drinking from a glass.

"Is that a common occurrence?"

The Dutchman smiled. "His is a convivial nature."

I was handed another glass of Hollands and invited to make a toast. "Happy days," I offered. The warm sensation as the gin went down was very agreeable.

"You said both porters lock up?" Holmes asked.

"Roberts turns the key to lock the door and activate the alarm. He withdraws the key, and Hobbs gives the dials a double spin to the left. That drops the gate, blocking the keyhole and starting the three timer clocks until a quarter to seven next morning."

The Dutchman shrugged. "Were I not the honest taxpayer you now see before you, I might wax the key, tickle the dials and, if the gods were in a good mood, short the alarm, but I'd give myself much more time for that, and more still to tackle the boxes than these fellows did." He gestured for Janssen to refill our glasses, but Holmes politely refused.

I hesitated.

"We have a last port of call," Holmes said mildly, and I put down my glass.

Holmes gestured to the mangled doors on the workbench. "Tell me about the safety boxes."

"The insurers requested a report." The Dutchman held up a safety-box door and turned it to show the inner locking mechanism. A metal sheet covering the lock was peeled away almost into an 'S' shape. "The mounting plates on all the box-door locks as originally installed were made of mild steel – a design fault or cost-cutting stupidity, I know not which. I warned the bank that the brackets could be buckled by an outwards pull, springing the deadbolt. After a lot of hemming and hawing, Mr Peters contracted me to replace the brackets with stronger metal, starting with the boxes not yet rented. They baulked at refurbishing all the boxes at once due to the inconvenience of requesting box-holders surrender their keys or open and empty their boxes while I worked."

He held up another door. The cover plate was the same dimensions as the previous one, but made of thicker steel and only slightly bent. "I replaced the brackets on all unrented boxes with these. The rented boxes were upgraded only when they needed servicing – when a key was lost, for example and I had to drill the lock. A tedious process. Three dozen or so have been replaced and tempered steel fitted.

"I made a new tip and tried the corkscrew device on a regular box and a stiffened one," the Dutchman continued. "I forced the regular, unreinforced box in two minutes. After eleven minutes of heaving on the strengthened one, the tip that fits inside the keyhole broke off just as it did for the thieves. It required a sledgehammer, a crowbar and a further eight minutes of hammering and levering to get the box open. And I know the weak points."

Holmes indicated a massively buckled door on the bench, stencilled '207'. "What of this box?"

The Dutchman turned the door over. The frame holding the deadbolt was warped, but the bolt was undamaged. "This was rented, but the box holder lost his key in June or July, and I had to drill out the lock. I replaced the plate with the heavier one." He held up a small, angled piece of metal. "This is the broken-off tip of the corkscrew. It was jammed in the lock, so the thieves had to jemmy the box open; it must have taken time and considerable effort."

"The contents were taken?"

The Dutchman shrugged.

Holmes ran his finger across the inside of the door, which was smeared with dust and smoke stains. "Would Mr Peters have known which boxes had been reinforced?"

"I gave him a list."

"Also the porters?"

"Probably not; I installed the new lock plates on Sundays, with an under-manager present."

"Why didn't the robbers just blow open the boxes with dynamite as they did with the vault?" I asked.

"Explosives are bloody dangerous in a confined space, if you'll forgive my language, Doctor, and they obviously thought their screw device would whip open the boxes in no time – which it did with the standard door. The device is ingenious." The Dutchman smiled. "I admire the gang's impertinence in blowing a hole in the vault roof at six on a Saturday morning with a dozen beat coppers within hearing distance, but either they didn't do their homework, or they had a different agenda to the obvious one. It's what my erstwhile colleagues in the Borough would call a rum do, Mr Holmes."

He signalled to Janssen to offer another round of Hollands. "Come, gentlemen, a last tot for the road." He grinned and raised his glass. "Cleanliness is next to Godliness, as the Good Book says."

Holmes smiled and lifted his glass.

We drank.

Janssen saw us to the door. "No hard feelings, Mr Holmes." He frowned, and we followed his gaze to the street outside. A police carriage had pulled up in front of the horseless carriage, and Inspector Jones and three police constables climbed out and hurried through the gate.

"Good afternoon, gentlemen," Inspector Jones said. "I see you are here before me, but it is no matter; we are not in competition. 'Justice rolls on like a river and righteousness is a never-failing stream.'"

"You intend to arrest Mr van den Boorn?" Holmes asked, a gleam of amusement in his eyes.

"Alias the Dutchman, yes, yes. We have opportunity and expertise, Mr Holmes, and motive is a given. If you will excuse me?"

Holmes and I stood aside.

———⋅◆⋅———

"The problem with jumping to conclusions," Holmes said as we boarded our cab, "is that you never quite know on what inadequate and precarious perch you will land."

"My dear Holmes," I said. "Have you any idea how irritating it is when you and one of your cronies smile knowingly at each other, suggesting that the answer to a conundrum is clear, when to me it is utterly opaque?"

"Cleanliness is next to Godliness? I'm sorry, old chap. The Dutchman was intimating that certain indicators suggest this was an inside job. Which it was."

"You suspect the porters?"

"I would not have a fellow with such dusty boots guarding my treasure." Holmes directed the cabby to Cornhill.

"Could the porters and the Dutchman be in league?" I asked. "Are van den Boorn and his servant really reformed, Holmes, or are they pulling the wool over their clients' eyes? And what does Inspector Jones know? He had a glint in his eye."

"A dust mote rather than a glint," Holmes said. "Talking of glints, I saw you noted the cigar humidor in the Dutchman's dining room. Many people smoke cigars."

"Not all have such an intimate knowledge of villainy or criminal records for larceny. The Dutchman's eyes were as red rimmed as Roberts' eyes were when we saw him this morning, and both stifled yawns. I suggest they were up to something last night. It strikes me that van den Boorn might be the mastermind, with Roberts, Hobbs and the boy as henchmen and the smelly servant up on the box of the coal cart, keeping watch."

"Who played the gas man who calmed the police?"

"Any one of the Dutchman's nefarious colleagues from the Borough. And we shouldn't discount the possibility the Marlborough people played a part in the affair. That manager fellow had a shifty look about him." I checked the time and made a note of the cab fare on my cuff. "I hope these expenses will be reimbursed." I looked up. "Who exactly is your client now?"

"The bank's insurers. I found their representatives picking through the debris when I returned to the bank to take a closer look at the boxes without Inspector Jones breathing down my neck. The insurers retained my services, and I suggested they employ the Dutchman to examine the box doors.

"You may recall," Holmes continued, showing his shirt cuff, "that while we were chatting to Inspector Jones outside your suspicious cigar shop, I made a note of the renters on his list whose boxes had been riffled. They are Lord Edward Hughes, the racehorse owner; Mrs Emmeline Jacobs, who I understand is a widow and temperance advocate; Colonel Raymond Duffy of polar expedition fame; Mr Oliver Trelawney, barrister, Señor Carlos Cervera Dardé and Mr Edward R. Waldron. I set enquiries in train on all these persons which show the first four box holders to be model citizens, at least from the criminal perspective, so I have put them aside for now. I have discovered no information on the last two gentlemen, aside from addresses in Fulham and Maida Vale, respectively."

"There were Spanish peseta coins on the vault floor," I said. "They may have come from Señor Dardé's box."

"That is a possibility."

None of the names Holmes had mentioned meant much to me, aside from that of Colonel Duffy, who had led a failed attempt on the North Pole in the mid-90s. Or perhaps to the South Pole.

"I interviewed the Chief Clerk of the New York and Continental," Holmes continued. "He was at his wits' end, desperately trying to reassure box-renters crowding the lobby and street outside. Word of the robbery had spread, and the scene was a madhouse; the gentleman's professionally sealed lips were thus opened to a useful degree. I was not permitted to take notes, but

I was able to access the relevant ledgers and correspondence. I got a glimpse of Señor Dardé's and Mr Waldron's statements of account."

Holmes passed me a list of payments and names. "Here is what I saw from memory."

"Señor Dardé's account shows little activity of late," I said, "but last year there were several transfers to an account at the Banco Financiero Internacional in Santiago de Cuba. There are several entries for large sums sent to Mr Waldron by Mr Augustus Revers and several titled persons. Is Mr Revers not the famous solicitor who acted in the Titchfield case and the Birchwood libel affair?"

Holmes nodded. "Further intriguing facts emerged from my perusal of the bank files. Every prospective renter of the London branch of the New York and Continental safety boxes must either be introduced by an existing holder or provide a banking reference. Señor Dardé was recommended by Mr Aleksandr Grigoryan."

"He mentioned a friend – an acquaintance rather – who had lost a considerable sum. Señor Dardé may be he. Perhaps he is another diamantaire."

"According to the bank's files," Holmes continued, "Mr Edward R. Waldron is a man of independent means who was introduced by a Mr James Carver of New York. The records show that Mr Carver irregularly transmits money to Mr Waldron's account at the London New York and Continental Bank, and Waldron transmits funds to Mr Carver at the bank's Manhattan branch – funds that roughly amount to ten percent of his deposits."

"An American," I said with satisfaction.

"Mr Carver's nationality and the nature of his business are not noted in the file, but he and Mr Waldron seem to have a business relationship in which Mr Carver gets a commission or share of Mr Waldron's income and perhaps vice versa."

"You suspect they are up to no good?" I asked.

"I have made an appointment with Mr Revers first thing tomorrow."

We passed along Cheapside, then Poultry, crossed the busy intersection at the Bank of England and got down at the pedestrian island below the statue of the Duke of Wellington.

Holmes nodded to a highly decorated jellied eel stall parked in the lee of the statue and surmounted by a large, coloured sign advertising 'Trotter's eels, periwinkles, whelks and oysters. Guaranteed fresh daily since 1066' and illustrated with images of smiling shellfish. "I thought we might take our tea here."

I raised my eyebrows. "I'm not sure I am ready for whelks for tea, particularly after the Dutchman's herrings. I don't want to come out in spots like PC Laidlaw's tardy relief constable."

"They do excellent tea, and Mrs Trotter's current buns are a well-established favourite in the neighbourhood."

"Since the Norman Conquest?"

"I believe the sign writer mistook an eight for a zero and Mr Trotter senior declined to have it rectified. The Trotters, *père et fils*, have been on this spot since 1866."

Holmes introduced the young man dressed in a chef's apron who occupied the serving hatch as 'Pony' Trotter. He leaned down and shook Holmes' and my hands with an iron grip, then swiftly produced two strong teas and a plate of well-buttered buns. We ate alfresco leaning against the podium of the duke's statue.

"I've often stopped off here when out late on a case," Holmes said. "Trotter's is one of the few places in the City open into the wee hours. They cater to bank clerks and passing trade in the afternoon and evening, then policemen, coal heavers, the night shift of Bank of England guards and consulting detectives till early morning. They are busy until three thirty or a little later."

Holmes nodded towards the building across the street. "What do you see?"

"The New York and Continental Bank on the corner. The front door and back doors are both visible, and the crowd has gone."

"And farther along the street?"

"The Salvation Army hostel, with a couple of tract girls shaking their collection boxes, and the facade and yard wall of the infamous Marlborough cigar shop."

"With streetlamps close by. PC Laidlaw ate his dinner on this spot at a quarter to three this morning, and there were doubtless other early morning diners from the Bank of England and elsewhere. The clear view from here in the bright lamplight constrained the timing of the robbery from three thirty, when Pony closed the stall, to about six, when the area begins to wake up."

We returned our cups and plates, and I whistled for our cab.

"We have done enough for today," Holmes said as we climbed aboard. "I have a good deal to catch up with, and Mrs Hudson has promised a joint for dinner."

Holmes and I dined splendidly, our roast beef complemented by a noble Portuguese claret, one of a dozen bottles a satisfied client had sent a few weeks previously, followed by a crusty rice pudding with jam and honey.

"Obviously DeBeers would not store their cache of diamonds under their own name," I said as we sat in front of the sitting-room fire with our coffee and evening pipes and dealt with our afternoon correspondence. "Perhaps Waldron is their account holder in the City and their Manhattan account is under the name of Carter. Payments into Waldron's account by Mr Revers and others may be for diamond purchases by prominent persons who prefer to keep their acquisitions confidential."

I puffed on my pipe as I considered the evidence Holmes and I had uncovered. "But what I don't understand—"

Holmes held up his hand, and I heard footsteps on the stairs.

I stood. "A penny gets you tuppence Inspector Jones is coming to you for advice."

Holmes glanced at the mantel clock and smiled. "You are throwing your money away, my friend."

I looked up eagerly as the sitting-room door opened, and Billy stood aside for a tall figure, a gentleman in his fifties perhaps, impeccably dressed in a slightly dated style. Billy made no effort to announce our visitor; he offered me the gentleman's card and shrugged an apology. "A foreign party, Doctor."

I took the card and waved the boy away.

Our visitor stood erect in the doorway, looking from Holmes to me. "Mr Sherlock Holmes?" he asked in a formal tone.

Holmes stood. "Good evening, Señor."

The gentleman bowed, sweeping off his silk hat in a courtly gesture. "Good evening, gentlemen. I am Carlos Cervera Dardé. I humbly apologise for disturbing you in your home at this hour, but I come on a matter of grave import for me, and if you will forgive me for being somewhat histrionic, for my country."

I settled Señor Dardé on the sofa and ordered Billy to fetch coffee.

"How can I help you, Señor?" Holmes asked.

"I understand from Mr Grigoryan that you represented his interests in connection with his deposits at the New York and Continental Bank. I would like to engage your services in the same context, but in more egregious circumstances."

"Your safety box was ransacked," Holmes said. "I trust the contents were fully insured."

"It was," Señor Dardé said in a weary tone, "and, lamentably, they were not."

Holmes nodded. "Perhaps you could give me some background to your situation."

Señor Dardé leaned back in his chair. "I am an exile from my native land, the island of Cuba, where I taught at the University of Havana and owned and intermittently published a newspaper at the repressive whim of the Spanish colonial authorities.

"I supported the revolution of '95 when we rose against our oppressors – machetes again maxim guns. By the grace of God, by October of '97, half the country was under our control and the other half was up in arms. Madrid offered concessions; they were on their knees." Señor Dardé sighed. "And then the Americans decided to help us."

The sitting-room door bumped open, and Billy entered with a tray. I helped him lay out the cups and saucers, and I offered our guest coffee, which he accepted.

"The Yanqui navy destroyed the Spanish fleet," Señor Dardé continued, "Colonel Roosevelt galloped up San Juan Hill, and their army, together with our troops, took Santiago. Spain sued for peace, and in a matter of weeks, the war was over. We had triumphed, but our joy turned to ashes in our mouths when the Americans excluded Cubans from the peace talks in Paris and even from the victory parades."

Señor Dardé smiled a wan smile. "And so, the Spanish yoke is thrown off, and we are independent – with the slight caveat of total occupation by the Americans. They deny any intention of annexing Cuba, and they run our affairs with a benevolently iron hand, ensuring American sugar and tobacco interests on the island are secure and profitable."

He stirred his coffee. "I and certain like-minded persons oppose this state of affairs. For us, American rule is no different, except in its trappings and fripperies, from being ground under the Spanish heel. We formed a society to further our aim of independence – by peaceful means while that option remains feasible. Since 1897 we have been gathering our strength, working towards the day when we can reclaim our heritage, our blood fired by the example of the brave Filipinos who have refused to bow down to their conquerors."

"And how is this connected with the robbery?" Holmes asked.

"Our movement's funds were stored in my safety box. We lost almost two thousand pounds in bearer bonds, and about three hundred in gold pesetas." Señor Dardé leaned forwards, and his hitherto calm voice gained a sharper edge. "I do not believe the robbery was a simple case of theft for gain. There have been persistent rumours in our community of American agents sent to dog us and frustrate our plans. What better way to achieve that end than bankrupt our movement?"

He shrugged. "We have few resources left, but I will gather what I can to meet your fees, Mr Holmes, should you agree to act for us in this matter."

Holmes steepled his fingers under his chin and was silent for a long moment. "I have been engaged by the bank's insurers, and you will understand that my first duty must be to them. However, you may rest assured, Señor Dardé, that while I cannot focus my attention primarily on the recovery of your funds, I have every hope that in discovering the truth of this convoluted case, your interests may be served."

"I am well satisfied by that assurance, sir," Señor Dardé said, rising from his seat. "Your reputation affords me hope that all will be well. I shall take up no more of your valuable time."

I saw Señor Dardé downstairs, and we parted with every courtesy.

"My goodness, Holmes, whom else can we expect on our doorstep?" I said as I returned to my seat by the fire. "Will racehorse magnates, famous lawyers, and polar explorers beat a path to our door? Shall I organise an orderly queue on the stairs?"

"You forget Mrs Jacobs, the temperance campaigner. She has a formidable reputation as a platform lady."

I helped myself to tobacco from the pouch and filled my pipe. "The Cuban and Filipino rebels welcomed American support in their efforts to eject their Spanish overseers, but now they are having the devil of a time getting their saviours to go home."

"I wonder where the Americans learned that trick?"

I frowned at Holmes. "Surely you are not comparing our empire with these sordid American land grabs in the Caribbean and Pacific? It is pure opportunism beneath a cynical cloak of altruism. Mr McKinley, the new Republican president, and especially his feisty vice president Mr Roosevelt, are ardent expansionists. Despite their lip service to arbitration and common sense, they have their eye on Canada, mark my words."

Holmes waved my concerns away with his pipe stem, and I subsided into my chair.

"So, we have yet another motive for the theft." I tallied them off on my fingers. "The DeBeers' diamonds, the Boer connection, and Señor Dardé's bonds, aside from the most obvious motive – simple larceny."

"The matter is becoming more convoluted," Holmes acknowledged, "but we are moving forward. I can offer categorical proof that will convince even Inspector Jones that the robbery was not just a smash and grab by the Dutchman's gang. At my suggestion, the bank's insurance company had the boxes photographed." He stood and took a large brown envelope from his desk. "They were kind enough to send me copies in the afternoon post."

He passed me a sheaf of photographs. One image showed the open, buckled door of safety box two zero seven and another the dusty and soot-blackened interior of the box.

"Notice anything?" Holmes asked me.

I leafed through the other images. "This box is much dirtier than the others. The dust and smoke obviously came from the explosion."

"The unopened boxes are clean inside; their doors fitted tight into their jambs, resisting the entrance of dust and debris. But the opened boxes are filthy – inside."

I gasped. "They were opened before the explosion."

"Exactly. And the doors were so badly bent they could not be properly closed again."

The doorbell rang.

"This will surely be the inspector," I said with a grin. "Or an Antarctic explorer."

The sitting-room door opened, and Billy stood aside for a stooped figure.

"Roberts!" I exclaimed.

The brash porter Holmes and I had encountered in the vault lobby was now a bowed, whey-faced, pathetic figure, his eyes even more red-rimmed and forehead beaded with sweat. He hesitated in the doorway, nervously clasping and unclasping one of his hands while the other clutched a carpet bag. Holmes curtly ordered him inside, and Billy closed the door behind him.

"You got my note," Holmes said.

Roberts looked down at his toes.

Holmes turned to me. "I ordered Roberts to attend here at eight to make a full confession of his part in the robbery on pain that I would take my evidence to the authorities."

"I didn't know what to do," Roberts said in a trembling voice. "I'm at my wits' end."

"You must understand that your fate is entirely in my hands," Holmes said in a flat tone. He took his churchwarden pipe from the mantel and filled it. "I can prove without a scintilla of doubt that you sabotaged the timer, opened the door, and helped your cigar-smoking companion first prise open the box or boxes he targeted, then break into other boxes as cover." He lit his pipe and settled into his chair. "Your only hope is to tell me everything and throw yourself entirely on my mercy."

"I will do so, sir," Roberts replied, looking down at his toes.

"When were you first approached?"

"Last Tuesday fortnight, sir, after work. I was in the Pope's Head having a bite of supper when a gent slid into the chair opposite and said, 'Roberts, how would you like to make a hundred pound in a simple day's work?'"

"He was an American?" I asked.

"My dear fellow," Holmes huffed, "kindly refrain from leading the witness."

"He was an American, sir," Roberts said. "Or at least he sounded like Mr Peters and the others I've met, though sharper toned, sir, snappish like. He never gave me his name or told anything about himself."

Holmes puffed a stream of smoke across the room. "Describe."

"In his thirties, sir, or forties, clean-shaven, dressed and bearing himself as a gentleman. He wanted me to get the key of a particular safety box, then let him in the vault, look the other way and keep watch."

"Which box?" Holmes asked.

"He didn't say, sir. I told him I had the master box key, but each renter had his own – you can't open the box without both keys. He talked around ways to get a renter's key, but there's no way I could think of. Anyway, I say, one box or a hundred, if I open the vault door, I'm done for. The suspicion would fall right on me."

Roberts licked his lips. "I never thought it was for real, sir. I thought he was having me on."

He leaned one arm against our dining table. "May I sit, sir? I'm a bit wobbly."

"You may not," Holmes snapped. "Continue."

Roberts took a breath. "The man says, how about if he blows the door open? That won't run, I told him. The door is the best-armoured part of the vault. You'd need so much dynamite you'd bring the building down on top of us, and the coppers would come running as soon as they heard the huge bang. He seemed to accept that, sir, and he gave me a half sovereign for my time. I never thought I'd see him again. Might I have a drink of something, sir?"

I stood before Holmes could reply. I fetched a glass, filled it with water from the carafe, and passed it to Roberts. He cast a look at the whisky decanter that I ignored, gulped the water, and thanked me.

"Two nights later, sir, and he was back," Roberts continued. "He said he'd blow a hole in the vault roof and jemmy the box with a device that would open the box doors in a trice. He had a plan to fool the police, but the timing was tight, and he wants to scarper right after the bang. I had to let him in through the door to open the box he was after, then he'd set off the dynamite."

"You insisted he attack more boxes as camouflage," Holmes said. "You wished to characterise the robbery as a safe-break and hide your involvement in the plot. You also insisted that only Mr Henry Clay, as I shall call him, knew of your part in the theft. And I expect you demanded more money."

Roberts nodded. "I asked for five hundred. We settled on two."

"Why did you bore through from the cigar factory?" I asked. "Why not simply steal a key or break in through the back door of the bank? And why did Clay give himself so little time in the vault?"

"Only Hobbs and Mr Peters have the front and back door keys," Holmes answered for Roberts, "and both doors are checked every half hour by the inspector's beat bobby. And as you saw, there is a streetlamp a scant two or three yards from each door, which are visible from the whelk stall."

Holmes puffed on his pipe.

I frowned. "Very well. I understand the time constraint imposed by the view from the stall, but why did they not attack on a Sunday? They would have been undisturbed for the whole of the day."

Holmes stood, stretched, and went to the sideboard. "You forget the Salvation Army, busy from an early hour on Sundays. Whisky?"

My eyes flicked to the abject figure of Roberts. "No whisky, thank you, Holmes. I'll stick with coffee."

Holmes helped himself from the Tantalus, settled back in his chair and addressed Roberts. "You donned a disguise: a false beard, an old coat and a flat cap to cover your uniform."

"I did, sir, from Petticoat Lane market. I didn't want the other men in the gang to know who I was."

"The gang arrived at the cigar factory on a coal cart," Holmes said. "At what time?"

"Four thirty, sir," Roberts answered. "We backed the cart to the wall of the cigar place and heaved over the sandbags and ladder. One of the gang jemmied a first floor window and opened the back door."

Holmes nodded. "So much for Inspector Jones's beat constables trying door handles. The most closely guarded square mile in the world, forsooth!"

"We smashed holes through to the bank lavatory," Roberts said, "then the gang laid the explosives while the American gentleman and me went through the door between the offices and the lobby – it's a self-locking Chubb that can be opened from the inside without a key. Mr Clay, as you call him, followed me down to the anteroom."

"How did you open the vault? What of the timer and the alarm?" I asked.

Holmes answered again. "At closing time yesterday, Roberts went through the motions of turning the key to lock the door and starting the alarm without actually doing so. His fellow porter spun the combination wheels as usual, setting the timer, but the door remained unlocked and the alarm was not activated."

I frowned. "If Hobbs spun the combination wheels, then the door could not be opened for about twelve hours."

"Roberts reset the timer at some time during the day when he was unobserved – for how long?"

"Till three in the morning, sir."

I leaned back in my chair. "Are you saying the door was unlocked? All the time you were trying to open it with the wheel, the key had not been turned, and the timer was not set. We could have simply pulled it open."

Holmes chuckled. "The crowbar disabled the wheel but had no other effect; the locking rods were drawn and the door was unlocked."

"Then what was the point of jamming the wheel?" I considered for a moment and turned to Roberts. "Was it a smoke screen? Were you trying to deflect attention from something else? The timer?"

Roberts took another gulp of water and looked to Holmes before he answered. "The plan was, after the gentleman got what he wanted, and we'd smashed open some other boxes as cover, I'd reset the timer, close the door and relock it, arming the alarm. I'd then spin the combinations, starting the timer. The gang would set off the explosion, put the ladder in place, and escape. I'd run upstairs, escape through the hole in the wall, throw off my disguise and walk around until it was time to go to work as usual."

He sighed. "Breaking into the box the gentleman wanted took far, far longer than he'd planned. He had a device he said would do it in seconds, but it broke, and he had to hammer and jemmy the door open. And then I had trouble with the empty safe boxes I'd planned to force as cover. The doors were too strong. We tried some rented boxes and managed to open a few. I took some stuff at random."

He picked up his carpetbag and emptied it on the table, spilling out banknotes in various currencies, coins, jewels and silver cutlery. "I never meant to keep the stuff, sir. I was going to drop it somewhere it could be found. I couldn't think of a safe place. So I left it in my bag in the utility room."

"It was under our noses," Holmes said. "The insurers will be pleased, but it will give them a headache deciding whose items are whose."

He addressed Roberts. "What box did Mr Clay attack?"

"I was busy with the boxes at the end of the vault, sir, but I'm sure he opened at least two boxes in the early numbers of two and three hundred range. He filled a valise with the contents."

Holmes rubbed his hands together. "We may imagine Clay's concern as the safe deposit opening time approached. Coming up to six, dangerously late, he called a halt. Having ransacked the box or boxes he targeted, opened several rented boxes, and damaged a few empty ones as a smokescreen to put the police and newspapers off the scent, he left to signal the detonation. How long did you have?"

"He would only give me ten minutes," Roberts said. "I told him it wasn't enough. I still had to rewind the clocks, reset the alarm and close and lock the door before the bang. He was jittery, sir; he said the explosive would go off at six ten, yay me or nay me.

"I hurriedly wound the clocks just enough to get them going, then I fiddled with the padlock on the timer, but I'd only a couple of minutes left by then, and I got scared. I ran out and pushed the vault door closed. A moment later, there was a tremendous bang.

The ground shook, the door swung open, and I was thrown off my feet as a cloud of dust and smoke spilled out."

Holmes chuckled, rubbing his hands together.

"I pushed the door shut again, but dust settled on the floor and tabletops, and the lobby stank of smoke and chemicals. I had to clean it up. I opened the utility-room door; there's always a strong draught of cold air down into the underground river and that cleared the smoke and most of the smell. Then I grabbed the mop and bucket and set to."

"You mopped the vault-room floor and cleaned the tables," Holmes said. "But dust also settled on the pump in the utility room, and on your boots. The contrast between Hobbs' guardsman shine and your dusty boots was my first indication that something was amiss."

Holmes leaned back in his chair and puffed on his pipe. "You still had to reset the timer, close the door, spin the locking wheel and lock the door with the key, and you had precious little time. Your colleague and the boy were due to arrive for work in minutes, and you needed the morning routine to be normal so that no suspicion would fall on you."

Holmes smiled. "The first thing the boy would do was trot downstairs and do what any messenger does on arriving at work —"

"— make the tea!" I smiled with him.

"That was Roberts' deadline. If the boy saw anything untoward, his goose was cooked." Holmes waived a languid hand for Roberts to continue.

"I was in a panic. I had no time to unlock the padlocks and reset the timer, so if I turned the key to lock the door, that would set the timer going for the eight hours I'd set. No-one could have fiddled that except me or Mr Peters – we're the only ones with the padlock keys."

"What did you do?" I asked Roberts.

"I opened the vault and jammed the crowbar in the wheel mechanism. I thought if I pretend the door can't be opened, I might have an opportunity to adjust the timer before the Dutchman arrived to fix the door and before ten when the bank opened, and the hole was found."

"The Dutchman, Hobbs, the boy and Mr Peters had no part in the plot?" I asked.

Roberts shook his head.

"There we have it," Holmes said. "You may sit at the table, Roberts. Doctor Watson will give you pen, ink and paper for your detailed confession. That done, you may have a glass of whisky to add to the several it is evident from your demeanour and the scent about you that you have consumed this evening. You will then you go home to await whatever fate has in store for you."

Roberts sagged into a dining chair. "May I—?"

"Begin with a full and minute description of Mr Clay," Holmes said, "then relate the events in order."

I helped Roberts with his narrative while Holmes sat at his desk and composed several telegrams and cablegrams. He called Billy, whose eyes widened when he saw the loot spread across the dining table.

Holmes instructed him to bicycle to the all-night telegraph office at Paddington Station, deposit the telegrams, then pick up a copy of the *Shipping News* from the station kiosk.

I insisted on a cab, as it was too dark for safe cycling. I handed the boy sufficient money and sent him on his way.

Roberts signed his confession, and I gave him his promised whisky before ushering him to the door.

"One more thing, Roberts," Holmes said. "You say Mr Clay wore a gold ring. With a stone?"

"No, sir, it was a seal ring with some words etched in."

"Could you read the words?"

"No, sir."

Holmes waved him away and slumped into his chair.

Roberts grasped my arm. "Eight years of loyal service at the Union Bank and nine months with the New York and Continental – will that count for nothing, sir?"

I sadly shook my head, led him downstairs and out into the street, a broken man.

Holmes was leaning against the mantel and reading the confession in the light of a wall lamp when I returned to the sitting-room. "A rara avis is our Porter Roberts," he said. "I believe this is one of the few confessions I have read that is not, at least in its essentials, a work of fiction designed to exculpate the scribbler's crimes."

"Two hundred pounds, Holmes," I said. "A king's ransom for a working man. One could say Roberts was led into temptation."

"Ha, I work for my bread and so do you. Compassion is all very well, friend Watson, but if an example is not made of these miscreants, no safety box with m'lady's *billets doux* or his lordship's *La Vie Parisienne* collection would be safe, to say nothing of DeBeers' diamonds and the funds of Cuban revolutionaries. What sort of anarchic world would that be?"

He tapped his finger against a corner of his mouth. "And yet." He tossed the confession onto his desk.

"Do you intend to pass that on to Jones?" I took my pipe from the rack and slipped into my usual seat.

"He disdains my help." Holmes passed me the tobacco pouch, and I filled my pipe.

"Yes, I feel for Roberts," I said. "Sympathy is a human emotion, and I am unashamed to admit it. But I also believe the rule of law is the foundation of civilisation. You talk of anarchism with disapprobation, my friend, yet in your make-up you must acknowledge a sceptical streak, an ingrained distrust of authority and hierarchy. You have donned the judge's mantel on more than one occasion and have not shirked from allowing a confessed felon to get off scot-free."

Holmes lit a spill from the fire and passed it to me. "I intend to show my deep respect for the Law by not treading on the redoubtable toes of the official investigator of the case, who has made perfectly clear he does not relish my interference. I will leave the matter in his capable hands. Roberts' fate, karma or kismet will take the unlikely and bewhiskered form of Inspector Athelney Jones."

"PC Laidlaw saw nothing suspicious," I said. "He missed all the clues that Leman, the omnibus driver, spotted."

"Laidlaw is even less observant than the common herd of constables." Holmes blew a vehement stream of smoke across the room. "What can we expect when police recruits are barely trained in anything more than polishing their uniform buttons and tying their boot laces in the approved manner? I have been advocating an elementary course of observation and detection for several years—"

"Why did Roberts deny cleaning?" I asked to stem the tirade I had inadvertently provoked and heard a dozen times.

"He could not admit he had departed from his usual routine and cleaned the anteroom before opening the vault door. When the door wouldn't open, it would have been odd if he'd mopped the floor before calling the manager."

"You believe Roberts when he says Hobbs and the boy were not involved?"

"I was certain they were not. The boy is a typical gangly, lazy specimen of adolescent London youth who could not be trusted to keep mum, and neither he nor Hobbs posed a threat to the robbers if the original timetable had been kept to."

Holmes took down one of his commonplace books and settled before the fire, making marginal notes, while I packed the contents of Roberts' carpet bag into a parcel – half expecting the doorbell to ring again.

"There are some Spanish pesetas," I said, "but not many, and no bearer bonds." A thought struck me. "Holmes, you deduced that our caller – the first caller Señor Dardé – was Spanish, yet his English was American accented. You greeted him as señor."

"He was the Spanish-speaking gentleman you bumped into outside the bank this morning."

Billy returned with the *Shipping News*, telegraph receipts, and change.

Holmes glanced through the sailing schedules, then leapt from his seat, took our Bradshaw from the shelf above his desk and flicked through it. "We have an appointment with Mr Revers at ten tomorrow. I suggest a few hands of piquet before calling it a night." He paused and gave me a questioning look. "That is, if you would care to accompany me – as I hope you will."

I puffed on my pipe. "Any time, my dear Holmes, and anywhere. I'll see the affair through to the end."

Holmes beamed. "You owe me a penny."

<hr />

I woke betimes the next morning and found Holmes had already left. A note on the dining table suggested I meet him at my club for breakfast at nine, so I contented myself with toast and coffee as I caught up with the news. The papers were full of the robbery in the City, with sparse facts and much ill-informed speculation and splutters of indignation. I sniffed at a *Times* leader summarising the new American president's inauguration speech and praising his moderation.

I was packing my morning pipe when the doorbell rang, and Billy showed up a half-expected and uncharacteristically unassertive visitor.

"Good morning, Doctor," Inspector Jones said, "I hope I am not disturbing you."

"Not at all." I ushered the inspector to a seat, not without an inward smile. "Mr Holmes is out on a case, I'm afraid."

Inspector Jones perched on the sofa, looking wan and ill at ease. He refused offers of refreshment.

"How go your investigations?" I asked.

"Well enough, Doctor," the inspector said, looking down at his toes. "These things take time, of course. Yes, Rome was not built in a day, or even several – softly-softly catchee monkey, as they say." He hesitated before he continued. "I received a parcel at the City Police Headquarters by messenger this morning."

"Holmes thought it best to pass the recovered loot to the insurers through you," I said. "It is evidence after all."

"Yes, yes, it is indeed, and my superiors are pleased." He hesitated again. "But they are understandably curious as to how the stolen items were found. I have managed to fob them off for now, but—"

"There was no note with the package or papers of any sort?"

Inspector Jones shook his head. "No, Doctor, it was addressed to me personally, but with no explanation. The parcel was sent from the district messenger stand in Baker Street at six this am, so I made the obvious assumption they were items from the bank robbery retrieved by Mr Holmes."

Holmes, I thought, was in a playful mood. "What of the Dutchman?"

The inspector looked down at his toes again. "I was misled by a report that Mr van den Boorn was in the City on Friday evening and was seen driving his horseless carriage near the scene of the crime. In fact, he attended a service at the Dutch Reformed Church in Austen Friars, and afterwards conveyed a party of Dutch reverends from the church to their lodgings in Marylebone. The vehicle broke down in Cavendish Place and had to be pushed from there to his home, a number of loungers and even police constables helping along the way.

The inspector sighed. "Boorn arrived home at just after five yesterday morning as attested by the local beat copper, who saw him in the street outside his house working on the vehicle's innards till at least six. An unshakeable alibi."

No wonder the Dutchman looked rather worn, I thought.

Inspector Jones shook his head. "Boorn has slipped my net, and I am at a stand, Doctor. I was hoping Mr Holmes might condescend to offer some guidance, or perhaps even share his findings."

"I have worked with Mr Holmes for many years and on a multitude of cases," I said. "In my experience, when an official cooperates with Mr Holmes rather than resenting his interference, Mr Holmes is extremely generous – usually bowing out at the conclusion of a case and allowing the official to take full credit for the solution and apprehension of the perpetrators."

Inspector Jones brightened. "I've heard that, yes indeed. Which is why I hope Mr Holmes did not take my jocular remarks in the early moments of this affair too seriously. It has always been my belief that what matters is the swift resolution of a case rather than who discovered what and any nonsense of credit." His face darkened. "Or blame. In the majority of investigations, collaboration is the key. 'Two are better than one; because they have a good reward for their labour.'"

I stood and checked my watch. "I am meeting Mr Holmes this morning. If you wish, I can convey to him your thoughts on cooperation." I smiled. "And I can certainly share with you my own research. An interview with Mr Grigoryan, the diamond dealer you met at the bank on the subject of DeBeers' diamonds and South Africa might be fruitful, as might a chat with the clerk at the tobacconist opposite Mr Grigoryan's office regarding *Henry Clay* cigar bands."

I saw the inspector to the door. "You must understand, Inspector, that Mr Holmes likes to play his cards close to his chest until he reveals them in a final flourish. Once the knots have been untangled, if I may mix my metaphors, his interest instantly wanes."

<hr />

I met Holmes in the lobby of the Junior United Service Club in Pall Mall as arranged, and I took him in to the members' dining room for breakfast. I was pleased to see that Cumberland sausages were again on the menu after a long hiatus without adequate explanation or apology. Holmes ordered the seafood kedgeree.

"I hope you don't come out in spots," I said.

Coffee was served, and I told my friend of the inspector's visit.

"I admit I had a moment of doubt when I heard the Dutchman was seen so near the scene of the crime late on Friday night," Holmes said, "but when the report mentioned he was in his horseless carriage, I instantly dismissed any notion of his involvement. Not only would no sane criminal trust his escape to such an unreliable contraption, his every move would be traced by the trail of gaping bystanders, gambolling boys and irate cab drivers with spooked horses he left behind him."

Our main course arrived, and we set to with a will. I was considering requesting more coffee when Holmes glanced at his watch and suggested I call for the bill.

As I paid, I was intrigued to notice George, a club pageboy, pass Holmes a folded note and exchange a few murmured words. I raised a quizzical eyebrow as we passed out of the dining room and, to my surprise, Holmes led the way across the lobby not to the entrance doors but to the magazine rack where he took a *Punch* for himself, handed me a *Strand Magazine,* and sat on a nearby sofa.

"I must apologise for suborning a page at your club," Holmes murmured as I sat beside him, "but, as you saw, we were circumspect." He smiled. "I also oiled the palm of the receptionist. A half crown bought me a list of foreign temporary members who have used the club facilities during the last three months."

"I could have furnished you with that information with a glance at the members' register."

"I wanted to be discreet. If I have misread the runes, which is perfectly possible, I did not want to spook our quarry. You know what a nest of gossips clubs are."

I restrained myself from reacting to Holmes' remark with a cutting riposte. A fellow does not like to hear criticism of his club, particularly if it is unfounded. The Junior United Service Club was not a hotbed of gossips, although I would not have said the same of our senior brother club in which valetudinarian colonels and generals spent their salad years picking apart each other's military blunders and retailing their own valorous deeds.

Holmes read my thoughts and gave me a contrite look that mollified me.

"What did you learn?" I asked from behind my magazine.

"Two gentlemen fit my description. Lieutenant Commander Nathan Butler of the United States Navy and Captain David Arthur Lamont of their Army. Both officers have stayed at the club for about a fortnight, and both requested the steward prepare their lodging and catering bills for payment today. According to the note I received from the boy, Captain Lamont is just about to leave the barber's salon."

Holmes nodded at a gentleman in a lounge suit who crossed the lobby to the reception desk. He was in his late twenties or early thirties perhaps, his fair hair oiled in a fashionable style and with the erect posture and smart gait of an officer. He spoke briefly to a clerk, who produced a sheaf of papers that the gentleman looked through before taking a notecase from his pocket and handing the clerk two five-pound notes. The gentleman accepted a receipt, passed the clerk what I deduced from his pleased expression was a generous tip, and marched towards the dining room.

I turned to Holmes, but he was already up and on his way to the reception desk. He had a brief word with the clerk and returned.

"Captain Lamont paid his bill to date and booked club accommodation for a further week," he said. "He was not my prime suspect; according to the barman, he smokes cheroots and does not wear a ring. And, unless his rebooking is smoke and mirrors, he is in no hurry to leave our shores."

Holmes smiled. "If you, friend Watson, had just carried out an audacious robbery in a foreign capital and the newspapers were baying for your blood, what would you do?"

"I'd make a beeline for the docks and the earliest steam liner either to the Continent or, if I were American, for home."

Holmes slipped his watch from his waistcoat pocket. "Lieutenant Commander Butler also called at the reception desk this morning and asked for his bill to be prepared. He is the more enigmatic of my two possibilities. He does not use the bar, and neither does he take his meals in the dining room. His room attendant knows almost nothing about him – his belongings are kept in a locked valise."

"The room attendants too, Holmes," I said with a touch of acerbity. "Do you have the whole staff of my club on your payroll?"

"Not just here, I have five other possibles under observation in other clubs and hotels." Holmes stood. "Butler is out and about, no doubt having breakfast or picking up some souvenirs. And we have an appointment at eleven."

We passed out of the club. Holmes stopped for a moment at a cabman's shelter a few yards along the street, exchanging a few words with a lounger, then he called a cab from the stand and directed the cabby to Chancery Lane.

"Lieutenant Commander Butler may be Mr Henry Clay," I said.

Holmes smiled. "I am somewhat out on a limb. The robbery showed few signs of being planned with precision, but Roberts described Mr Clay's erect bearing and clipped authoritative tones, which suggests a military background. If we accept the possibility that Señor Dardé's safety box was the target, then the involvement of an American official agent becomes more likely." He hesitated. "And there is another nebulous clue that I hardly like to mention."

"You think the ring Roberts and the omnibus driver described may be a gold signet ring commonly worn by a graduate of an American military academy," I said with some satisfaction.

Holmes smiled. "There is no fooling you, my dear Watson."

"But how would an American officer, in all likelihood newly arrived in this country, conjure up a gang of London safe crackers at a few days' notice? Was this a long-matured plot or were all the safety-deposit staff involved – Roberts, Hobbs and the boy?"

"Long matured? A possibility if Señor Dardé's notion of surveillance of his group by American agents is correct, but I have my doubts. I have a notion on how the robbery was planned that I will put to Mr Clay when we find him." He tapped on the cab roof. "Stop opposite the safe deposit, Cabby."

Holmes and I got down outside a solid block of offices. Workmen across the road were erecting scaffolding over the massive, arched entrance of the Chancery Lane Safe Deposit Company and positioning a sign advertising the company's range of safes and strongrooms.

"Guarded night and day by military patrols," I read.

"Inspector Jones would not approve."

We crossed the pavement, entered a chill, marble-floored lobby, and gave our names to a porter.

"This morning the insurers offered an interesting snippet of news that arrived on their overnight telegraph cable," Holmes said, his voice echoing as we followed the porter up a sweeping marble staircase. "The Manhattan branch of the New York and Continental Bank was robbed yesterday as it closed for the day. A score or so of deposit boxes were opened."

I clutched the banister and gaped at Holmes. "But that's extraordinary!" I cried.

The porter gave me an admonishing look.

"What infernal cheek, robbing two branches of the same bank on two continents – a madcap plan," I said in a more tempered tone. "This increases the probability the real target was the DeBeers' diamonds kept in safety boxes under the name of Waldron in London and Carver in New York. The American officer who planned the robberies might be a renegade or not even an officer at all, perhaps with links to Mr Marick Peters and South Africa. The Boers are at the bottom of this, Holmes. Only they could mastermind such a scheme, mark my words."

"You have a certain reputation, sir," Holmes said.

"As do you, Mr Holmes," Mr Revers replied in a faint Scots burr. He sat in an elegantly appointed room behind a wide mahogany desk. He was exactly as I had seen him depicted in a *Spy* cartoon in *Vanity Fair*, a gentleman of middle age, clean-shaven, impeccably dressed and groomed, who regarded us over half-moon pince-nez with grey eyes that sparkled with intelligence.

Shelves along the oak-panelled walls of the office were lined with rows of hefty books identically bound in green Morocco.

The pen set on his desk was onyx, and his telephone instrument and oil lamp were enamelled green. Holmes and I sat in olive, buttoned-leather chairs, and a potted aspidistra between the green-curtained windows continued the colour scheme.

"You will have heard of the robbery at the New York and Continental Bank," Holmes said.

Mr Revers smiled. "To which robbery do you refer, Mr Holmes?"

Holmes returned his smile. "Both."

"The news from New York was on the telegraph tape at my club at breakfast time." Mr Revers stood, opened a cabinet behind him, and extracted three glasses and a decanter. "Whisky? It's a malt from the Stralochy distillery near my home town in Perthshire – long gone, I'm afraid, but my father laid down a few cases."

Holmes and I accepted, and I sipped the rich, peaty whisky with deep pleasure.

"I'm surprised we have not had any direct professional dealings, Mr Holmes," Mr Revers continued. "I recommended you to one of my clients when my negotiations with the late and unlamented Charles Augustus Milverton failed, and he declared he would send certain letters to the lady's husband."

"Blackmail," I said. "Milverton was a professional blackmailer."

"So it was alleged, Doctor. My client ignored my advice to seek your aid and took matters into her own hands. Her solution was a touch felonious for my taste, but she achieved more gratifying results than I or even you, might have obtained for her."

"Five bullets into the fellow's chest," I said.

Mr Revers spread his hands. "Terminally conclusive for Milverton. Alas, as always in these cases, when he bowed out, others took his place."

Mr Revers refilled our glasses. "You will understand, gentlemen, that if I am to be of service to those who request my advice, I must maintain absolute discretion." He indicated a short stack of envelopes on his desk. "I received a package this afternoon delivered by district messenger. On enquiry by my clerk, we found the parcel was deposited at the messengers' office in the Strand by a waiter from one of the clubs in Pall Mall. I did not investigate further. The envelopes contain documents, letters and, in one case, photographs."

"I assume the contents might be problematic if they fell into the wrong hands," Holmes said.

"They are incendiary. The public stature of several persons of note would be diminished if the matters contained in these documents became common knowledge. I intend to pass the papers to the interested parties for disposal."

"The payments you made on behalf of your clients to Mr Waldron related to similar documents?" Holmes asked.

Mr Revers leaned back in his chair. "I cannot answer that."

"Then I will make that assumption."

"You are free to do so, Mr Holmes. In which case I must presume you may make the same conjecture regarding the services rendered in New York in relation to Mr Carver's activities by Attorney Zachary Dufay of Gottleib, Dufay and Bannerman with offices at 2200 Nassau Street, New York, telegraphic address, 'SUBPOENA.'"

I made a note.

"Are you aware of the details of the robbery in the City?" Holmes asked.

"As I heard it, the robbers burst through a wall, planted explosives on the floor above the vault and smashed a hole in the roof by which they extracted the contents of several safety boxes. I assume their haul was considerable."

"What would you say if I suggested that one of the gang's aims was to possess the contents of Mr Waldron's safety box and that the New York gang targeted Mr Carver's box for similar reasons?"

Mr Revers glanced towards the stack of envelopes. "I might reply, in a purely speculative remark unalloyed with any juristic assessment, that the process of extraction seems excessive. Could not the contents of Mr Waldron and Mr Carver's safety boxes have been accessed by stealth rather than brute force?" He held up his hands. "I may be entirely wrong in that suggestion. My experience of the rough and tumble elements of criminality is limited to a brush with a would-be mugsman in a dark alley in Glasgow in which I hope and pray the fellow came to no lasting harm and repented his evil ways."

He sipped his whisky. "The persons for whom the documents I received today are of consequence are, for the most part, public figures in the United States, some with considerable responsibilities and authority. However, I think it improbable to the point of absurdity that any of them could command the resources to conduct a criminal enterprise dynamiting the New York and Continental in London." He considered. "The attack on the branch in New York is another matter."

"Could not these blackmail fiends be arrested, and their filthy trade suppressed?" I asked. "They suborn servants to collect information on their employers or even steal their personal letters."

"I was obliged to meet Mr Waldron on behalf of my clients," Mr Revers said with a moue of distaste. "He informed me that, unlike Milverton, his papers were kept in a place immune from interference, and he intimated, or perhaps even warned, that certain photographs in his possession secured him from both legal and more direct moves against him."

Holmes stood. "Thank you."

Mr Revers saw us to the door of his office. "It is mere gossip," he said, "but a rumour swirling around the breakfast tables at my club this morning suggested the gang got away with an emperor's ransom in DeBeers' diamonds."

Holmes and I made our way downstairs and out into Chancery Lane.

"Waldron and Carver act in concert," I said. "They secure each other's secret files on either side of the Atlantic, so their caches of compromising material are safe from attempts to repossess them."

A newsboy passed us waving the late-morning papers in the air and screaming, "Extra! New Yankee president, all the latest!"

"What has Mr McKinley to say?" I asked him.

He grinned. "Cost you a penny to find out."

I accepted the boy's logic, purchased a paper, and scanned the columns for the text of the new president's inauguration address. "Here we are. Mr McKinley refers to the arbitration between us and America on the Canada and Venezuela issues. He says, 'I cannot but consider it fortunate that it was reserved to the United States to have the leadership in so grand a work.'"

I shook my head. "American leadership, forsooth! Arbitration is all very well, Holmes, but Mr McKinley's vice-president, Mr Roosevelt, has a bellicose reputation. He was a major instigator of the unnecessary war with Spain, and he is intent on building up American naval strength – against whom? And what will that mean for Anglo-American relations?"

I looked up as a red-faced pageboy on a bicycle weaved through traffic and skidded to a halt beside Holmes. I recognised George from my club. He leaned towards Holmes, and between pants and gasps, murmured a message. Holmes passed him a coin, and he saluted and wheeled away at a more sober pace.

"Anglo-American relations?" Holmes said with a grin. "We are about to do our bit in that regard."

<hr />

Our cab deposited us at Waterloo Station, and on enquiry of a porter, we made our way to platform nine for the twelve-thirty boat train to Southampton, the American Eagle.

"Why didn't we just follow Lieutenant Commander Butler from my club?" I asked Holmes. "We'd know how he was making his getaway."

"I have no direct evidence against Butler, and, as I said, there are several other Americans in London who might fit Roberts' description of Mr Clay. But I must confess to you that, like Waldron and Carver perhaps, I am guilty of suborning not only the page, receptionist, barber and room attendant at your club, but also the smoking-room waiters."

"In a good cause," I said, suppressing a spurt of indignation. "And does the Lieutenant commander smoke *Henry Clay* cigars?"

Holmes smiled. "He does – with the band on, which gives us hope. But we may still be on a fool's quest. I have seldom been less sure of my man than today; the runes may be read in a number of ways. Still, Lieutenant Commander Butler is, according to your page, on the move with his bags. Let us see."

We stood beside the wrought-iron gates at the entrance to platform nine with a clear view of the London and Southwestern train. Far down the platform, the massive engine huffed and puffed, emitting clouds of steam as if anxious to set off for the south. A stream of porters dragged trolleys stacked high with steamer trunks to a string of baggage cars attached to the back of the train.

"The American Eagle delivers first-class passengers to the North German Lloyd liners at Southampton," Holmes said. "NG Lloyd is the only steamship line operating from Britain to the United States on Sundays." He shrugged. "The trail here is faint, and the scent almost imperceptible, but it seemed worth a trip across town."

Holmes and I observed every male passenger who passed through the gate, making allowances for disguises as we tested each against Roberts' description of Mr Henry Clay. Many of the passengers were in family groups, but a score or so of single gentlemen passed us, most with valets and porters trailing them. None fit the description given by Roberts and Leman.

"He may be travelling with female company, Holmes," I suggested. "Or even dressed as a female! These foreign agents are sly devils." I glanced at my watch and frowned. "The train leaves in eleven minutes."

Holmes held up a pair of train tickets and gave me a wry look. "We can get a refund. I have my people enquiring at likely hotels and clubs within a mile radius of the bank. They may unearth Mr Clay's lair."

I nudged Holmes. "Is that who I think it is?"

The lounger from the cab shelter outside my club sauntered past us. He stopped to light his pipe, discreetly indicating with his pipe stem a heavily built, clean-shaven gentleman in a long overcoat and top hat with a newspaper tucked under his arm. He marched past us with an assured and jaunty gait, his stick swinging, followed by a porter hefting a large valise. The gentleman had his ticket clipped, and he passed through the barrier.

Holmes slipped a coin into the lounger's hand and nodded to me. We followed the gentleman and porter towards the train. I craned looking for a ring, but our quarry wore black leather gloves.

The porter opened the door of a first-class compartment, heaved the valise onto the rack above the seats and stepped out. The gentleman tipped him and climbed aboard.

Holmes and I joined him in the compartment. Holmes sat by the window, and I took my place in a deeply upholstered seat beside my friend, facing the gentleman. He opened his paper, the *New York Times*, I was pleased to see.

Not having a newspaper to hide behind, I gazed out of the platform-side windows at the hurrying passengers, at the empty track on the other side, and at the framed coloured prints of seaside resorts fixed above the seats opposite. The minutes dragged, and I restrained myself from checking my watch until at last the guard's whistle blew and the train jolted once, then again and twice more. A cloud of steam enveloped the carriage as we moved, slowly at first, then gathering speed, clattering and screeching across a series of points before curving along a viaduct with smoky rows of Lambeth workmen's houses on either side.

The gentleman opposite me dropped a corner of his newspaper. "Pardon me," he said in a cultured American accent, "May I smoke in this compartment?"

I observed him with intense interest. He was pale and fine-featured with a neatly clipped moustache and short auburn hair – in his mid-thirties or early forties, perhaps. His eyes were clear, his mouth in a half smile, and he regarded Holmes with an open expression at odds with any thought of him as a criminal mastermind.

"Smoking is permitted on all trains by parliamentary legislation," Holmes said. "Gentlemen refrain when ladies are present unless they give us leave. Since we are in exclusively masculine company, you may smoke as you wish, Lieutenant Commander."

Our fellow passenger looked puzzled for a moment, then his face darkened. "May I ask whom I have the pleasure of addressing?"

Holmes introduced himself and me.

"I have heard of you, Mr Holmes. I understand you are a private agent, not connected with the regular police."

"That is so. Although I work closely with Scotland Yard from time to time. I have been engaged by the insurers of the New York and Continental Bank to enquire into the robbery that took place there early this morning."

Lieutenant Commander Butler removed his gloves, took a cigar case from his pocket, and offered *Henry Clay* cigars. I smiled when I saw the heavy gold ring, engraved with letters and symbols, on the ring finger of his left hand.

Holmes accepted a cigar and removed the band. I spurned the offer and lit a cigarette from my case. Butler lit Holmes' cigar and his own, the band on, with a patent oil match.

"Something of great value was in one of the riffled safe boxes," Holmes said in a musing tone. "There is speculation it was the DeBeers' diamond cache, but I believe the missing something has a value other than monetary; I further suggest that whatever is missing has very considerable power."

Butler laughed what sounded to me like a hollow laugh. "Power? You think the robbers released a disagreeable mummy from his slumbers, or discovered a cursed gemstone – a second *Koh-i-noor*? A fascinating notion; but are you not letting your imagination run away with you, Mr Holmes?"

"Incriminating documents," Holmes said in a languid tone, "embarrassing photographs—"

Butler's smile faded.

"—contained in box number two hundred and seven."

Butler folded his newspaper and tossed it onto the seat beside him. "This is interesting, Mr Holmes, but what has it to do with me? And how do you know my name?"

"The robbery played out like this," Holmes said softly. "The robbers arrived at the cigar shop at about four thirty yesterday morning disguised as coal heavers. They were surprised by the appearance of PC Laidlaw, late on his beat due to an altercation with a drunk. Their leader quickly dropped down and pretended to examine the shoe of the offside horse – farthest from the pavement – while one of the men on top chatted with the policeman."

"The leader was an unlikely coal man," I said, "far too clean and wearing an elaborate gold ring." I glanced at the lieutenant commander's hand. "We suspected he was an American from the cigar stub he dropped in the vault. He had to keep mum to avoid betraying his accent."

"One robber kept cave in the shop doorway," Holmes continued, "while the leader, the bank employee Roberts, and the others entered the cigar factory and bored through to the bank. Then the watcher moved the cart, joining the nightly stream of coal carts to and from the depot by circling the city block. Coal vans run back and forth through the City all night."

"Roberts opened the vault door," I said, "while the gang prepared the explosives. The leader attempted to open the target box. The plan was to use an ingenious corkscrew device to open that and a few others. An hour must have seemed plenty of time. But he was unaware, for Roberts did not know, that most unrented boxes and the target box had been reinforced making them difficult to open. Several upgraded boxes were attacked with the prying device, and all but one successfully resisted. That box was forced open after a very considerable effort."

Butler puffed on his cigar and said nothing.

"It took far longer than expected to open the blackmailer's box," Holmes said. "Time was ticking away while the gang, unable to do the work, ordered their late supper."

"Pie and mash," I added.

Butler frowned.

"A delicacy much favoured by persons living in the East End and the poorer districts of London," I explained. "The inspector in charge of the case deduced from their eating habits that the thieves must be local. I wonder how they were recruited."

Holmes waved the interruption away with his cigar. "The box was finally forced just before six. Mr Clay removed the contents and, very much later than planned, the explosion was triggered, and he made his getaway. An omnibus driver saw the coal van still outside the bank doors at six-ten." He considered the ash at the end of his cigar. "Box two-oh-seven was rented by Mr Waldron of 12 Ranleigh Gardens WC. Mr Waldron is a professional blackmailer."

"A compelling story, Mr Holmes, worthy of inclusion in one of your penny dreadful magazines," Butler said. He paused as with a long, shrill squeal, the train negotiated a tight curve. "Again I ask, what has it to do with me?"

Holmes drew a paper from his pocket. "Roberts has confessed. He will be able to identify you despite the fake beard you wore."

"We knew you were an American because of your *Henry Clay* cigars," I said, not without a touch of self-satisfaction. "They are unobtainable in this country."

"My cigars?" Butler tapped the ash from his cigar in the ashtray attached to the compartment door. "I bought a box of twenty at the White Star terminus in Liverpool."

Holmes chuckled, and I was put somewhat out of countenance. "And your ring," I said, "the mark of a graduate from your military academies."

Butler glanced down at his hand. "A class ring brings a fellow luck – usually." He addressed Holmes. "May I ask what your intentions are?"

Holmes took out his watch. "You will arrive in Southampton in less than two hours. I believe your ship sails at six, tide permitting, and the pilot is dropped about an hour later. You would not be hard to find. The Scotland Yard inspector in charge of this case will receive the evidence I have accumulated, and he will enjoy an invigorating voyage on a fast boat from the port of London to rendezvous with your ship within British waters."

"You will stir up a hornet's nest, Mr Holmes, here and in the States."

Holmes smiled. "Particularly in New York, I would imagine, where the safety box of Mr Waldron's associate, Mr Carver, was ransacked at the same time as his."

Butler was silent for a long moment, drawing on his cigar and looking out on the London suburbs racing past the window. "I am prepared to give you my version of certain events," he said at last, "but I require you to keep this matter entirely confidential."

"My duty is to my client, the insurance company," Holmes answered. "I can make no such assurance."

Butler sat back in his seat. "Restitution for the insurance companies has been set in train, and the New York and Continental will be discreetly compensated for the damage."

"Here and in New York?" I asked.

"The Manhattan vault was not blown open; it was robbed by an armed gang who kidnapped the chief cashier and forced him to open the vault. Only the boxes were smashed open."

"I suppose an armed robbery seemed more appropriate for New York," Holmes said. "And it had the advantage of being considerably less messy."

"You must understand, gentlemen," Butler said, "that I had no part in the inception of this sorry affair, and I warned my superiors that it would be an enterprise fraught with danger. It was instigated by the British. An agency tasked with the protection of a prominent person, part of your Special Branch, I believe, was concerned that in an inevitable eventuality, photographs purloined by unscrupulous persons might cause embarrassment."

I frowned.

"I contend Lieutenant Commander Butler's obtuse statement can refer to only one distinguished figure on this side of the Atlantic," Holmes said, "the Prince of Wales, now, after his mother's death in January, King Edward the Seventh."

Butler smiled a wry smile. "I made no such reference, sir."

Holmes tapped his finger to his lips. "What might have prompted such a concern? The death of the Queen was a seismic upheaval, but not unexpected. However, the accession would have been more problematic if photographic evidence of the new king's philandering and sexual escapades with Parisian—"

"I say, Holmes," I said.

"—courtesans were made public. His activities are known and winked at by his aristocratic chums and by the elite for obvious reasons, but we are in a new century, which I believe we may call the age of the common man. More men are educated and franchised than ever before. They are avid newspaper readers."

"No newspaper would dare—"

"You underestimate the ingenuity of our scandal mongers, Watson. And particularly of those on the Continent and in America. I am not saying that photographs of the new king in, let us say, interesting circumstances in Montmartre, would be published by the regular press. But consider the plethora of radical, anarchist publications that infest Paris."

Holmes smiled at the lieutenant commander and raised his eyebrows.

"Photographs may exist of champagne baths with Parisian good-time girls," he answered, "and bedroom romps, perhaps taken through a peephole."

I frowned. "How is that possible in the dark?"

"The gentleman may prefer to perform with the lights burning."

I gaped at Lieutenant Commander Butler. "But that's – that's utterly – I do not believe for a single moment that His Royal Highness, His Majesty, a person of the highest breeding and now our monarch, would leave the — I say, Holmes, this is no laughing matter."

"The photographs were Waldron's guarantee of immunity," Holmes said, recovering his composure. "He kept them safe in his associate's vault in New York, where he thought them immune from interference from British agencies. Thus, the reciprocal agreement: our people organised the robbery here in

London, with an American officer in command." Holmes smiled at the lieutenant commander, who bowed. "And the Americans recruited New York villains to execute the Manhattan job. No doubt one of our spies ran that show."

The carriage was plunged into darkness as the train entered a tunnel. Only the glow of Holmes' and the American's cigars and my cigarette were visible.

The lieutenant commander's cigar brightened as he drew on it. "There was a certain urgency on both sides. Your Queen was aged and unwell, and on our shores certain events were on the horizon."

Daylight streamed in the windows as the carriage sped out of the tunnel.

"We must consider, Watson, who of great public stature on the other side of the Atlantic might be compromised if his indiscretions were spilled into public domain by the newspapers," Holmes said. "The Americans were going through their regular self-inflicted mayhem with the presidential election, but Mr McKinley is an unlikely possibility for our victim; he is conventional to a humdrum tee. His running mate, however, has an ardent, enthusiastic nature."

"Unwarranted speculation," Butler huffed.

"Mr Theodore Roosevelt caused quite a stir as police commissioner and then governor of New York, making many enemies, then even more of a sensation in Cuba leading the Rough Riders up, and perhaps down, San Juan Hill. I believe he will not accept the post of vice-president as a sinecure. He is a man of action."

"I expect great things." Butler smiled. "The Navy expects great things."

"Mr Roosevelt is not, as far as I am aware, a philanderer, or in the thrall of any other vice that might debar him from public office if it were made public," Holmes said in a musing tone, "but he experienced a family tragedy in his recent past concerning his younger brother, Elliott."

Lieutenant Commander Butler narrowed his eyes but said nothing.

"Elliott Roosevelt fathered a son with a young servant girl. His older brother engaged a detective who specialized in likenesses, and after reviewing his evidence, the Roosevelts settled $10,000 on the child. In '94, Elliott's alcoholism escalated to the point that he was consuming numerous bottles of champagne and brandy daily, and in a drunken fit he jumped from a window. He survived but then suffered a seizure and died of heart failure."

"The fact that the vice president's younger brother committed suicide has not been hidden by the Roosevelt family," Lieutenant Commander Butler said in a frosty tone.

"The young man's tragic death was reported in your newspapers and picked up by papers here and in Europe. Your papers were reticent, and largely sympathetic, but the publication of, say, hospital or police reports offering evidence of laudanum and morphine addiction and of outbursts of violence by his brother would be deeply wounding to the new vice president's family and would feed a scandal. His enemies would not hold back from suggesting a family weakness of intellect or propensity towards feeble-mindedness, alcoholism, drug dependence and, most damaging perhaps in the view of a predominately Christian electorate, self-murder. While he was police commissioner and governor, such matters were perhaps moot, but now he is second in the land."

Butler drew on his cigar and said nothing.

"There we have it," Holmes said, leaning back in his seat.

"I predict an almighty stink if this devil's pact of yours becomes public knowledge," I said.

"It's in both countries' interests that it should not do so," the lieutenant commander answered. "And I hope that you and Mr Holmes will do the right thing by your new monarch and bow gracefully out."

"First you must reassure me on several points," Holmes said. "No box holder must suffer financial loss from the robbery."

Butler tapped his cigar ash into the ashtray. "We agreed with your people that the intrepid detectives – your Scotland Yard man and an agent on our side – will recover the goods through their sleuthhound skills, or the insurance companies will be discreetly reimbursed."

"I assume your American investigator is of the same calibre as our Inspector Jones?"

"We seconded our man from the Department of Fisheries. His detective experience is composed of chasing unlicensed anglers. It's planned that both he and your man will be steered in appropriate directions in due course."

"What of Waldron and Carver?" Holmes asked. "I presume they worked in tandem, trawling for information here and in America that would compromise their victims and sharing the proceeds."

"That is so," Butler answered. "Papers recovered from their boxes are either being examined or have already been returned to the victims or would-be victims anonymously through discreet legal representatives here and in New York. I doubt we will find enough evidence to prosecute – not without the cooperation of the victims – but the blackmailers don't know that. I very much hope they are shaking in their nefarious boots."

Holmes nodded. "Very well. My second proviso is that no employee of the bank will be censured. Roberts may retire with his ill-gotten gains."

"Agreed."

"Lastly, I require the bearer bonds and gold you purloined from the safety box of Señor Dardé shall be returned through me together with, let us say, five hundred pounds in compensation. You may requisition that sum from the United States or from Her Majesty's government as you wish. That to be paid within three banking days from today."

Butler stiffened, and his face clouded. "Surely you do not condone insurrection, sir."

"I do not, but like many heavily loaded words, that term is liable to interpretation."

"Cuban independence is guaranteed by my government – in due time."

Holmes held up a restraining hand. "We, and perhaps our respective governments, may differ on this question, Lieutenant Commander, but your new president advocates arbitration over conflict."

Holmes turned to me and raised his eyebrows.

I considered. "Señor Dardé's group is a patriotic association of Cubans who desire their independence. As long as they proceed by peaceful means, they are protected under the laws of England."

"There speaks the voice of reason and fair play," Holmes said, "notions that I am sure will bind our two great countries in friendship no matter what petty differences may divide us. You will kindly oblige me, Lieutenant Commander, by returning the gentleman's funds with compensation."

Lieutenant Commander Butler stood, took down his valise and handed Holmes a brown-paper-wrapped packet.

Holmes glanced at his watch. "I believe the train stops briefly at Basingstoke. Watson and I will hop off there and wish you bon voyage, sir. Meantime, might I borrow your newspaper?"

———— ◆ ————

I picked up the afternoon mail from the hall table at our lodgings.

"I say, Holmes," I said. "Here's a letter addressed to 'The Meddling Oaf' at our address. Who could that possibly be?"

"Open it and see." Holmes took the stairs two at a time.

"The writer is incensed," I said as I followed my friend into the sitting room. "He believes you masterminded the New York and Continental robbery in which his safety box was ransacked. He says, 'You may think you have bested me, Mr Holmes, but we will see who has the last laugh.'" I passed the letter to Holmes. "The missive is unsigned."

"We may hazard a guess as to the identity of my disgruntled correspondent. He gives me too much credit; I had never heard of him, at least under the name of Waldron, before yesterday. Perhaps I should send him a reply giving credit where it is due and have him direct his venom to the Home Office and the White House."

"There's no return address."

"I have his contact details. But no, we will let him stew. People of Mr Waldron's ilk cannot bear being ignored." Holmes threw the letter into the fire.

"I wonder if he has heard the news of his American partner's discomfiture."

"The robbery was a madcap scheme." Holmes took his pipe from the mantel and slumped into his chair. "If I had been consulted, I could have suggested at least four far simpler alternatives that would have done the job without dynamiting a rather elegant building in central London."

I smiled. "If Roberts had polished his shoes and dusted the pump more efficiently, would you have deduced the robbery was a fake?"

Holmes waved my question away with his pipe stem. "My dear fellow, you are going to say that my deduction was a fluke, and I solved the case by accident. Really, this is a bit much. All crimes, or almost all crimes, leave evidence, but not all evidence is observable to the crass observer."

"Such as Inspector Jones."

"Precisely. Am I to be pilloried for drawing the correct conclusions from those elements of the scene of the crime that escape lesser investigators?"

"I am not demeaning your achievement, old man. In fact, I applaud it; I just wondered."

Billy pushed open the sitting-room door and entered with a tray of tea things. "Which, Mrs H asks if you'll be in for dinner tonight as it's steak and kidney pudding and the suet needs making up in good time."

I looked to Holmes, who shrugged. "Yes," I said. "And ask Mrs Hudson whether she could manage a rhubarb tart for dessert. The one she made on Tuesday was excellent."

I poured the tea and passed Holmes the bread and butter and the honey jar. "I understand DeBeers have closed their account at the

New York and Continental, as have many other clients. I feel sorry for Mr Peters and the other bank employees. And the shareholders, of course. They have been badly used by our authorities and the Americans."

"There are no shareholders," Holmes said. "The bank is private. Ownership is murky and the files are convoluted, but the New York and Continental is rumoured to be wholly owned by John Pierpont Morgan, the multi-million-dollar American financier."

"That makes me easier in my mind. He has so much money he may not even notice any loss."

Holmes lathered his bread with honey. "If only a fraction of what I have heard about Morgan is correct, he will notice, and woe betide the perpetrators. As Inspector Jones and Deuteronomy might have it, 'Their day of disaster is near and their doom rushes upon them.'"

TA-RA-RA-BOOM-DE-AY

AN ATTENDANT SHOWED HOLMES and me to a private box close to the stage and offered menus. I waved mine away and indicated a bottle and glasses on a side table.

"I pre-ordered a bottle of the house red."

The attendant looked down his nose at the bottle and withdrew.

I chuckled. "What airs these fellows give themselves."

The house lights were still up, and Holmes surveyed the ornate auditorium. "The Tivoli Palace of Varieties is well named. The chamber is graced with an eclectic frolic of gilded Indian gods, elephant's-head pillars, and Moorish arches. Are we in Calcutta or Casablanca?"

He glanced at the programme. "No dancing dogs or whistling tramps, but we have the usual motley crew of *lions comiques* and seriocomical *artistes*, of whom the famous Miss Lottie Collins is the leading light." He turned to me. "My dear fellow, kindly explain what I am doing here."

I poured Holmes a glass of wine. "It's quite a serious situation. In a recent review of her performance, *Stage News* characterised Lottie's – that is, Miss Collin's dance as vulgar. She naturally demanded a retraction—"

"Yes, yes, a sordid scuffle that sullied even the august pages of *The Times*. What of it?"

"The court case comes up on Monday, *Collins* v *Stage News*. If Miss Collins loses, the Lord Chamberlain will be constrained to ban her performance, forcing the Tivoli management to remove her from the billing with all the consequences that follow – loss of employment, income, reputation and so on."

"Again, my dear fellow, kindly explain what that has to do with me."

"Well, the thing is, some of the chaps at my club are aficionados of the halls—"

Holmes smiled. "Stage-door johnnies."

"—and they formed a committee of support, do you see? And since it is public knowledge that you and I, that is, we are...."

"You offered to drag me aboard."

"I thought I might ask your opinion, no more. Several highly respectable persons appear for the defence. Mr George Bernard Shaw is a defence witness, and the Earl of Canby and the Argentinian ambassador have offered their support."

Holmes did not seem impressed.

The theatre lights went down. "I know you are immune to the charms of the halls," I said over the start of the overture, "preferring your motets and so on."

"On the contrary," Holmes replied. "I am very much alive to the cultural roots of music hall among the jongleurs, minstrels, and jesters of the medieval period, the forerunners of the *Commedia dell'arte.*"

I frowned. "Quite."

The Tivoli chairman banged his gavel and introduced the first act as a tribute to our boys fighting the followers of the Mad Mahdi of Khartoum. Two lines of ballet girls in native dress and carrying spears marched on stage. They formed a double line and presented their spears in salute as a lady in white tights, an officer's tunic and a white, sequinned bearskin, skipped onto the stage and led the audience in a rousing chorus:

> *We've fought with many men acrost the seas,*
> *An' some of 'em was brave an' some was not:*
> *The Paythan an' the Zulu an' Burmese;*
> *But the Fuzzy is the finest o' the lot."*

The troupe paraded back and forth waving union flags, eliciting loud cheers and whistles from the audience.

> *So 'ere's to you, Fuzzy-Wuzzy, at your 'ome in the Soudan;*
> *You're a pore benighted 'eathen but a first-class fightin' man;*

"Miss Brooks plays the officer," I said. "She carries it off very well, I think."

"Fuzzy-wuzzies." Holmes sighed. "Mr Kipling has a lot to answer for."

The troops formed a line and marched off to thunderous applause, and the chairman called for silence as he introduced 'Our one and only Miss Lottie Collins!'

She entered without fanfare, wearing a restrained costume of a dark, brocaded dress, black evening gloves, and a wide-brimmed hat worn slantwise, Duchess-of-Devonshire style. She sang a sweet melody in slow time,

> *A smart and stylish girl you see,*
> *The Belle of High society;*
> *Fond of fun as fond could be-*

When it's on the strict QT.
Never forward, never bold,
Not too young and not too old,
Not too timid, not too bold,
But the very thing I'm told,
That in your arms you'd like to hold.

After a moment's pause, a bass drum banged, cymbals crashed, and Lottie cried,

Ta-ra-ra Boom-de-ay!

and burst into motion, leaping, spinning in a frenzy of whirling petticoats, lunging and doubling up before springing into the air, her scarlet-clad legs flashing in the limelights as she repeated the phrase.

She raced around the tight stage, each circle more animated and energetic, the audience cheering and singing,

Ta-ra-ra Boom-de-ay!

A thunder of drumbeats and to an elemental roar from the audience, Lottie performed a spectacular high kick with a final cry of,

Ta-ra-ra Boom-de-ay!

"What did you think of it, Mr Holmes?" Miss Collins spread skin cream across her brow and began wiping off her makeup.

"The song?" Holmes accepted a cigarette from a rhinestone-encrusted box proffered by Miss Collin's lady dresser. "The verse is at first rational, if trite." He assumed a considering air as I lit his and my cigarettes with a match. He puffed a stream of smoke across the tiny dressing room. "Then, in the vapid refrain, reason is abandoned in the senseless howl that accompanies your frenetic dance."

Holmes and I sat close together on flimsy gilt chairs amid a tumult of brightly coloured fabrics, a riot of dazzling Pierrot costumes, puff-sleeved flamenco dresses, flounces of lace and feathers and a plethora of hats of varied styles and ample proportions. Miss Collins sat with her back to us at a dressing table piled with pots and flasks of make-up and before a brightly lit mirror. Her dresser squeezed between us hanging up garments and tut-tutting at marks and tears.

"Your dance is a hybrid of Bacchic frenzy and Parisian *can-can*," Holmes continued. "It is a farrago of motion made more extravagant by its performance not to the beat of Apache tom-toms, but to the strains of a mediocre pit band in a London music hall."

Miss Collins paused in her toilette and regarded Holmes in her mirror with raised eyebrows. "But what did you *think* of it?"

"It was athletic."

Miss Collins nodded. "You're not wrong, Mr Holmes. It's the mad rush and whirl of the thing that makes it go. I get round a forty-foot circle twice in eight measures. I've sprained my ankle a dozen times already."

She chuckled. "I first sang it at a matinée in '92, and such a storm of applause followed! I didn't know what I'd done, but I was determined to do it again."

She stood and kicked her leg between Holmes and me almost to ceiling height, filling the tiny room with billows of Liberty's scarlet silk and white lace petticoats.

"Ta-ra-ra-BOOM-de-ay!"

We left the dressing room and pushed through a crowd of gentlemen in evening dress and young officers in uniform crowding the dusty corridor, all clutching bouquets of flowers or boxes of chocolates.

A fearsome imp in page's uniform guarded a line of scuffed dressing room doors marked with faded stars. After sufficient pecuniary inducement had been provided by each gentleman, the boy tapped gently against a door, whispered the suitor's name and either opened the fortress gates or sent the unfortunate fellow away in ignominy.

The gentlemen glared at Holmes and me as we sauntered by.

A line of young ballet girls dressed in the scanty frippery of the chorus line tripped past us, and I started as I heard my name called. A young blonde lady stepped from the line and greeted me with a peck on the cheek.

"May I introduce Miss Brooks," I said, feeling myself flush pink. "She is the principal dancer of the chorus, and understudy to Miss Collins."

Holmes bowed. "A pleasure to meet you, Miss Brooks."

"The very same, I'm sure, Mr Holmes," Miss Brooks answered with a winsome pout. "Johnny has told me all about you."

She winked, and Holmes blinked at her, and then turned to me and smiled. "Ah yes, Johnny Watson."

I reddened more brightly.

Miss Brooks nodded towards Miss Collins' dressing room. "You've been paying court to Her Imperial Radiance, then."

I mumbled something deprecatory, smoothed my moustache, and avoided both Holmes' and Miss Brooks' eyes.

She laughed. "You won't get far with her ladyship, gentlemen. She requires her followers to wear a strawberry leaf coronet and robes of ermine at the very least."

She put her hand on my arm. "All right for Thursday, Ducks?"

"Actually, I, ah, might not be free. I have a prior—"

Miss Brooks pouted and flounced away. The crowd of gentlemen parted to let her through to her dressing-room door, held open by the grinning page boy. She paused in the doorway, turned and blew a kiss at me, or perhaps at Holmes; no, definitely at me. I offered a tiny wave in return.

Holmes raised an enquiring eyebrow.

"Billiards. Miss Brooks partners me against Miss Chambers – one of the ladies you saw on stage in the parade – and Major Henderson of the Royal Engineers. The Star Tavern has a private billiard room one can hire."

Holmes and I passed through the backstage corridors to the stage door and out into the mellow Spring evening air.

"Mr Holmes, sir?" A young man in a curled-rim bowler with an eager expression pushed through the knot of loungers on the pavement and faced Holmes.

"*Stage News*, sir." The man poised his pencil over an open notebook. "Will you be appearing for Miss Collins at the trial, sir? Any comment after viewing the performance?"

Holmes peered down his nose at the young reporter. "The matter is *sub judice*."

A photographer and his assistant hurriedly manoeuvred a camera on a tripod towards Holmes.

"If you wouldn't mind just—" The cameraman shooed me to one side.

"Wait, this is Doctor Watson," the reporter said, "the author of Mr Holmes' memoirs." He turned to me. "What are your thoughts on the dance, Doctor, from the medical point of view? Some medicos have suggested high kicks and leaps are injurious to the health of the dancers, and that the female body is not constructed for intense physical movements."

A flash blinded me, and I blinked and rubbed my eyes as Holmes took my arm and propelled me through the crowd to the cab rank.

"I didn't know you were a balletomane, my dear fellow," Holmes said as we drew away from the theatre in a hansom.

"No more am I," I answered, shifting uncomfortably on the hard seat. "The so-called 'ballet girls' of the chorus at the Tivoli or any other music hall have no relation to the classical ballet. For that you'd have to go to Covent Garden or Drury Lane. The chorus are merely decorative."

"They certainly exhibited little skill this evening," Holmes said. "I'm not an aficionado of the ballet, but I think it a shame that not a single English prima ballerina has graced our stages. Can it be true that our home-grown Terpsichorean talents are so weak that we must depend entirely on French and Italian imports?

"And I have to admit I am in two minds whether to support or condemn Miss Collins. I admire her energy and sense of rhythm, but having a half-dozen servant girls marching arms-linked along the pavement on their Sunday afternoon off screeching that 'boom-de-yay' nonsense or 'Knocked 'em in the Old Kent Road' – their current favourites – is more than a little irritating to quiet-loving citizens such as myself."

I smiled. "Strange, Holmes, I would have characterised you as a sworn enemy of monotony."

———◆———

Our breakfast the next morning was interrupted by an imperious ring of our doorbell, and Billy poked his head around our sitting-room door to announce the presence in our waiting room of the famous, or perhaps infamous, Mrs Ormiston Chant.

Mrs Chant's controversial contribution to the regulation of public decency was her campaign to rid music halls of impropriety, vice, and alcohol by lobbying the Theatre and Music Hall's Committee to refuse to renew licences to halls and theatres offering entertainments that she deemed offensive.

She had incurred the ire of predominantly male theatregoers by having the notorious second-floor gallery of the Empire music hall cleared of unaccompanied ladies, many of whom, it must be admitted, were of a certain sort, thus provoking a near riot.

I stood and picked up my coffee cup and a slice of toast. "I'll get out of your way, Holmes."

"You'll do nothing of the sort," Holmes said firmly. "I have no doubt that this visitation concerns your music hall shenanigans."

I subsided into my chair and gulped my tea as Billy cleared the table.

Mrs Chant was not the harridan I expected; at least she did not look the part when she was shown up to the sitting room. She wore a demure, grey, puffed-sleeved gown with a fashionably ornamented hat, her complexion was clear, and her eyes sparkling with vitality. She sat primly on our sofa, ignoring an offer of tea. I noticed a wide mourning band on her arm.

"I saw your name on a newspaper vendor's placard as appearing for the defence in this sordid *can-can* action, Mr Holmes," she said after our mutual introductions. "I could not believe my eyes."

"Miss Collin's dance is hardly a *can-can*," I suggested. "It is a variation of the well-known skirt dance that has been a feature of the music halls for some years without adverse comment: without widespread adverse comment."

"I directed my remarks to Mr Holmes, Doctor." Mrs Chant turned to Holmes. 'Surely you would agree that we have no right to allow on the stage that which, done in the street, would compel a policeman to take the offender in charge."

"You are in the right, madam," Holmes said. "I certainly believe that any tramp whistlers, dancing-dog handlers or fuzzie-wuzzies who infest our streets should be instantly locked up."

Mrs Chant frowned. "This is hardly a matter for frivolity, Mr Holmes. The members of the Ladies National Association and the British Women's Temperance Association stand firm against Miss Collins' abomination."

She stood. "But I see my representations in the name of public order and morality are falling on stony ground." I jumped up and Holmes levered himself up from his chair.

Mrs Chant turned to me. "I had expected more from a member of the medical profession, sir. Do you not agree, Doctor, that the excitement, the unreality, the sensationalism, the costumes of the ballet girls' occupation distance all feminine sobriety and practical domesticity?" She poked me in the chest. "*Deny it who can,* the calling of a ballet girl is in itself a recognised lure to the depraved of your sex."

She stalked to the door and tapped the mourning band on her arm. "I wear this as much for the death of Christian values in our society as for poor General Gordon killed by the Mahdi." She opened the door. "The whole question of indecency on our public stages would be solved if men, and not women, were costumed in such an unseemly fashion and made to prance in lurid ways. Men would refuse to exhibit their bodies nightly in these sordid displays."

Billy appeared in the doorway with a tray of tea things. Mrs Chant batted him away and thundered downstairs. The street door opened and shut with a bang.

Billy gaped at me.

"Lay the tea things on the table, Billy," I ordered, "and see what Mrs Hudson can do in the matter of toast and boiled eggs."

Holmes and I settled into our respective armchairs.

"What a very excitable lady," I said.

Holmes indicated a stack of letters on the floor at his feet. "Unsubstantiated reports of my support for Miss Collins have prompted a vituperative correspondence on both sides of the issue."

He tossed the letters into the fire. "In fact, I have decided to appear as a witness."

"In support of Miss Collins as the newspapers suggest?"

Holmes smiled.

———◄○►———

Our cab dropped Holmes and me outside the imposing neo-Gothic edifice of the Royal Courts of Justice in the Strand, and we were assailed by an ear-splitting cacophony.

An orchestra crammed into a wagon parked on the pavement and festooned with banners advertising the Tivoli Theatre of Varieties played, 'Let's All Go Down the Strand (have a banana)'. On the opposite side of the street, a Salvation Army band and chorus opposed this with a rousing 'There is a Fountain filled with Blood'.

Chanting and singing demonstrators waving placards supporting or reviling Miss Cohn and the music hall in general, and gawkers filled the street on both sides.

Holmes and I pushed through the crowd to the wrought-iron gates of the carriage yard in front of the court. A young lady in a lavender dress and ample hat planted herself before me, waved a 'Votes for Women' banner and shook a collecting box. I smiled and attempted to pass her, but she countered every attempt to evade her, and at last, encouraged by the chafing of a good-natured crowd, I gave in and dropped a coin into her collecting box. She leaned in close – a delicious whiff of musk perfume – pinned a small pink rosette to my lapel and smiled a most winning smile. I gaped like a guppy and felt myself reddening.

Holmes had carved his way through the throng to the gates. I sidled past the young lady and pushed through to him. On examination of his witness summons by a stalwart police sergeant in charge of a half-dozen constables, we were allowed into the courtyard.

We stood under the magnificent Gothic arched entrance of our great cathedral of law.

"I see you have embraced women's suffragism," Holmes said over the hubbub from the street, raising an eyebrow at my rosette and sniffing. "Or perhaps you have embraced a suffragist?"

"Holmes!"

"Today of all days, my dear Watson, we must not be prudish." Holmes surveyed the street packed with cavorting ballet girls and the massed ranks of uniformed Salvationists. "Even severe disciplinarian General Booth of the Salvation Army has his lighter moments; it was he who quipped that prostitution is the only avocation in which the apprentice is paid more than the seasoned professional."

"I say, Holmes—"

Holmes looked over my shoulder and smiled. "Inspector."

Inspector Lestrade of Scotland Yard joined us, shook our hands, and turned to the melee in the Strand. "We have forbidden the theatre musicians from playing either the 'Marseillaise' or 'Ta-ra-ra Boom-de-ay' close to the court precincts," he said. "And the Salvationists must stay where they are and not march up and down, impeding the roadway." He shook his head. "Not that anything can pass along the Strand with the mob tight packed in the street."

"The Marseillaise?" I said with a grin. "Do you fear a descent on the courtroom by a tumult of French boulevardiers and prima ballerinas determined to free Miss Collins from the shackles of our prim-and-proper bourgeois judiciary?"

The inspector sniffed. "The trial is a civil not a criminal proceeding, Doctor. There is no danger of Miss Collins being shackled or imprisoned. The police are here solely to keep order. We are neutral in this sorry business – unless provoked." He offered cigarettes from his case. "The music ban was not my decision, but I can understand the concern of the Powers-That-Be. I don't know which are worse, the theatricals, the suffragists or the Salvation Army."

He struck a match against a Gothic column but paused in lighting his cigarette and focussed narrow-eyed on a group of men in black clothes and bowler hats on the opposite pavement surrounding a tall clergyman holding a staff topped with a black crucifix. A white-haired military officer stood beside him. "Actually, I do know."

"Reverend Gaunt," Holmes said.

"And General Reid-Aladyce, MP, the hero of the Ashanti War," Lestrade said, "who recently introduced anti-immigration legislation to the House. He blames Jewish bankers and gold merchants for the South African unrest, and wants Jewish immigrants fleeing the Russian and Polish pogroms sent back where they came from. Reverend Gaunt blames the Jews for everything from murdering the Saviour to the death of General Gordon."

He lit his cigarette and flicked out the match. "Miss Collins is of Jewish extraction – her birth name is Cohn, and one of her ancestors was the *Baal Shem* of London. Several theatre impresarios are of that faith."

Lestrade checked his watch and blew three long blasts of his whistle. The sergeant at the gate acknowledged the signal with a wave, and he opened the gate sufficiently wide for people to pass through one-by-one. I saw Miss Brooks in her mauve dress caught in the crush, and I waved, but she didn't see my greeting.

Reverend Gaunt handed his cross to an attendant, and he, General Reid-Aladyce and several of their followers crossed the street to the gate and bulled their way through the crowd struggling to enter. They pushed through by main force, and were let in.

Holmes and I followed the stream of people across the magnificent central hall of the Courts and along a side passage to the courtroom allotted for the case. An usher directed the inspector and Holmes to seats at the front of the gallery, and I was allowed to sit with them. Mrs Ormiston Chant was farther along the row, and I avoided catching her eye.

The court struck me, as it must do most spectators, as cramped. Bewigged lawyers huddled on benches tight under the clerks' tier and judge's podium and spectators packed into steep tiers around the witness box. The jury benches were empty.

"Both sides have agreed to let the judge decide what a jury would or should have concluded," Holmes said. "The lack of a jury to seduce by their rhetoric will hopefully limit counsels' histrionics."

I heard a fuss behind me, and I turned. A group of young ladies high up in the gallery had unfolded a banner of the National Central Society for Women's Suffrage. Raucous shouts came from a lower section in which Reverend Gaunt and General Reid-Aladyce sat with a half-dozen black-clad bruisers. A pair of court officials bustled the suffragists out to cheers from the theatrical section of the crowd, and jeers from Gaunt's men.

We stood as the bailiff tapped his staff on the floor and the judge swept in and took his place. His Lordship peered around the court over half-moon glasses and spoke in a weary tone. "I am disappointed that the parties in this nugatory dispute have been unable to find a common ground for conciliation or have not sought the arbitration of other judiciaries with appropriate authority. That being the case, I am prepared to rule on the matter. I will tolerate no partisan or emotional displays."

"Other judiciaries?" I murmured.

"The learned judge perhaps refers to the *Beth Din*, the Jewish rabbinical court," Inspector Lestrade answered. "Both Miss Collins and the editor of *Stage News* are Jews. He suggests the case is a spat between co-religionists."

The bailiff called all parties in the matter of *Collins v Stage News* to order, and the counsel for the complainant opened the proceedings with a mercifully short speech declaring his intention to provide the judge with the opinions of persons of impeccable reputation and worth in the community who held that Miss Collins' performance was indeed vulgar.

He called Mrs Ormiston Chant, who rehearsed the arguments she had offered during her visit to our lodgings.

"Have you personally seen the performance in question?" the judge asked.

"I most certainly have not!"

The judge shook his head and scratched a note. Counsel for Miss Collins waived cross-examination, and Mrs Chant was dismissed.

The prebendary of St Paul's Cathedral and another religious worthy who spoke in a hoarse whisper and whose name and position I could not catch, decried the diminution of orderliness and piety in modern life and in the pastimes of the young in particular. In each case the judge asked whether the witness had seen Miss Collins' performance, and again the answers were negative.

The lively mood of the spectators was dampened by the dreary back and forth between the *Stage News* counsel and his lacklustre witnesses. Even the judge seemed disengaged from the proceedings as he leaned back on his throne with his eyes half-closed.

"The defendants don't seem to be making much of an effort," I murmured to Holmes.

The editor of *Stage News* was the last witness for the paper. Mr Mayer too admitted that he had not seen the Tivoli performance before his journal printed the review, but he stated that the reporter who wrote the critique had, and that he himself had subsequently attended the show. He contended that Miss Collins' dance was vulgar, and it exhibited no mitigating artistic merit.

A roar of approval came from the Salvationists and Reverend Gaunt's supporters, which was quickly drowned by counter-cheers from the theatricals. The usher stilled the hubbub with furious application of his stave on the floor.

Vapid cross-examination of Mr Mayer by Miss Collins' barrister made no dent in the editor's position. The judge interrupted him. "The witness has characterised Miss Collins' performance as vulgar. I should like to hear his definition of the term."

The counsel perked up. "Could you tell the court what exactly you mean by the term vulgar?"

The editor frowned. "Tending towards the indecent. Of dubious morality and inciting depravity."

The judge leaned forward and addressed Miss Collins' counsel again. "I wonder what element in the lady's dance incited the witness to depravity."

The question was asked, and the witness floundered for an explanation.

He was dismissed and *Stage News* rested their side of the case.

Mr George Bernard Shaw, a slim, bearded man in a brown Norfolk jacket, took the stand as the first witness for Miss Collins. Counsel established that he was a music critic and playwright, and that he had visited the Tivoli on several occasions and seen Miss Collins' act.

"The performance is a most instructive example of the value of artistic method in music-hall singing," Mr Shaw said in nasal tone with a faint Irish accent. "Miss Collins' perfect self-possession and calculated economy of effort carry her audience away. She articulates her words with ringing brilliancy and with immense assurance of manner. The dance refrain, with its three low kicks on 'Ta-ra-ra' and its high kick on 'Boom' (with *grosse caise ad lib.*), is the simplest thing imaginable."

I frowned. "*Grosse caise?*"

"Bass drum," Holmes murmured. "Ta-ra-ra-Boom!"

The judge sighed. "If I might cut to the bone, Mr Shaw. Would you or would you not, in your professional opinion as a -" He frowned down at his notes. "- as a 'music critic', class Miss Collins' performance as vulgar in the sense of the term adumbrated by the previous witness?" He glared at the witness over his pince-nez. "A single word answer, if you please.

"No, Your Honour, I would not."

Holmes was called, and counsel established his name and occupation without provoking the usual eruption against 'paid sneaks' from the bench.

"Am I right in saying that your detective work requires you to visit the very lowest slums and courts of London and deal with some of the most vile and wretched of its denizens?" Miss Collins' attorney asked.

"You are. I also deal with some of the most vile and wretched denizens of Belgravia and Park Lane."

"What is your opinion of the song in question?"

"I need not speak to the artistic merit of Miss Collins' performance as Mr Shaw has very eloquently covered that."

A squawk of laughter came from the public gallery, instantly suppressed by the bailiff.

"I will say that Miss Collins appears to be in fine athletic training, and she carries out her performance with a combination of perfect sang-froid and the unsparing vigour. I saw nothing that would tend to deprave the mind of the beholder, unless that person's mind were already predisposed to vice, in which case I doubt he would require help from Miss Collins when there are far more titillating spectacles on view in public houses and gin palaces throughout the metropolis."

"Thank you. Then, given your experience in rookeries and criminal dens would you describe Miss Collins' performance of the Ta-ra-ra-boom-de-ay song as vulgar?"

"I would not. However—"

"Thank you, Mr Holmes." Miss Collin's counsel sat.

"You were about to say, sir?" the judge asked, peering at Holmes over his spectacles.

"I find one element of the performances I witnessed at the Tivoli vulgar in the extreme. The young ladies in the *corps de ballet* who appeared in earlier part of the evening's entertainment were clearly recruited for their looks rather than Terpsichorean skill. They are semi-skilled workers, rows of commonplace dancers, individually uninteresting (from the artistic point of view), wearing costumes encrusted with glitter and teetering under elaborate headdresses, who have been trained to perform nothing more elaborate than a simple hop and twirl. These so-called ballet girls are massed and depersonalised; they do no *pointe* work; their role is simply to be decorative, to provide allure and spectacle. That is both vulgar and dehumanising. It is no wonder that women desire the vote."

A roar of approval came from the theatrical spectators, and boos and catcalls were heard from Reverend Gaunt and his attendants. The Salvationists looked to their leader, a stern gentleman in a befrogged uniform and cap with a luxuriant walrus moustache. He remained silent, and so did they.

The *Stage News* barrister waived his right of cross-examination. In fact, he had made no significant contribution to the proceedings thus far.

Miss Collins took the stand, and after detailing her career, she answered the key question from her counsel.

"No, it is not vulgar in the least. My idea of the song is that it represents a shy young woman who takes advantage of the absence of her elders to have a harmlessly lively time by herself."

She turned to the judge. "You wouldn't credit it, Your Honour, but I sprained my ankle a dozen times in the dance that accompanies the song." She swung her leg up and rested it on the edge of the witness box, lifting her dress several inches and exposing her ankle. "I'm not sure my health would permit my thinking of ever putting it on again."

The judge leaned forward, adjusted his pince-nez and smiled. "Surely not, my dear lady?"

Reverend Gaunt sprang from his seat. "Jezebel!"

General Reid-Aladyce stood with him. "The Jew theatre owners corrupt our youth! The Rothschilds, Carte and the rest degrade English womanhood. They are parasites and predators, snatching the innocence of English maidens and the jobs and comforts of our honest English folk while Britannia's sons in the Sudan give their all for freedom and decency."

A roar of approval came from the black-clad bruisers. The theatre folk raised a spirited counter-cheer and the Salvationists and Suffragist ladies again seemed nonplussed.

I frowned. "Does he mean Mr D'Oyly Carte, the Gilbert and Sullivan impresario? Is he Jewish?"

"I have no idea." Holmes shrugged. "Facts are not central to the tenets of General Reid-Aladyce's argument."

The usher banged his stave in vain, and the judge's admonitions were drowned by a discord of competing cheers and jeers. His Honour threw up his hands and stalked out.

Amid the pandemonium, I noticed two young members of the Salvation Army on their knees before the witness box, praying aloud for the Almighty to strike Miss Collins down with a lightning bolt.

The young reporter from the Tivoli ambushed Holmes and me at the door of the courtroom. "The judge has delivered his verdict from his chambers, gentlemen, twenty-five pounds damages and costs against *Stage News*." He grinned. "A famous victory for Miss Collins. Any comments, Mr Holmes, sir, or you, Doctor?"

"You are much underfoot, young man," I said.

"I make up for my limited expertise by the application of zeal, Doctor. I aim to rise in my profession by being where the news is."

"Your employer lost the case."

"*C'est la vie*, sir. Win or lose, the trial will generate good copy."

Holmes and I nodded curtly and passed into the great hall.

"You showed remarkable knowledge of the ballet girls' plight in your evidence, Holmes. I was not aware that *you* were a balletomane."

"No more am I. But for every glittering Lottie Collins there are a hundred Mavises or Florences who remove their makeup and tinsel at midnight after gruelling hours on the boards and late-night rehearsals, and who traipse across the Waterloo Bridge or along the Ratcliffe Highway to the East End to their cold and inhospitable garrets. One must be aware that behind the footlights may lurk an all-too-human tragedy."

I shook my friend's hand. "I heartedly agree."

A young lady in the fetching uniform of a Salvation Army captain skipped to me and offered a Union flag pin and a collecting box. I slipped a coin into the box, and she smiled a charming smile and pinned the flag to my lapel, opposite the pink rosette, her face inches from my own. I reddened.

Holmes raised his eyebrows.

"Like Switzerland, I adhere to a policy of absolute neutrality."

Holmes and I stopped at the entrance to the Courts and surveyed the Strand, where chaos reigned with even more abandon than in the courtroom. At the one end of the street, Reverend Gaunt stood on a pillar box and ranted against licentiousness. On the other, the Salvationists massed, singing hymns and waving banners, and the Suffragists formed an orderly rank holding their placards high. In the middle, the theatricals celebrated, the theatre orchestra playing a lively tune as a line of ballet girls linked arms and marched along the Strand whooping, high-kicking, and chanting,

> *"Sister 'Ria of the Army soon began to tire*
> *So she sold her tambourine*
> *Now she's nightly to be seen*
> *Dancing in the ballet at the Old EmPIRE."*

The Salvation Army band, unabashed, retorted with a spirited rendering of 'Onward Christian Soldiers'.

I spied a flash of mauve in the crush of Collins supporters, and I darted forward. "Miss Brooks!" I gently tapped the young lady on the arm.

She turned. She was not Miss Brooks, she was a younger girl, and with longer blonde tresses under her expansive hat. "Pardon me, Miss." I bowed and returned, feeling rather crestfallen, to where Holmes stood by a pillar.

"We are done with this nonsense," Holmes said, checking his watch. "Let's leave before things get ugly. We can walk to the Savoy and a quiet luncheon."

A white-faced police constable pushed through the crowd to Holmes and whispered in his ear. Holmes' eyes narrowed. He beckoned to me, and we followed the constable back into the courthouse and along a side corridor to a door guarded by a court usher. Water seeped under the door and pooled in the corridor. A sign showed this was a ladies' retiring room.

Holmes pushed open the door. The floor of the lavatory was flooded. Inspector Lestrade stood in front of an open cubicle, notebook in hand. He stepped back, and Holmes and I looked inside.

The body of a woman lay spread-eagled on the floor of the cubicle, her lemon-yellow and grey striped dress and pink petticoats pulled over her head, revealing her drawers.

I knelt and examined the woman, lifting her dress from her face. I started back, ashen-faced. "Miss Brooks!"

Her tongue protruded from her mouth, and a silk stocking was tight around her neck.

Holmes laid a hand on my arm. "There's no need for you to examine the lady further, old man. A police surgeon will be on the way."

I nodded and stood back, taking deep breaths, while Holmes knelt by the body.

Lestrade surveyed the lavatory. "The washbasin has a stocking stuffed into the drain, and the tap was running." He emptied the wicker bin onto the floor. "Rags with traces of make-up – I suppose you would expect that in a ladies' lavatory." He turned to me. "When did you last see the lady?"

"At the Tivoli yesterday," I answered in a hoarse tone. "I thought I saw her in her mauve dress when we arrived at the court today, but I must have been mistaken. Then just now, as we left, I saw a lady who looked like her, but she was younger, just a girl." I shook my head. "What fiend did this?"

"These ballet girls swap clothes all the time," Inspector Lestrade remarked.

Holmes held up a clump of long, blond hairs. "These were clutched in her right fist." He and Lestrade peered at the hairs, and Holmes rubbed them between his fingers. "Not human. From a wig perhaps."

I looked down at the body. "Has her own hair been cut? Chopped more like. It's usually tightly pinned back, not loose as now."

Holmes stood. "Do you mind if I keep some of these hairs for analysis?" He borrowed an evidence envelope and divided the blonde hair between himself and the inspector.

I leaned back against the cool tiles and gave Lestrade as many details as I knew of Miss Brooks' circumstances – surprisingly few, in fact. I understood she lived in Lambeth, but I did not know her address, age, or any family details.

Lestrade offered cigarettes from his packet. "We'll wait till the street clears; no need for a fuss. I've sent for a stretcher and a police ambulance. I have my men searching for witnesses."

Holmes and I retreated outside and smoked in the busy hall where the work of the court continued.

"We might leave this matter to the official police," Holmes said quietly.

"No, Holmes, I appreciate your concern, but no. I implore you to use all your skills to find who did this. I will not rest until the beast is brought to justice."

"Very well."

Two barristers in court dress and wigs passed us. "The defendant in the case attested her husband was the meanest man she knew," one said to the other. "She said he frequented the shunting yards and made faces at the firemen in the passing engines, so they would throw coal at him."

Holmes and I exchanged glances. "Ravenscroft," Holmes said, holding up the evidence envelope. He led the way towards the entrance, passing the young reporter as he hurried along the corridor, the cameraman struggling behind him with his heavy equipment.

<hr>

Our cab stopped in Serle Street, Lincolns Inn Fields, outside the venerable shop of Ravenscroft, peruke maker to the judiciary.

The manager teased the fibres Holmes had recovered from Miss Brooks' hand. "This is horsehair, the material we use for our barristers' and judges' wigs, but we use darker shades than this. You will understand that no new barrister wishes to advertise his inexperience by wearing a bright new wig." He shook his head. "No, gentlemen, this is not from one of ours." He returned the hairs to the envelope and passed it to Holmes. "You might try a theatrical wig-maker; Clarkson's are the best known, of course."

"It was worth a try." Holmes said as we left the shop. He called up to the cabby. "Wellington Street, Soho."

<hr />

"Good afternoon, Mr Holmes. How lovely to see you again."

Bearded, dapper in his dress and extravagant in his gestures, the proprietor of Clarkson's ushered Holmes and me through the main chamber of his emporium. Masks and wigs were in profusion, either on mannequin heads set along the counters or on standing figures in theatrical costumes. Grotesque masks, outlandish hats, Indian feather headdresses, beards, and moustaches and banks of make-up pastes and powders were displayed on shelves. Paintings, photographs, and testimonials of actors of the past and present covered every inch of the walls.

Mr Clarkson posed under a glittering plaque listing the dozens of international medals and awards his products had garnered. "Here is my sanctum, gentlemen; I insist on attending to all the chief business myself." He smiled at Holmes. "The study of hair and how men have it cut is surely basic to the detective method. As a man's hair, so is his mind. And people are so very strange."

I knitted my brows.

"Wig making, mask-making," Mr Clarkson continued, "these are only a few of the details of my work. If you want a false ear, a false nose, a false chin to wear on the stage, I am at your service. Nothing connected with the art of make-up comes amiss to me. Ladies' wigs a yard long or a Jack shepherd of half-an-inch – just name your requirements, and I obey your commands."

He lowered his voice. "And if Nature or illness has been unkind to a gentleman or lady, one does one's best to supply the deficiency. Some men can wear a wig and you would never know. Others, no matter how perfect the product I supply, somehow let the fact be patent." He smiled a self-deprecating smile. "To enumerate the multifarious calls upon my talents would be a labour of Hercules. I am the recognised universal provider."

Mr Clarkson frowned, looked over my shoulder, muttered a brief "excuse me" and pushed past me. "Mr Irving," he called, "how lovely to see you again!"

I glanced at Holmes. "That man is in drink."

Holmes smiled. "Or inebriated with himself." He took my arm and led me behind a counter laden with unguents, through a green-baize-covered door, and along a shabby, ill-lit corridor lined with doors. He knocked at one and entered. A young man with over-long, flaming-red hair sat before a brightly lit mirror in a small cubicle similar to a theatrical dressing room. An array of paints and lotions lay on the dressing table before him, and portrait sketches, photographs, and images torn from magazines covered the walls. He looked up from combing the glossy black tresses of a female wig on a mannequin head.

"Mr Holmes, sir. What can we do for you today? Aged clergyman, is it? We've just received a consignment of fine, grey hair from Peru that will make convincing Dundreary weeper whiskers."

Holmes turned to me. "This is Raymond, who usually sees to my needs in the article of whiskers and false noses – disguises generally – when the owner of the shop is busy."

"As he usually is," Raymond said with a pout. "Willy Clarkson has an active social life."

Holmes took the clump of hair from its envelope and held it up. "I need your expert opinion on this."

"Coarse horsehair, bleached, and dyed blonde." Raymond squinted at the fibres close to the gaslight. "Theatrical, Mr Holmes: greasy with make-up." He wrinkled his nose. "The low end of the profession. You won't get any of the boys on the boards wearing this stuff."

I wrinkled my nose. "Female impersonators."

"How is that different from the male impersonators who are so popular at the Tivoli?" Raymond asked in a cold tone, his hands on his hips.

"Might there be a connection with the Tivoli?" Holmes said.

"No, no, Mr Holmes, this is not Tivoli-style. We supply them and all the better halls. Was I you, I'd look south of the river, not up West. Maybe the smaller pub halls or specialist clubs."

Holmes slid a half crown onto the dressing table, and we said our goodbyes.

"I trust Raymond's judgement," Holmes said as we came out into the street. "But we'd best double-check. The Tivoli may use another supplier as well as Clarkson's."

———◦○◦———

Mr Lane, the stage manager at the Tivoli, fingered the hairs. "Could be from a prop wig, but tracking which one would be an impossible undertaking. Had you the whole wig, it'd be lettered with our name, but as it is...."

He shook his head and sighed. "We had a visit from a police detective, but we could not offer any assistance. A tragedy, gentlemen. Miss Brooks was coming up in her profession. She started at the back of the chorus line, but she was noticed, moved to the front, then offered a solo part as the Captain. With Lottie thinking of giving up the skirt dance, her chance had come. She will be missed by the whole company."

Mr Lane hesitated. "I spoke with the theatre owner, and if it is not inappropriate, Mr Holmes, the Tivoli would like to engage you to investigate the death of poor Miss Brooks. A note with that request and enclosing a cheque is being prepared."

"I am engaged in the case by Doctor Watson, and I intend to cooperate with the police investigation."

"Then perhaps, without presuming, we might become co-sponsors?"

Holmes turned to me and raised his eyebrows.

"Of course."

"No payment is necessary," Holmes said. "Have there been any threats against Miss Brooks or any other member of the cast in recent days?"

Mr Lane shrugged. "No more than the usual. The *poses modèles vivants* at the Palace Theatre in Cambridge Circus get the most attention, mostly from the National Vigilance Association. The attempts by Mrs Ormiston Chant and her cohorts to partition the promenade there and evict the unaccompanied ladies caused a minor riot. With us, they bluster and threaten to have our licence revoked, but don't interfere with performances. I hope today's verdict with take the wind from their sails. We get the odd crazy, as you'd expect, but I don't know of any actual violence offered to our people. The stage-door johnnies are a nuisance, but they are harmless, as far as I know."

Mr Lane frowned, stood, and went to the window. "What's that noise?"

Holmes and I joined him. A group of black-clad men were in a half-circle on the pavement in front of the main entrance to the theatre. Reverend Gaunt stood in the centre, holding his cross. The men pumped their fists in the air and chanted slogans against Miss Collins and the Jews.

Mr Lane spread his hands. "I spoke too soon, gentlemen."

Holmes and I thanked him, and we were escorted to the main entrance. The sky was grey, and a light drizzle pattered on the pavement in front of the theatre on which Reverend Gaunt and his supporters stood. One brute held a placard with a threat to burn Miss Collins at the stake scribed in lurid red letters.

A Victoria was parked a little way along the street with its hood up and a top-hatted gentleman inside, his face in shadow. A wreath of smoke curled from the cigar in his hand.

"Those that live by smut shall die in ignominy," Reverend Gaunt cried. His men displayed another placard with a sketch in crayon – a revolting caricature of a hook-nosed man in a silk hat with his hands around the neck of a semi-naked girl.

I raised my stick and started towards the men. Holmes laid a hand on my arm.

"There was nothing sordid about Miss Brooks," I said. "She was a gentle soul."

A hansom drew up, and the young reporter from the Courts jumped down and helped his photographer set up his apparatus in the road facing Gaunt and his men. At a sign from the clergymen, three of the toughs crossed the street and attacked the reporter, beating him to the ground. The photographer was knocked aside, and his camera smashed,

Holmes and I raised our canes and sprang to their defence. I snapped mine over a thick-necked bruiser who was about to kick the young man on the ground. Holmes whacked another on the knee with his stick, and while he hopped away, howling, he felled the third with a straight left to the jaw.

Reverend Gaunt screamed an order, and he and the remaining followers charged at us. As Holmes and I turned to face them, a police van turned into the Strand at the gallop and pulled up between us and the black-clad thugs. A sergeant and a half-dozen constables jumped down and spread across the road. Reverend Gaunt snapped another order and his men fell back, snarling and shaking their fists.

Holmes conferred with the sergeant, and I propped the reporter up and dusted him off. He helped the photographer pick up the debris of his camera and tripod.

I looked up as the mysterious Victoria trotted past me, and I recognised General Reid-Aladyce looking straight ahead and blowing out a stream of cigar smoke.

"Never say die, Doctor," the young reporter said when I enquired whether he was injured. He wiped blood from his nose with his handkerchief. "Can I have your comment on the verdict?"

I smiled. "You are a very persistent and possibly very foolhardy young fellow. Very well. I consider dancing to be a form of exercise, and like all exercise it should be performed with moderation and care lest the muscles be strained. That applies equally to men and women."

The reporter returned my smile, closed his notebook, and stuck his pencil behind his ear.

"And if I may say so, Mister?"

"Daladier," the reporter answered.

"If I may say so, Mr Daladier, you might care to take a course of exercise and muscular development if you intend to face off Gaunt's bruisers again."

He grinned. "I'm wirier than I look, Doctor."

"A rather charming, irritating young man," I said as Holmes and I boarded a hansom. "In fact, he is a mere boy; he looks about sixteen. I suppose I'm at an age when policemen and newspaper reporters look like schoolboys."

A page ran out of the stage door shielding an envelope from the rain with his cap. Holmes extracted a telegram from the envelope, read it, and called up to the cabby, "Scotland Yard."

"We attempted to put the dress on the body, as you suggested, Mr Holmes." Inspector Lestrade indicated one of two dresses laid out on a trestle table in an otherwise bare room at the back of the New Scotland Yard building by Westminster Bridge. "It would not fit."

He lifted the second dress to the light of the gas lamps. "If you compare it with the other, one of Miss Brook's costumes from her dressing room at the Tivoli, you can see her regular costume is at least one or two sizes larger than the yellow dress she was found in. That is why that dress was only pulled down to her waist. The lady for whom this yellow dress was made has slimmer hips."

"The killer tried to change her clothes," I said. "What for? It seems absolutely demented, as if the abominable crime itself were not vile enough."

"Did you have any luck with the hair?" Lestrade asked.

Holmes summarised our findings at Clarkson's, and Lestrade nodded. "Theatrical, that accords with our analysis; but not from a major hall that's interesting."

He opened his notebook. "I have Miss Brooks' home address in Lambeth. Would you care to accompany me, gentlemen?"

———————◆———————

At just after six in the evening, Waterloo Bridge was busy with office clerks and shop attendants heading towards their homes on the south side of the river in increasingly heavy rain. A dozen or more young girls came in the opposite direction, heads bowed, and coats held tight closed, making haste through the downpour which must have saturated their flimsy skirts. Mud and ordure from horse droppings covered the hard pavement, unpleasant and cruelly uncomfortable to ill shod feet.

"Ballet girls heading for the halls," I said.

The police van pulled up outside one of a long row of terraced houses, each with a fenced patch of front garden. A police constable in a cape standing by the gate of one house saluted Lestrade, and a group of burly men leaning against the wall of the house watched through narrowed eyes as the inspector led Holmes and me to the front door. A small metal plaque was affixed slantwise to the doorpost.

"The *mezuzah*," Lestrade explained.

I raised an enquiring eyebrow.

"A kind of house blessing."

"You seem well up in these matters," I said.

"I was on the beat in Spitalfields for four years – the streets I patrolled were mostly Jewish. The Jewish youngsters could be wild, but we seldom got an older Jew as a thief; with the cockney men, once a thief, always a thief." He indicated the unkempt and overgrown front garden of the cottage. "Their front gardens are neglected, but the inside will be spotless; exactly the opposite of the cockney."

We were let in by a boy and shown into a small parlour. As Lestrade has surmised, the room was clean but strangely devoid of furniture apart from a few stools. Dark-bearded men in caps and women wearing headscarves sat in silence on stools or on the floor. The curtains were tight drawn, the gas was unlit, and a pair of candles cast flickering shadows over the walls. A black cloth covered what I presumed was a mirror or picture above the fireplace.

Inspector Lestrade introduced himself, Holmes, and me, and asked to speak to Miss Brooks' father.

A middle-aged lady stood and led us along a passage and into a stone-floored kitchen. "I am Anna's mother. My husband is with the rabbi, making the arrangements. The funeral is tomorrow."

"What does Mr Brooks do for a living?" Lestrade asked.

"He's a horse butcher." Mrs Brooks pressed a handkerchief to her eyes. "We weren't happy when Anna got a job on the stage. I'd hoped she'd get a refined position as a nanny to a good family or as a typewriter in an office. But she was so overjoyed. We celebrated when Anna got a place in the front row – the front row girls are paid more. And then again when she got her solo part; she was getting nearly two pounds a week."

She sobbed into her handkerchief. "Anna was so proud."

"Did she have any particular friends or acquaintances?" Inspector Lestrade asked. "I refer to male friends."

Mrs Brooks looked up, red-eyed. "Anna was not that type of girl."

"Who are those men outside?"

"Men from my husband's work and *shochet* brought by the rabbi. He said the Christian priest has his butchers dressed in black, so he brought these men to defend us. There's a rumour the priest will attack the funeral procession on its way to the cemetery, so the rabbi is keeping the time and place a secret." She shook her head, "What kind of world is this when innocent girls are murdered, and these people attack us? What for do they hate us?"

"I knew Miss Brooks," I said. "I would like to attend the funeral, if it is permitted."

"You are welcome, Doctor. Come at nine tomorrow. My husband and the rabbi are arranging the procession and everything. We're not orthodox, you understand, but I try to get to the *shul* most weeks."

Inspector Lestrade requested an account of Anna's doings over the past month or so, a list of her friends and acquaintances and of anyone who might wish her harm. Mrs Brooks was unable to offer any useful information, insisting that her daughter was a good girl and universally loved.

We climbed back aboard the police vehicle and set off, passing an organ grinder who had set up his cart on the pavement farther long the street surrounded by a group of little girls dancing to the music. A bare-armed woman darted out of a house, shushed the organ and led the children away.

"Odd that they didn't have a single photograph of Miss Brooks on display," I said.

Holmes leaned forward. "There's a paperboy."

I bought the afternoon editions, and passed newspapers to Holmes and the inspector.

"I see the forgery in the Dreyfuss case has been exposed," I said, "and the Dervishes in the Sudan have attacked General Kitchener's column."

"A single paragraph on the Brooks murder is in the stop press," Holmes said.

"Reverend Gaunt has been arrested for affray, disturbing the peace and criminal damage to the Tivoli theatre carriage outside the court," Inspector Lestrade said. "His men tried to overturn the musician's carriage. The article prints his deranged rants that Jewish bankers and 'imperialist Judaism' are behind the South African unrest. He says Jewish-owned theatres showing half-naked Jezebels are undermining the moral fibre of our young men so they will be easy meat for the fuzzies and the more robust, God-fearing Boer farmers if it comes to war again."

"A potent mix of prurience, misogyny, anti-Semitism and patriotism," Holmes said.

"The papers give this religious maniac a pulpit," Lestrade said. He read from his paper. "'The reverend was brought before the desk sergeant and searched; his prayerbook was hollowed out, hiding a curved dagger and a palm pistol.'" He shook his head. "Yet he was released on his own recognisance."

The inspector's tone hardened. "We had complaints that Gaunt has been following ballet girls home, threatening them with hell and damnation. I checked his file; the reverend was arrested in

Swansea five years ago for a vicious attack on a prostitute, but she declined to testify."

<hr/>

The following morning, Holmes and I followed the funeral cortège in a cab along a circuitous route to the cemetery. Tough-looking men on horseback and in carriages guarded the procession until it turned through a pair of ornate wrought-iron entrance gates and stopped outside an unimposing red brick building.

The same boy who had opened the door of the Brooks' house the day before introduced himself as Miss Brooks' cousin and ushered Holmes and me into the building. He bade us wash our hands at a fount by the doors and keep our hats on.

The tiled-floor room was almost bare save for a lectern, benches and memorial plaques attached to the walls, with stained-glass windows above incorporating Star of David motifs. The boy drew our attention to charity boxes built into the walls.

Men clustered at one side of the hall and women on the other, and a rabbi led the party in prayers, but there did not seem to be a formal religious service.

A bowed, grey-haired man detached himself from a group, made his way to us and was introduced by the boy as Miss Brooks' father. He addressed Holmes.

"You are Mr Holmes, the detective in the newspapers?"

"I am."

"The copper says you are hunting her murderer." He held out his hand. "Thank you for that, sir. You see we are not wealthy, but I will pay what and when I can."

"That is taken care of," Holmes answered. "The Tivoli theatre and her friend, Doctor Watson, have engaged me."

Mr Brooks shook my hand. "I shouldn't have let her go up West. We were that worried about her all alone after her friend Sarah up and disappeared."

Holmes frowned. "Disappeared?"

"Sarah Abrams, as lived in Coral Street near Waterloo Station. She was Anna's friend; they were both doing the ballet together. She didn't come home one night last January, and she's not been seen since."

Mr Brooks was called away.

Inspector Lestrade joined us as the congregation filed out, and, after washing our hands again, we made our way along an avenue of trees towards the burial area. The cemetery was sparsely wooded, consisting of an open expanse of grave plots subdivided by grids of paths, lacking the ornamental landscaping seen in Christian cemeteries. There were few flowering plants, and I realised that I had seen no floral tributes or wreathes.

"This seems almost perfunctory compared to the pomp of our English observances," I said.

"Christian ceremonies are in part to comfort the living, Doctor," Inspector Lestrade said, "but that's impossible when Jewish tradition requires immediate internment, so close to death."

The ceremony proceeded at the graveside.

"How many other girls, Inspector?" Holmes asked.

The inspector looked down at his toes. "We have two other open cases. We're trying to keep a lid on, Mr Holmes, so I was constrained from informing you."

The mourners returned to their carriages, and Holmes and I joined Lestrade in his police van. We turned out of the gate and the inspector rapped on the roof and called to the driver to pull up.

A group of black-clad men gathered on the opposite side of the road, holding placards with the same vile images I had seen outside the Tivoli. In their centre stood Reverend Gaunt, clutching his crucifix staff.

Lestrade jumped down, took the bridles of our horses, and guided the police van across the road, stopping in front of the demonstration, shielding it from view. Holmes and I got down and stood with Lestrade as behind us the family carriages came out of gates and trotted away.

I was no more than a dozen feet from Gaunt, who regarded us with a slight smile, his long moustaches as ridiculously sinister as a pantomime stage villain. Neither he nor his men said a word or made any move against us. I resisted the urge to break another cane over the reverend's head.

When the funeral carriages had passed, Lestrade, Holmes, and I climbed back into the carriage and set off.

"Did you notice the last carriage that followed the funeral cortège?" Holmes asked. "A Victoria with its hood up."

"General Reid-Aladyce?" I suggested.

"It was too far to tell."

We drove south along the same route we had followed to the cemetery, but halted on the south side of Waterloo Bridge.

"The Bridge of Sighs, gentleman," Lestrade said. Holmes and I followed him down to the police landing stage and into a large hut on stilts set into the foreshore. We clambered up a set of wooden stairs and found ourselves in a dingy room with a bath to one side and a pot-bellied stove in the centre. A hook on a pulley hung from the ceiling.

A male corpse in a sodden scarlet uniform lay on a trestle table, and another soldier sat in a corner of the room with his head in his hands, quietly weeping. A police constable adjusted a camera on a gantry above the table and set off a flash stick with a muffled boom and a cloud of smoke.

"We photograph the Drag these days," Lestrade explained, "and develop the pictures in our own darkroom."

He opened a roll-top desk, took out a slim file and spread out a sheaf of photographs. "This is how the two bodies were found, strangled, with stockings still in place around the necks. One washed up against the Westminster Steps, the other at Wapping."

A bearded sergeant offered steaming mugs. "Beef tea, gentlemen? We make it as a reviver for the half-drowned, so we add a dash of rum, Navy fashion." The sergeant beamed at me. "Don't you remember me, Doctor?" I was with Inspector Bliss in the old floating station at Blackwall at the time of the Ripper murders: the Abode of Bliss, as us youngsters called the boat." He held out his hand. "Sergeant, as was Constable Andrews."

"I'm pleased to see you again, Andrews," I said. "But I could wish for better circumstances."

Inspector Lestrade held up a photograph. "The first one found in February, the lady we now know is Sarah Abrams, wore rose-red petticoats, so we assumed she was a prostitute." He indicated the second photograph. "The second in April, Eva Margolis, was in cheap clothes, had traces of scarlet rouge on her lips, and her fingernails were long and smooth, not cracked and chipped as those of a servant or manual worker would be, so we came to the same conclusion. Both women were blonde, and missing clumps of hair."

He sipped his beef tea. "The Thames police pull a dozen or more bodies from the river every week, more than half of them women. The two strangled women had no identification on them, and what with their dress and our assumption they were on the streets, we were naturally wary of making a fuss. No-one wants to reignite the Ripper madness. What I don't understand is why their relations don't come forward to say the young ladies are missing.

"After Miss Brooks' murder we enquired at the Tivoli and found no less than five girls from the chorus left without notice and without forwarding addresses in the past year, none of them reported to us. We tracked down the relatives of the two we found and got a positive identification for Margolis and Abrams.

Lestrade looked down at his toes. "I must offer my apologies, Mr Holmes, for keeping mum about the two other ladies, but you'll understand the department's reticence over the matter when you recall the Ripper circus. Now we've made the connection with Miss Brooks, Abrams, Margolis and the Tivoli, we have a copper on the stage door, and we set a watch on the likely johnnies. We've asked the management to send the ballet girls home in four-wheelers late at night."

"Committing murder in daylight in a crowded court building does not suggest the killer is shy or cautious," Holmes said. "He may strike again despite your precautions."

Inspector Lestrade slipped the photographs into a desk drawer. "Assuming our man is attracted to water for disposing of his victims, we're maintaining a twenty-four-hour watch on the upstream bridges."

"The floor of the ladies' lavatory was flooded," I said.

Lestrade nodded.

"Do you have addresses for the other two victims?" Holmes asked.

Lestrade scribbled a note.

"Did the killer target Miss Brooks, or would any girl who went into that lavatory have been in danger?" I asked.

"I wish we knew, Doctor," Lestrade answered. "All we can say is that the three victims were ballet girls associated with the Tivoli, and three identical murders make it certain he's choosing his victims from that source." He balled his fist and struck the desk. "It's the same problem we had with Jack. The killer may have no connection with the girls; he may just lie in wait for any who strike his fancy. That makes him devilish difficult to track."

"He is a devil," I said. "And he must be destroyed."

<hr />

Holmes and I made our way back to our lodgings and found Mr Daladier in the waiting room.

"You again," I said as he followed us upstairs to the sitting-room. "Are you dogging us, young man?"

"I thought I should show you this, Doctor." He held out a photograph. "My photographer found his way to the gallery above the gatehouse of the Law Courts, and he took pictures of the crowd yesterday. I was looking through them when I noticed you, Doctor."

I borrowed Holmes' magnifying glass and peered closely at the photograph.

"There you are, pushing through the throng towards a young lady," Mr Daladier said "You can see the stripes on the lady's dress.

A dress of that style is missing from Miss Brooks' wardrobe; I spoke to her friends at the Tivoli, and they say she wore it the day she died."

Holmes leaned against the mantel and lit his pipe. "Thank you, Mr Daladier. You have been helpful."

The young man pouted, reminding me of a smacked puppy. "Don't I deserve a quote, gentlemen?"

"You may say that Mr Holmes is proceeding with enquiries that he hopes will lead to an early conclusion to the case," I answered. "And you would do well to eschew sensationalism, particularly with regard to Miss Brooks. Fanatics like Gaunt and Reid-Aladyce attempt to tar the Tivoli dancers with a broad brush of wickedness and depravity, which is very far from the truth. Think also of the girls' relatives."

"May I mention the photograph in my piece?"

"Since it's your property," I said, "I can't stop you. In fact, it might flush the lady out if she is an innocent party."

Billy saw the reporter to the door, and I studied the photograph in the light from the argon lamp on my desk. "I don't see Reverend Gaunt or General Reid-Aladyce."

"Lestrade says Reverend Gaunt was under close observation the whole morning, either in court or the street outside," Holmes answered.

"And General Reid-Aladyce?" I asked.

"He slipped out during the mayhem at the end of the trial."

"Was he under observation?"

"A sitting MP? I doubt it. It would have been more than Lestrade's job is worth to dog him." Holmes frowned. "Lestrade kept the lid on the two earlier murders. Have you seen any mention of them in the papers?"

"No."

Holmes leaned back in his chair, tapped his finger to his lips in a characteristic gesture and sat silently for ten minutes or more before he looked up. "Ask Billy to fetch a cab, would you?"

<hr />

The rain had eased, and the street was quiet, with just a pair of toughs on guard at the gate of the Brooks' house; the windows were close-curtained, and no were lamps lit.

Holmes stalked to the front door, knocked, and spoke briefly to Mrs Brooks before returning to the cab. He rubbed his hands together. "They sold what photographs they had of Anna to pay for the funeral."

"Who to?"

"A brown-haired young man who didn't look old enough to work for a newspaper. He contacted them on the evening of the murder and paid ten shillings for six photographs of Anna." He called to the cabby. "Wardour Street."

"Daladier bought the photographs – what of it, Holmes?" I asked. "He's an eager-beaver reporter; it's not strange for him to pursue a story and request details and photographs of the victim in what would be a sensational case."

"And yet there was very little about the murder in today's papers and no photographs. Let's see what Daladier's employer has to say."

"Look at this, gentlemen," Mr Mayer said as a page showed us into his office, "A dozen letters today – one asking us to kindly pass the enclosed dried pansy to the ballet girl third from the left in the chorus line of *Aladdin* at Drury Lane. Or this, enquiring whether we can assure the writer that the lady who posed as Venus in the *vivantes plastiques* display at the Empire is wearing a *maillot*."

I frowned.

"A body stocking." Mr Mayer shook his head. "We are plagued with communications from gentlemen who are obsessed with their ballet pets. They endeavour to find all about them, worrying and annoying respectable editors with questions as to their ages, addresses, preferred flowers or chocolates and other minutiae respecting them.

"What does it matter whether they rehearse of a morning in their common walking dresses or whether they are painted and decorated? What does it betide anyone save themselves and their intimate relations that they reside over the Surrey side of the water, and cross and recross the bridge at Waterloo in their journeys to and from the theatre? For some reason that journey excites the fevered imaginations of these fellows."

Mr Mayer sat back in his chair. "How can I help you, gentlemen?"

"We are investigating the murder of three ballet girls. We believe you may be planning an article on the subject."

"Eh? We're a theatrical paper. We don't cover murders or social issues. Try the *Pall Mall Gazette*."

"One of your reporters has knowledge of the murders, Mr Daladier."

"Daladier? Yes, he's freelance." Mr Mayer smiled. "I expect he portrayed himself as a house reporter to give himself more gravitas; it's common enough."

He offered cigars from a humidor and took one himself.

"The boy's enthusiastic, he knows the halls, and he's cheap, so we've had him provide colour or background pieces. He's had some experience, even a scoop. He got the *Morning Post* an interview with General Reid-Aladyce after the final battle with the Ashanti, when their king was deposed and we annexed the place. General Reid-Aladyce was the hero of the hour, but he was notoriously tight-lipped and publicity shy and no one could get an interview. Daladier did somehow; it was quite a coup at the time. I'm surprised he wasn't offered a job on one of the dailies."

"Was he the reporter who wrote the Lottie Collins piece?" I asked.

Mr Mayer smiled a rueful smile. "To be perfectly honest, that was me. And you might say I got what I deserved."

"Do you have Daladier's full name and address?" Holmes asked.

"I might have." Mr Mayer swivelled his chair and consulted a ledger on a shelf behind him. "We by-lined a couple of stories. One was on ballet girls, as I recall. Yes, here we are, E C Y Daladier. Sorry, no address." Mr Mayer frowned. "I recall he told me the initials stand for 'Efion something Yves'. One presumes the young man is of French extraction. That may explain his odd behaviour."

Holmes leaned forward. "Odd?"

"One of the typewriting girls found him in the ladies' lavatory one Saturday evening," Mr Mayer answered. "He was putting on lipstick. He said it was for a lark as he and some of his fellows were going to the Empire dressed as ladies. I told him it was no laughing matter, and that he'd get himself arrested if he carried on in that fashion. I reminded him of the fate of Boulton and Park."

"The actors who dressed in women's clothes?" I said. "Weren't they exonerated?"

"Acquitted, yes, but the taint was on them. Who would employ or associate with a pair like them? Their flaunting themselves in women's clothes was an affront to our national character, a sign of moral weakness. And don't think the Boers weren't watching. Would they have dared rise up against their lawful masters if they were not convinced our manhood had been undermined by such displays as those at the Tivoli and Empire?"

"Do you have a bank address for Mr Daladier?" Holmes asked.

"We pay cash."

"What of his photographer?"

"He provides his own photos." Mr Mayer stood. "I've not had dealings with him for weeks. I nodded to him at the court, that's all."

"Why are these mashers so focussed on girls who live south of the Thames?" I asked as Holmes and I made our way into Wardour Street.

"I believe it is the titillating contrast between the unattainable, in their view, tinsel and rhinestone clad fairy on the stage and the reality of the ill-clad and low-paid, and thus obtainable young girl struggling through the rain to her lodgings in Lambeth that piques their interest."

"Dastardly," I said. "And terribly sad."

Holmes hailed a cab. "Daladier visited Anna's bereaved family, and he bought photographs, but he has not written an article or sold the pictures – at least we've seen nothing in the likely papers."

"His piece may have been rejected."

"Not by the *Illustrated Police News* or the *Pall Mall Gazette,*" Holmes answered. "They would jump at the story. He could make his name as a reporter. Why has he been so reticent?"

"It is odd. And if he dresses as a lady for a lark, he would wear a wig," I said. "But how could such an open, charming young man perform such heinous acts? It beggars belief."

Holmes directed the cab to the East End homes of Sarah Abrams and then Eva Margolis.

"The same story," he said as he returned to the cab. "Both contacted within a day or so of the girls' disappearance. The families sold photographs of their daughters after being told they would be used in missing persons reports in national newspapers. The buyer fits Daladier's description."

"How did Daladier become aware of the disappearance of Sarah Abrams and Eva Margolis?" I asked.

"Exactly. He visited the victims' families soon after the murders. How did he know of them?"

"He may have an informant in the river police. It's common enough."

"For a veteran reporter with the *Morning Post* or the *Illustrated Police News,* perhaps. But Daladier is a freelancer for *Stage News,* a minor theatrical paper. And the police did not know the names of the first two victims until after Anna's murder."

I considered. "No, I can't believe he could be responsible for the murders, Holmes. I'm sure Daladier will have a simple explanation. We have no address, but perhaps we could find the photographer."

Holmes shook his head. "There are literally scores of studios in a mile circle from here; there must be a dozen on the Strand alone."

"The boy will turn up again: he usually does."

Holmes checked his watch and tapped on the roof of the cab with his cane. "Wellington Street." He settled in his seat. "Clarkson's will be shutting up shop in ten minutes."

Holmes buttonholed Raymond as he stepped out of the employees' entrance of the wig shop. "I need you to take me on a tour. We are looking for a young man who dresses in lady's clothes."

Raymond drew back. "You can get into trouble for that."

"He may be already in a raft of trouble, but not for dressing inappropriately." Holmes held up a half sovereign and raised an eyebrow.

"Only for you, Mr Holmes," Raymond said, taking the coin. "And as long as it's between ourselves."

We got down from the cab outside a nondescript smoke-blackened building behind Waterloo Station. A staircase led down to an unmarked basement door. Holmes led the way into a long, low room with a black-and-white-checked linoleum floor and on one side a marble-topped counter backed by a mirror with glass shelves lined with spirits and wine bottles. A stuffed, pink-dyed, Manx cat stood on one end of the bar below a hand-written sign, 'Le Chat Rose Rusé.'

A half dozen ladies in colourful evening gowns and wide hats sat at tables, chatting or playing cards, glasses of beer before them. They looked up as we entered and conversation stopped. The only patron at the bar, a bald, middle-aged man in a frock coat, slipped from his seat, clapped on his bowler, and stalked, head-down, for the exit.

The barman was of the usual thin-moustached, slicked-down-hair variety. He smiled a greeting to Raymond and nodded to Holmes and me. "What's your pleasure, gentlemen?"

"Three whiskies," Holmes ordered.

The barman giggled. "The bottles are just for show, sir. We're a beer house."

"Three beers, then."

The ladies resumed their chatter.

"We are looking for a young man—"

The barman smiled.

"—or a young lady, about this tall, slim with brown eyes and possibly in a blonde wig. A talkative young person with a habit of smiling and a gold tooth here." Holmes pointed. "My friend and I are not with the police."

The barman continued to smile at Holmes for a long moment. Holmes slid a half crown onto the bar, which was instantly covered by the barman's hand and slipped away.

"You mean Petite Yvette?"

"Perhaps."

"Yvette Etrilles we call her, or Petite Yvette as she calls herself."

Holmes slid another coin onto the bar. "Address?"

"She lodges three streets away with Lady Buxton."

"What motivates these people, Holmes?" I said as we climbed aboard our cab. "This silly dressing up is the stuff of nursery games. I am with Mr Mayer, to a degree. I cannot see those effete young men facing the Mad Mahdi's hordes with the bayonet, or yet standing against the stalwart Boers if it comes to a fight in South Africa."

The cab set off. "And Mrs Chant may also have a point, at least in relation to the signboards outside the Empire music hall in Cambridge Circus. The management maintains that the nudes on their posters are 'classical', painted by old masters like Rembrandt and so on, but the passing newsboy or young office clerk doesn't know about all that, and he may be disturbed. The more so if the young man goes inside and is subjected to the live presentation of the painting on stage with ladies and gentlemen wearing only—"

Holmes smiled. "*Maillots.*"

I wrinkled my nose. "Body stockings."

The door of the lodging house was opened by a middle-aged lady in hair curlers, holding a plump tortoiseshell cat in her arms. "Can I help you, dearies?"

"Lady Buxton?"

She patted her hair. "My young girls call me Lady Buxton, because I come from Buxton, which is in the North, and I am always ladylike in my demeanour. I have my standards, gentlemen, and I expect my young ladies to abide by them. Which means no gentlemen callers." She made to close the door.

"We wish to see Miss Yvette Etrille on a matter of business."

"That's all right then," the landlady said, ushering Holmes and me into a hall decorated in dark green wallpaper with swathes of green paisley fabric framing doors and the posts of a staircase. She led us into a dimly gas-lit sitting room crowded with dark furniture. A white cat lounging on an Ottoman hissed at us and fled behind a tall, potted aspidistra.

"I try to oblige, being on the boards myself at one time (you may remember Adele the Hoxton Warbler) whether it's an extra kipper for breakfast come audition day or a pinch of tea of an evening after a show."

"Is Miss Etrille at home?"

"Yvette is one of my regulars. She keeps a room, but she's so busy I hardly ever see her. She's got herself a lovely part at the Tivoli, the lucky girl. And principal boy in Aladdin at the Drury! I do so love it when my girls come good." She chuckled and nudged me with her elbow. "Aside from getting the rent arrears paid up!"

"Is she in?" Holmes persisted.

"I'll have to call her. Her room's at the top of the stairs, and the gyp my knees give me you wouldn't believe, gentlemen."

Holmes smiled. "We wouldn't dream of putting you to such trouble, my dear lady. We've come about the Tivoli engagement – we'll just be a jiffy. The top floor on the right, was it?"

"On the left."

There was no response to our knock.

Holmes knelt, took a roll of silk from his pocket, spread his picklocks and swiftly unlocked the door.

The room was larger than I had expected from the pokey hallway and narrow stairs outside. It was divided by a screen into a sitting room and bedroom. A green-baize-topped table and two chairs furnished the sitting area, which smelled musty, principally of burnt oil. Holmes tried to light the oil lamp on the table, but it refused to light, and when he shook the chamber, it was clearly empty. I lit a match, checked the walls, and found a pair of gas mantles on either side of the cold fireplace.

I lit both. In their light, the walls of the room, papered with the same dour wallpaper as the hall downstairs, glowed with colour.

Bright posters and other pictures were pasted over every inch of wall space, most of them from what I could see, with French text.

"Political and theatrical," Holmes said, "concerning the Dreyfuss case and advertising the Moulin Rouge and other Montmartre shows."

I peered into the bedroom and lit a lamp, illuminating a huge poster pasted to the wall above the bed featuring a man, presumably Emile Zola, pointing at the viewer with a banner above reading 'J'Accuse!'.

Photographs and sketches of Captain Dreyfuss cut from magazines showed him at his trial for treason and languishing on Devil's Island after his conviction. Other pictures were of Marie Lloyd, Lottie Collins, and a dozen more English music hall favourites, together with French artistes I was unfamiliar with.

I lifted the lamp and opened a tall wardrobe that, aside from the single bed and a small bedside table, was the only piece of furniture in the bedroom area. I gasped and stepped back.

"Holmes! Ladies' dresses – there must be a dozen here. My God, Holmes, is that Miss Brooks' mauve dress?"

Holmes laid his hand on my arm.

I pointed wordlessly to hanks of long, blonde hair that hung from a coat hanger. On a shelf was a mannequin head with a half-finished blonde wig on it.

Holmes teased the hair. "Human."

I sat back on the bed. "I don't understand," I said. "How could a young man like Daladier do something so heinous? It beggars understanding. It's the stuff of nightmares."

Holmes held his handkerchief under the gaslight. "I swabbed this from the door handle. There are signs of a struggle."

"Blood."

"Visitors?" Lady Buxton said. "About four it was. Two men came to the door dressed as oriental gentleman, for the Aladdin pantomime, they said. They had a hamper of clothes and props they wished to leave with Yvette. I said no gentlemen are allowed upstairs, but they requested ever so nice. The hamper was heavy, they said, and Yvette being so petite would need help getting it up to her room. Are you sure you won't have a glass?"

I politely refused, and Lady Buxton sipped her sherry and continued. "They asked me to fetch a jug of beer from the public at the corner to help celebrate Yvette getting the part, but, funny thing, when I came back, they were gone. They left a half sovereign on the table though, and I had the beer all paid for, so that was all right.

"Don't forget to sign the visitor's book," she said as she followed Holmes and me into the hall. "I have Vesta Tilley and a paw print from Rollo the Waltzing Pekinese."

"Reverend Gaunt is swarthy," I said. "He's ex-Indian Army, and he carries a curved dagger in his prayer book."

"I need a *Who's Who*," Holmes answered.

"The Junior United Service Club has the run."

We left my club, and Holmes directed the cab to Salisbury Square, where we stopped outside a dignified town house with a Victoria parked at the curb. A liveried coachman lounged by the horses' heads smoking a pipe.

An Indian butler in native dress enquired our business and let us into the hall, where he requested we wait while he informed his master of our visit. He returned after a few moments and saw us into an elegantly furnished study.

General Reid-Aladyce, a tall white-haired figure, stood before the empty fireplace, smoking a cigar. He wore evening dress, and an opera cloak was draped over an armchair with a top hat laid on it.

Holmes introduced himself and me, and the general raised an eyebrow.

"You do not approve of private detectives?" Holmes asked.

The general smiled. "On the contrary, I think every person in the kingdom should take a leaf out of your book, Mr Holmes. We must be on the watch for depravity in our neighbourhood, even in our intimate circle. A moral militia must be formed to stamp out abominations like the alleged entertainments at the Tivoli and replace them with wholesome, spiritually uplifting, and enlightening productions."

He indicated the opera cloak and hat. "I have tickets for 'The Union Jack' this evening at the Adelphi, so you will oblige me by being brief."

"I understand a reporter named Daladier interviewed you on your successful Ashanti campaign," Holmes said.

"He did nothing of the sort. The fellow made the interview up. I abhor the notion of public scrutiny of my private affairs. These newspaper scribblers have no sense of decency. Look at the nonsense the press is writing about Reverend Gaunt." He rocked on his toes and heels. "The so-called interview was frivolous nonsense; my views were trivialised and simplified to the point of caricature. I ignored it."

The general leaned an elbow on the mantel and puffed on his cigar. "The war was unfortunate, but necessary. The Ashanti fought for their right to run their own affairs and keep outsiders out of their territory. Naturally, the English public disdained them, assuming because they must be backward, uncouth and stupid: in fact, nothing could be farther from the truth. Their general fought a tough, cleverly conceived defensive battle before their capital Kumasi, but he was doomed to failure because I had maxim guns and artillery, and he had not. No soldier who was with me on that campaign would have doubted the Ashanti's courage or skill at arms.

"The king's palace in Kumasi would, in terms of size, have rivalled Buckingham Palace, and inside we found many artworks and a library containing books in several languages." General Reid-Aladyce shrugged. "We ransacked the palace and blew it up. Why? Because we have the power. The Anglo-Saxons are the dominant race in the world, and for that to remain the case, other strong, manly, but technologically primitive peoples like the Ashanti, the Zulus and the Dervishes must be mastered.

"That at least some of the idiots in government have come to understand, but what they do not see is that we are diluting the racial purity that is the fundamental source of our power. Just as America was, so England is now the rubbish tip for the scum of Europe. The destitute, diseased, verminous and criminal foreigner who dumps himself on our soil and property rates simultaneously must be expelled along with those who entice him to these islands.

"Our nation has been infected; we must not be afraid to cut out the pestilence and cauterise the wound with fire and white-hot iron." The general pursed his lips. "Through legal means, naturally. My efforts to educate the ninnies in Parliament have not been entirely unsuccessful."

"Your colleague, Reverend Gaunt, does not restrict himself to legal methods," I said. "He is a thug."

"True." The general shrugged. "There is an old saying that politics acquaints a man with strange bedfellows."

"Doctor Watson and I are part of a police investigation into the murder of three women associated with the Tivoli Theatre," Holmes said.

General Reid-Aladyce tapped his cigar ash into the grate. "I heard of the incident at the Law Courts from an acquaintance in the police. Most unfortunate. One feels for the family, of course, but it must also be admitted that these girls put themselves at risk. They flaunt themselves in indecent raiment and with louche behaviour without a thought for the dangerous passions they may engender."

"Miss Brooks was a kind, innocent young lady," I said.

Holmes put his hand on my arm.

"As I said, one feels for the family in individual cases." The general puffed on his cigar.

"I saw from your entry in *Who's Who* that you are a widower with a son, Edward," Holmes said. "I met him just the other day."

"You are mistaken. Edward is with the expedition mapping the North-West Passage. He sailed for Nova Scotia several months ago."

"Do you have a photograph of Edward?" Holmes asked.

The general's eyes flicked to a painting of foxhounds that hung on the wall above an escritoire. "I do not."

"The reporter who wrote the article on you was named E. C. Y. Daladier."

"What of it?"

Holmes turned to me. "Would you kindly say that name backwards?"

"Backwards? Ah, reidaladyce: Reid-Aladyce!"

The general drew on his opera cloak, picked up his silk hat and tugged a bell pull hanging by the fireplace. "Your questions are becoming intrusive and tiresome, Mr Holmes, and I have an engagement. Abdul will see you out."

The Indian butler appeared in the doorway.

"I think you may find the questions of the official police even more bothersome, General. The investigating officer in this case is dogged in pursuit." Holmes bowed, and we turned to follow the servant out.

"A moment." The general indicated the painting of fox hounds that hung between two bookcases. "Do you hunt, gentlemen? No? You must understand that every now and then, the master of hounds finds a whelp in the litter who will not follow the pack. He cringes away from the hunt. In other respects he may be a well-set-up dog with an immaculate pedigree, but there is nothing to be done, the whelp has to be put down or his weakness will infect the rest of the pack – bad apple and so on. It is a question of selection of the fittest, an inexorable law of Nature."

"What has this to do with your son?" I asked.

The general bowed. "Good evening."

"The North-West Passage," Holmes said as our cab pulled away. "Not an alluring prospect for Daladier, I suspect, nor for Petite Yvette. You saw the light patch on the wallpaper where a painting has been removed and the smaller one of foxhounds substituted?"

"You think that was a painting of the general's son?" I asked.

"We will never know, but it seems likely."

"His father may have merely sent him to Nova Scotia as he said." I frowned. "Or he may have had his Indian followers do away with him."

"Lestrade will make representations to the Nova Scotians," Holmes answered, "and he will scour London."

I shook my head. "And that's it? We can do no more to bring the fiend to justice and give Miss Brooks' family solace in their grief? And why did Daladier kill Miss Brooks and the other girls? Was he was trying to please his father in some twisted way? Did he tell the general what he had done? We did not find the photographs he bought from the grieving families; were they sent to his father as proof of his devotion to their cause? Perhaps they were acting together. Or was Daladier secretly against his father's beliefs?"

I considered. "His attacks seem to be motivated by a pathological jealousy of the ballet girls. The fact he took their clothes and clumps of their hair suggests he was trying to ape them in some depraved way." I shook my head. "General Reid-Alladyce's hound analogy was correct. If his son killed those defenceless, innocent girls, he is a despicable coward who must be put down. We think back to the beast in '88, of course. Are these monsters born with some innate foulness in their nature, or are they made by their upbringing? I cannot imagine what vile notions Reid-Alladyce infused into his son."

Our cab pulled up short of Trafalgar Square, and the cabby flipped open the hatch. "Something's up gents."

A continuous roar came from the direction of the Square, and the street ahead of us was thronged with people dancing and waving their arms.

"I imagine we have won a battle," Holmes said, "or perhaps a war."

I leaned out of the cab. "I can't see a newsboy's sign." I stood up on the running board. Trafalgar Square heaved with people.

A woman ran up to the cab. "Gi'us a kiss, Duckie!"

"I will do no such thing. Have a care, woman, venereal disease is spread by mouth-to-mouth contact."

The cabby turned the cab, and we took a circuitous route home through minor streets. Jubilant crowds were also out in Baker Street, and Holmes and I had to step down at the station, a block from our lodgings. A police constable lounged in a shop doorway smoking a cigarette, and Holmes asked him what was up.

"We've revenged the death of General Gordon at a great battle with the Dervishes in the Sudan," he said, hiding his cigarette behind his back. "God save the Queen."

"So, the Mad Mahdi's hordes are defeated," I said as Holmes and I made our way through the throng. "I can understand the crowd's elation, but this demonstration would give pause to an observer who thinks he knows the habits of the phlegmatic, imperturbable English."

A man in a battered top hat sat on a coal cart outside our lodgings playing the tuba. He began 'Ta-ra-ra-boom-de-yay' and the crowd roared its approval and sang along. Women and men alike leapt and high-kicked with abandon.

"The tune is without meaning," Holmes said, "but the sudden absurd jolt of its high note makes it a jeering, ludicrous affront to civil discourse. Just now, it is simply the voice of the crowd asserting itself, and they are happy enough. Heaven help us and them if a demagogue arises to lead them in another direction, against whatever minority he chooses to blame for our ills."

I surveyed the crowd, shook my head, and added a heartfelt, "Amen."

A REQUEST

I hope that you enjoyed this book, the eighth compilation of
novellas and short stories in the Sherlock Holmes Singular Tales
series.
A review on Amazon or Goodreads would be very much
appreciated.
To receive an email on upcoming and new books, please join my
mailing list at mikehoganauthor.com

ABOUT THE AUTHOR

Mike is British and lives on Mersea Island on the East Coast of Britain. He writes novels, plays and screenplays. He is an avid Holmesian and a Monty Python and *Frasier* fan. His obsessions are Shakespeare, Ancient Rome, and the Royal Navy. Among his favourite modern writers are Patrick O'Brian, Mary Beard, Robert Harris, Stephen Ambrose, Rick Atkinson, Gore Vidal, and Tom Wolfe.

Contact Mike at mikehoganauthor@gmail.com.

SHERLOCK HOLMES

THE TESLA TELE-AUTOMATON AND OTHER STORIES

MIKE HOGAN

SHERLOCK HOLMES NOVELS

The Scottish Question
1888, Autumn of Blood: The Thames Torso Murders in the
shadow of Jack the Ripper

OTHER NOVELS

Hamlet & Me
Alternative Facts
Romulus and the Pope

THE SHERLOCK HOLMES AND YOUNG WINSTON
TRILOGY

* The Deadwood Stage
* The Jubilee Plot
* The Giant Moles

NOTE ON SOURCES

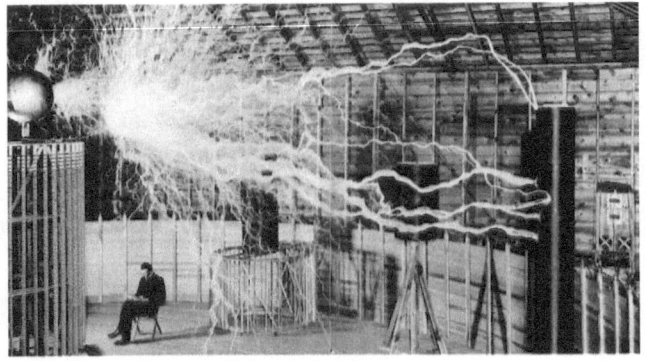

'If you only knew the magnificence of the 3, 6 and 9, then you would have the key to the universe.'

'The feeling is constantly growing on me that I had been the first to hear the greeting of one planet to another.'

Nikola Tesla was famously eccentric, and in later life his mental demons overshadowed his brilliance. But perhaps we should look at his legacy and be more impressed that he accomplished so much.

Tesla was granted over a hundred patents during his life; he invented, predicted or contributed to the development of remote control, neon and fluorescent lights, wireless transmission, computers, smartphones, laser beams, x-rays, robotics and alternating current, the basis of our present-day electrical system.

Tesla at the 1898 Electrical Exhibition at Madison Square Gardens

Ta-ra-ra-boom-de-yay

The origins of the song and accompanying dance are obscure and controversial. Lottie Collins bought the rights to a version of the lyrics in America, where it had supposedly originated in a St Louis bordello, sung by black performer Mama Lou.

The seemingly respectable young woman (a belle of good society) singing the opening ballad suddenly bursts through the bounds of propriety with a breathtaking display of high kicks, leaps and lunges as drums pound out the beat, cymbals crash, and she and the audience repeat the meaningless refrain. It took music-hall London by storm, and the moral backlash was inevitable.

The song has entered the British national psyche, often used as a gesture of defiance – although the melody was once adopted as a campaign song by the Central Conservative Committee.

Lottie won her lawsuit in 1897 against the editor of Society, who said her song 'A Little Widow' was in 'gross bad taste which is not redeemed even by the singer's ability and rose-red petticoats.' She died in 1910.

Anti-Semitic groups thrived in late-Victorian and Edwardian Britain. Captain William Stanley Shaw formed the British Brothers League in 1902 to campaign against immigration. Member of Parliament William Evans-Gordon led moves to pass an Aliens Act to restrict immigration, of which Winston Churchill wrote at the time,

'The bill ... proposes to establish in this country a loathsome system of police interference and espionage, of passports and arbitrary power exercises by police officers who in all probability will not understand the language of those upon whom they are called to sit in judgement.'

William Le Queux, who wrote popular yarns about London pogroms and foreign invasions, claimed that European Jewry owed its loyalty to Germany: 'the Jews have worked for the triumph of the Teuton everywhere'. Invasion fears of conquest by a Continental enemy added to anti-immigrant sentiment.

For a graphic depiction of similar groups in Paris at the time of the Dreyfuss affair see the excellent series *Paris Police 1900*.

www.ingramcontent.com/pod-product-compliance
Lightning Source LLC
Chambersburg PA
CBHW020313200626
46814CB00006BA/2225